The
Girl
Who
Didn't
Go

THE GIRL WHO DIDN'T GO

A Private I. D. Mystery

Stephanie Elliott

Orange Blossom Press Co.

ISBN: 9798856865966

Cover design by: Stephanie Elliott
Library of Congress Control Number: 2018675309
Printed in the United States of America

ORANGE BLOSSOM PRESS Cᴼ

for moi. keep up the good work.

STEPHANIE ELLIOTT

In Case You Were Wondering

Nobody ever tells you when you're getting pummeled, and I mean, really and truly getting your ass absolutely kicked: that you stop caring about stuff. Not just about some things, but about *everything*.

Your only thoughts are something along the lines of 'Stop hitting me. Why are they still hitting me? I'd really like them to stop hitting me' and so on.

You don't worry about who's going to look after your cat or whether you got that bill paid, or if there's going to be a new season of your favorite show. You don't care if your kid ever gets to school on time again, or if your package has been delivered to your house. You don't care if you ever get to see another sunrise.

You only want it to be over- and you don't care what it takes to get there. You'll say anything, do anything, try anything. Even if your arms are pinned and your legs can't move and you can't focus for the blows. You might even get to a point where you don't mind dying, because it might be preferable to all this pain. That's your brain going into shutdown- it's like, okay, well, we had a good run, let me send you some endorphins to give you a nice, easy exit. One way ticket to Sleepyville, choo choo!

I've heard that old trope about how when you're about to die, your life flashes before your eyes. That would have been nice actually! I had a good life. I'd have enjoyed seeing my son's smile when he was little again - all crooked and goofy. I'd have liked to smell my Granpop's cinnamon bread or scratch my childhood dog's ears. Or hell, I'd even have settled for the time I drank that jock under the table in college, and all his teammates carried me on their shoulders chanting my name. I felt like a million bucks right then, well, I mean, I did until I projectile vomited all over the place.

But I got totally dicked over! All I could see, as my eyes rolled back into my head and the darkness started to close in, was the goddamn sign on my office window, that I still needed to have repainted.

Total. Bullshit.

Several Weeks Earlier

'Ma! Hey, Ma!' Robbie's voice called up from the foyer at the bottom of the stairs. 'Hey, yo Ma!'

'Shut up or you'll wake Chuck,' I whispered loudly, leaning over the railing on the landing. 'What are you doing standing down there and yelling?'

'Sorry, I didn't see his van, I didn't know he was home,' he said, climbing the stairs two at a time, his legs long and thin like a grasshopper's. He was ridiculously tall, like his father. Being reminded of my ex made me try to remember when the last time was that we spoke, and I couldn't quite. I wondered how his new wife was doing, who he basically left me for- she was a yoga instructor from California. I wasn't mad about it. She's nice.

'Quit fuckin' yellin'!' Chuck hollered through his apartment door, and I winced.

'Sorry,' I called back, waving Robbie into my apartment. 'Why didn't you call first?' I asked, closing the door quietly behind him.

'Cuz we were just driving by, so I pulled over. I wasn't planning to visit.'

'Well when you put it like that, thanks. What's up? Are you mad at me?' I craned my neck to look up at his face. I usually made him sit in a chair so we could talk with our faces closer together but I'd only just gotten out of bed. I was tired and not in the mood for whatever this was.

'Yeah I am!'

'Oh, christ, why *now*?' I went into the kitchen and turned on the coffee machine.

'I want you to stop dragging Becky into your work,' he said.

"Dragging'?'

'Yeah! I mean, I knew she helped you sometimes but I didn't know you were making her do so much for you!'

"Making her'?'

'Stop just repeating what I say!'

I sighed as I shook coffee grounds into the reusable pod. A few buttons later, hey presto, coffee was brewing. 'Don't you know it's not cool to be a mean, annoying mother-in-law anymore? Becky and I get along great, and she only does what she *wants* to do. I don't know what else to tell you, but I'm not *making* her do anything.'

'Ma, that last guy you dealt with got really nasty. He could have hurt you! I don't want Becky to get involved in that shit. You know how I feel about all of this anyway. It was *your* choice to go into this business, a choice I'm still not crazy about, and Becky only wants to feel included... she just wants you to like her.'

'I *do* like her; she doesn't need validation from me.'

'That's right, I don't,' Becky interjected, the door slowly closing behind her. Her face told me she was *also* done with this shit.

'Ugh, I told you to wait in the car!' Robbie cried, gesturing toward the door.

'Oh, yeah, like a dog? Please.' Becky rolled her eyes. She joined me in the kitchen and filled another pod, then helped herself to a mug from the high cupboard. I only kept her and Robbie's favorite mugs up there because I couldn't reach them anyway. She hit the buttons and her coffee brewed. 'I *like* helping your mom.'

Robbie continued. 'I just want you to spend time doing... something else. You can look for another job.'

'Ha! Another *job*? Your mom doesn't *pay* me.'

'What?'

'Yeah, no, I don't pay her,' I said.

'I like the work. And besides,' Becky said, waving a hand around, indicating my apartment. 'It's not like she has a ton of money anyhow.' Then to me, she said 'No offense.'

'None taken. You're right.' I stirred my coffee and took a sip, glancing up at Robbie who I could tell now knew he was losing this battle.

Robbie groaned. 'Becky, you have *two* degrees. You can do *anything*.'

'I have a job! You know my windchimes are selling like crazy.'

'Still?' I asked.

'Oh, yeah,' she smiled at me. 'You know how they're really good at repelling bears? Well another region in northern Finland has caught on- we can't *keep up* with the demand.'

'That's amazing.'

Robbie was exasperated. 'Okay, well, I mean, I just don't want you running around after philandering husbands and wandering through the shit parts of town looking for wayward teens.'

'I'm not sure why you think you get to tell me what to do?' Becky said coolly, flipping her long wavy blonde hair over her shoulder. 'If I want to do some occasional pro bono internet research for your mom's detective agency-'

'Private investigations-' I interjected.

'-whatever. I'm going to do it.'

'Fine. Fine. Just, promise me you won't go after these people, like, in real life.'

'Sure, sure. Whatever. Now can we please go?' She carried her coffee mug as she headed for the door. 'Thanks for the coffee. Do you want anything from the market?'

'Yeah, actually- can you get me a bunch of the usual stuff?' I rummaged around in a lower cupboard and handed Robbie a canvas shopping tote.

'You got it. I'll leave it downstairs on the steps and send you a text,' Becky said.

I raised my coffee mug in reply, and Robbie, who was already halfway down the stairs, yelled up 'Bye, Ma,' his voice loaded with irritation.

'Don't worry about him,' Becky said, rolling her eyes again. 'He'll get over it.'

'I know,' I smiled.

A little over an hour later, I received a text from Becky that my groceries were on the step, and I went down to retrieve them. The canvas tote was packed full of fresh fruits and vegetables, and she added a little jar of specialty honey too.

I held the door open with my foot as I heaved the heavy bag inside with my right arm, cradling my nearly useless left arm against my chest.

Back in my apartment, I sorted and washed the produce, then prepped my breakfast: a kale blueberry protein smoothie. Yes, it's as terrible as it sounds.

I go to my physical therapy, and to my boxing lessons, even if I can only really fight with fifty percent of my arms. I keep my apartment clean and run on the weekends. I drink a lot of kale smoothies. So, Robbie mostly leaves me alone about my private investigating.

At least he did until Becky took an interest in helping me out occasionally, and now I suspected I'd be getting some fresh grief now and again.

A New Case

I was keeping busy on an otherwise wide-open day by cleaning up the hard drive of one of my laptops when a woman pulled her car into the parking space to the side of my building.

She walked with hurried steps to my office door. I closed

everything I was working on and stood up to greet her when she came in.

'I'm looking for uh, D. Ostrov- Ostro-'

'Oshtrovsky.'

'Are you them? The private investigator?'

'I am. Can I help you?'

'Yes, please, I hope so. It's my niece. My niece is missing.'

The woman was older than me by about a decade and was exactly what you'd expect an aunt to look like. Her clothes and shoes were high quality, but comfortable and casual, and her graying brown hair was cut in a sensible bob. Her designer handbag was enormous, and made a loud thud when she set it down on my desk.

'Did you call the police?' I asked, sitting again and gesturing toward a chair. She sat down hard and let out a huffy breath.

'Yes, of course! That's the first thing I did, I've just come from there- I was at the station for hours.'

'What did they say?'

'They said that she's *not missing*. That she left on her own- that there's nothing wrong.'

'Okay. Let's start at the beginning. What is your name?'

'Lennette. Lennette Golding, I'm from Nebraska, I just arrived this morning.'

'Alright, Mrs. Golding-'

'Just call me Lennette.'

THE GIRL WHO DIDN'T GO

'-Lennette, did you come because you were concerned about your niece?'

'No- that's just it-' Her words came fast and breathlessly, and I could tell she'd already told this story, probably a few times. 'I visit every six months. Like clockwork. She was expecting me. She wouldn't just take off when she knew I was coming into town. My trip was planned; it's almost the same thing every time. I treat her- we do a spa day, we go out to eat, do a little antiquing in Wetherville and watch movies 'til late. Drink a lot of wine. Spend too much money. That sort of thing.'

'That sounds nice. Why do the police think she's not actually missing?'

'They ran her credit cards or ID or something, I'm not sure. They said her passport was used, that she got on a plane and is currently en route to Mexico.'

I frowned, but kept my thoughts to myself. *That was fast.*

Jennette looked panicky. 'What, what is it? I can tell you are thinking something.'

'It's, er, nothing. I'm assuming you're not getting any replies from your niece's mobile phone?'

'That's just it- I *am*.'

Now I was confused. 'Okay, Lennette, I'm not sure what you're expecting here. She's replying to you, she's used her passport, she's an adult. Maybe she just went, you know, spontaneously. Maybe a love interest is whisking her away on some romantic retreat, and she got so caught up she forgot you were coming.'

'No.'

I was not seeing a case here, but I had to admit something about it felt off. Maybe it was just because she was so adamant. Her mouth was set in a defiant line, and she looked at me directly in the eyeballs. I sighed. 'Alright, why do you still think there's a problem?'

'I don't *think* it, I *know* it. For one thing, the text messages. They're not like her at all. They're brief, and monosyllabic. Look, look at how she *normally* texts me.'

She held up her phone and scrolled back through a longwinded text chain that showed lengthy conversation with complete sentences, full word use, almost no abbreviations or shortcut phrases. These ended two days prior. Then the most recent ones, which were exactly as she'd described- brief, blunt and dismissive. Plenty of acronyms. No in-depth answers, and some messages were completely ignored. One that stood out to me was Lennette asking *Are you okay?* And getting no reply for hours. The reply was cool, distant and noncommittal. That was yesterday morning.

'I assume you've also tried calling?'

'Of course. And it just goes straight to voice mail. I've left numerous messages.'

'I see that you don't discuss your trip in the recent texts- you didn't mention it at all.'

'Right, well, we'd talked about it a week back- I can scroll through and show you-'

'That's okay.'

'And we emailed about it, a few days ago, I don't remember exactly. I forwarded her my itinerary, we talked about our plans. I always go to sleep as early as possible for a few nights before I travel here so I can adjust a little better to the time difference. Janelle knows this, so she'd email me during the day while she was at work. According to her they frown on personal phone use at her office.'

'Makes sense. But, the short messages, they could be indicative of her heading to the airport, maybe in and out of cabs, lots going on, perhaps she will get in touch with you when she lands?'

'That's the other thing- she's positively *terrified* of airplanes. She would never, ever, ever fly. *Ever.* That's why I come to her! That's why I come here, every time.'

'Maybe she just took a Valium?' I was reaching, and she knew it.

'Absolutely not!'

Geez. I get it, I get it! 'Alright, I'll take your case. Let me get some preliminary info from you. And I'll give you an invoice with my fee schedule.'

'That's fine, it's fine, just show me where to sign the paper and I'll write you a check.'

'First things first,' I said, waking up my laptop, 'What's your niece's name?'

'Janelle Stevenson.'

We spent a few moments going over identifying information, addresses and background about her niece. Janelle was an only child, and her parents, Lennette's brother and his wife, had been deceased for years. The wife passed from cancer when Janelle was little, and the father died from a heart attack a few years ago. Lennette and Janelle had always been close, but since her brother's death, Lennette made it a point to stay in consistent, loving contact with Janelle, like a second mother. She sent me several photos of Janelle from her phone, which I saved to the file as well as to my own phone.

'You said the police checked her credit cards, did they give you the printouts?'

'No, but I read them and I have an excellent memory.'

'Okay, what did you see?'

'The ticket was purchased on Savan Airlines, and the resort was called La Bastian. It's a hotel and spa. I looked it up while I was at the station, it's in Puerto Vallarta.'

'Let's call the resort, and see if we can get your niece-'

'It's not my niece. I don't know who it is but it's *not her*.'

'Sorry, let's see what the resort says about *whoever it is* that booked the room, and when they arrive we can try to get them on the phone. I'll check the flight schedules. Help yourself to some coffee or water or something,' I said, gesturing toward the kitchen off to the side of the office.

'Thank you, thank you,' Lennette said, standing and walking across the room. She quietly fixed herself a cup of coffee and asked me if I'd like one too. I shook my head.

'It looks like there is only one flight today on Savan Airlines that can take you to Puerto Vallarta; it has a connection in Charlotte. The plane on the second leg is due to land in about... um... thirty-five minutes. Give it another hour or two after that to collect luggage, get a cab or rent a car, and arrive at the resort. So, while we wait, tell me more about your niece.'

The Apartment

'I'll do you one better than that,' Lennette said, pointing a finger at me while she spoke. 'I'll take you to her apartment.'

'That's a great idea. We can talk on the way.' I shut down my laptop and locked it in my desk drawer, then grabbed my coat and watchman's cap and followed her out the door.

I sent Becky a text message to tell her what was up and

where I was going, and she responded with a double thumbs up, which meant she turned on the tracking software we had linked between our phones. Can't be too careful.

Lennette insisted on driving; on the way to the apartment, she told me more about Janelle's habits and interests, dating life, names of friends and so on.

'Does she have any pets?'

'No, she has allergies.'

'Gotcha.'

Janelle's apartment was in a rental community comprised of a series of ten or so white stucco buildings lined up in tidy rows along new streets named things like 'Partridge Place' and 'Sparrow Row'. It was previously an industrial area that had been overhauled and the condos were an improvement over the run-down factories that had been here for years, even though they had very little personality and were probably way overpriced.

Minimal landscaping between the buildings lent a sparse feeling to the place, but it was clean and tidy, and I'm sure was brightened up nicely with flowers and such in the spring and summer. The parking and common areas were well-lit and easy to navigate. The community was too new for it to start showing wear and tear; it appeared to still have responsible landlords; well, give it a decade or so and it would probably start to look like crap the way they always do.

Lennette led the way, walking swiftly, and pulled out a mess of keys and keyrings from the bottomless purse, flipping through them until she landed on the key to Janelle's apartment.

A small pile of mail was on the floor under the door slot, but it wasn't possible to tell exactly how many days worth there was. Lennette collected it and placed it in a tidy stack upon the table inside the front door.

Upon entering, my first impression of Janelle was that she seemed rather, well, *normal*. Her decor was friendly and inviting but wasn't anything that stood out; it was mostly items purchased from standard home stores, with the exception of a few affordable antiques, probably acquired during her outings with Lennette. Nothing customized or artisanal. I was struck by how easy it was to sound judgemental, but in order to understand as much as I could about a person, I needed to make rapid analyzations of what I could see, and from what I was looking at, Janelle was just a plain old normie.

She only had a few books that were popular titles, some romances and a few mysteries. She had a small television resting upon an affordable stand. Her furniture matched- clearly it was purchased as a set. She made an effort: her throw pillows and rug coordinated, and her end tables had well-used coasters. Scented candles in glass jars were scattered around the apartment, some had been burned, others had not.

Her dining table was small and old but clean; when I ran a finger along her kitchen counters I detected no crumbs or residues.

The dishwasher had been run recently even though it was mostly empty; the plastic containers inside had a few marks from dried water droplets on them, but they were cold to the touch. The sinks and tub were dry, as were all of the towels.

The trashcans were empty and had fresh liners, and the bed was made. Curtains and shades were closed, and one lamp was on in the living room. The thermostat was programmed to stay at a low temperature.

Everything was set the way one would do it when planning to be away from home for a few days or more.

I glanced at Lennette. She was watching me, with her eyes as wide as dinner plates. I could feel her anxiety pulsating in the air. When Janelle failed to pick her up from the airport, she'd hired a car and driven herself here. She had told me on the way over, that she'd taken one swift look around, hadn't touched anything, and went straight to the police station.

No doubt she'd seen everything I was seeing, and was terrified I would tell her there was nothing to worry about, and she would be left alone to fret. Her sheer terror was so palpable that I became convinced there was something wrong, the problem was, now I had to find out what it was.

I frowned and walked down the hall and went back into the bedroom. I stood at the foot of the bed and closed my eyes for a second, then opened them again and looked at the room under the assumption that there *was* something wrong.

Everything seemed so right, so tidy, so carefully done. The apartment practically screamed 'on vacation'. It was perfect.

But... one phrase began to whisper at the back of my mind, until it was positively screaming inside my skull- *too perfect*.

I needed to find something that was missing. Or that *should* be missing. Something that either should be here or shouldn't. I had no idea what. But I knew I needed to find it. Sure sure. No worries.

I opened the closet, the drawers, the nightstands. I looked at them as though I was Janelle, living there every day, going about my business.

I checked her underwear, socks, toiletries. I checked the hamper and the medicine cabinet.

'Lennette,' I called, 'what is Janelle allergic to?'

She appeared at the doorway to the bedroom. 'So many things. Pet dander, pollen, some medications. Do you want me to make a list?'

'No,' I said, pulling out an item from the medicine cupboard and holding it up. 'But would she ever travel without this?'

Lennette's face went pale, and tears filled her eyes. She shook her head and held out her hand, and I gave her the Epi-pen. 'No, she would never leave without this,' she said quietly. 'If she did, she could potentially die.'

'Does she have a spare? Say, one that she would keep in her purse so she can leave this one here?'

Lennette shook her head. 'She had to use one last week because of an ingredient in her takeout that wasn't supposed to be in there. The pharmacy gives her two at a time. She takes it with her wherever she goes, and when she comes home, she puts it in here- I told her... I said 'pick a spot where it will be, all the time, anytime you are home. Like, when you put your keys on the same hook all the time so you never lose them. That way, when you're in a panic, you don't have to try to remember where it is'.'

'That's good advice.'

'If she was going to travel, she'd take two of them with her.' Lennette wiped tears away from her face. 'Something terrible has happened, hasn't it?'

'We don't know anything for sure yet. But we'll figure this out,' I said quietly, touching her arm. I felt I already knew the answer to what I asked her next, but I needed to hear it.

'Is she always this tidy? Does her apartment always look like this?'

At my question she broke out in loud sobs, everything she'd been holding in came out at once. I grabbed some toilet tissue and handed her a wad of it to use to blow her nose.

'No!' she cried, 'It's always a mess! Well, like, you know, not *dirty*, but there would be toothpaste in the sink, or used coffee mugs, or clothes piled on the chair, or shoes all over the floor! She cleans up before I come visit, but not like *this*.'

'Lennette, I am going to need you to try to think. You need to think about everything you know about Janelle's life. Right now I'm going to start tearing this place apart. I want you to stay calm. You might feel like I'm being invasive, or rude, or intruding on her privacy. So I want you to be prepared to feel that way. I'm going to be as thorough as possible, and I'm going to see things that may be embarrassing. Do you understand? Do you think you can help?'

She nodded, and threw her tissue in the trash can. 'Yes. Yes. I can do it. What are we looking for?"

We walked together toward the living room. 'We can start with paperwork: pay stubs, receipts,' I said, 'anything we can use to paint a picture of Janelle's life and track her movements over the last few days. I don't see a laptop. Do you know if she has one?'

'Yes she does, but, I don't see it anywhere.'

'Okay, what's the name of the company where she works?'

'IEE or EIA or something like that? It a few letters strung together; they do importing or car parts, or something.. I can barely think straight right now.'

'It's okay, we'll figure it out. Let's get started, you let me know if it gets to be too much for you.'

'I'm fine, I'm fine... Let's do it.'

'I'm going to call in some help.'

Becky, My Intrepid (Unpaid) Assistant

Becky had the uncanny ability to find anything on the internet. She was savvy and determined in ways that even I found bewildering.

I'm not one of those people who can't handle new tech- in fact, I manage just fine on my own, and have decent computers, phones, cameras and other devices that are helpful in my line of work. I used bugs and trace programs and surveillance equipment of all sorts. And I have two computer whizzes who I consult sometimes; both of whom were clients at first, who've come through for me more than once.

But when I tell Becky I need to find out what someone has been doing online, she's able to find things that surprise even me.

And lately, since her windchime business took off and was largely self-regulating, she found she had more time on her hands. Well, what am I gonna do when she asks me if she can help out around the office? Say no?

At first I think she just wanted somewhere to sit and knit without feeling lonesome. Robbie and Becky met in law school, and married in a courthouse in Colorado; most of her family was from the Pacific Northwest, and she didn't know anyone here on the east coast when they first moved here.

I didn't particularly enjoy ruminating on that time in my life; the two of them chose this region to live and set up Robbie's legal career based on the fact that I'd been nearly done in. While I was fine hiring a nurse for my care once I was free to leave the hospital, they decided to come to look after me, and stayed on once I'd recuperated despite my objections. They initially stayed in my house, but Robbie's commute was too far, so they bought their house closer to his office and I moved with them.

Robbie helped me navigate all my legal and medical paperwork, the sale of my home, and the eventual purchase of my building. The idea was to give me someplace small which I'd be able to manage the care of on my own, while also bringing in a little income. Moping around by myself in my new building led me to make the decision to open my agency, instead of renting out the office space as I'd originally planned.

Becky made friends locally in the subsequent years but by that point, coming to my office to hang out with me had become a regular routine. No complaints. I was used to a noisy bullpen at the police station, or having a partner with me most of the time. I didn't much like the quiet hours alone, either. A lot of the people she made friends with were corporate business people or lawyer types; they spent their days in offices or courthouses, with busy schedules. She socialized regularly with her peers but found many of her days had unoccupied hours.

When they first moved here and bought their (at the time) ramshackle house, Becky scoured all the local shops for windchimes for their porch but ended up hating the noises they made. She complained about it so much it made me cross-eyed. For the life of me I couldn't figure out why she was devoting so much time and effort to something that seemed so frivolous. But then, she told me about her grandmother, who had a set of chimes in her garden for her whole life; and Becky just wanted something similar to the sound they made. But they'd been a handmade set, brought over from Ireland when her grandmother had emigrated. They were impossible to replicate. Well, nearly impossible. She spent a year designing and redesigning windchimes.

Meeting with metalworkers and carpenters. Sourcing materials and testing prototypes. She was relentless. I never wanted to hear about or see or talk about another goddamn windchime again. But once she had the design right, she set up contracts with manufacturers and distributors. And now? I admit, she really created a beautiful product. I had two sets hanging from my apartment fire escape; they made the most incredible sound. And, well, apparently the bears in north Finland were no match for them. Mindboggling. So, it's like I said. When Becky is determined, nothing gets in her way.

The way she put it, law school made her never want to practice law. So, windchimes it is. And knitting. And home renovations.

I knew she wasn't totally disinterested in practicing law; but she always resisted Robbie's suggestions that she take the bar exam, and frankly he knew better than to push it. They weren't hurting for money, and she wasn't someone I'd call idle.

She handled nearly all of their home renovations herself; one morning I walked into their foyer, to pick up some items she'd gotten for me from a specialty shop an hour away, to be greeted by a toilet sitting in the hallway. She had decided *that* was the day the old tile on the powder-room floor *had* to come up, and she'd removed the fixtures, sledge-hammered the tile, repaired the sub-floor and laid new tile herself all before Robbie got home from work that evening. I ordered us up some lunch and reminded her to take breaks occasionally. The best help I could give her when she was eyeballs deep into a home reno project was to get out of the way.

Their house looked amazing, well half of it anyway was like a magazine spread.

But currently, in the kitchen there were no counters or cabinet doors, and there was a folding table next to the stove to use as a surface for food prep. A few sets of shelves served as a pantry and last time I was there, a metal folding chair was holding the coffee pot and the toaster next to a wall so they could be plugged in.

There was a sunroom on the back of the house that had so many broken glass panes that it practically rained inside every time it rained outside. The floor was made of slate tiles that sometimes had a bit of ivy or morning glory vines that poked up from the crawlspace below, until Becky got around to pulling them up before they could do any more damage.

Some of the unused bedrooms were stripped down to the bare plaster and their windows had no curtains, but it was comfortable and quiet, which I had first-hand knowledge of, for that's where I spent my time recuperating. And damn that incredible wallpaper in the foyer blew me away every time I went over.

I knew whatever Becky did with the rest of the house would be amazing, and I didn't mind spending the occasional weekday, when my case load was slow (dead) travelling with her to various home improvement stores for this or that.

The Search Begins

Becky arrived at Janelle's apartment a short time after I phoned her, and at my request, began searching for any information she could find about Janelle online, starting with the names of the companies and organizations whose paperwork I found. Lennette and I weren't getting far with the small amount of paperwork we found in a filing cabinet beside the couch.

I assumed like most people, Janelle managed most of her life online. I myself use mostly paperless billing and accounting, so I wasn't surprised at how little we actually were able to glean from the filing cabinet.

Copies of the previous years' tax returns, some random mailings from her banks or insurance companies detailing account or policy changes, the paperwork for her apartment lease, her car. Not much that could tell me how she spent her every day life.

Her kitchen had standard groceries, some produce in the fridge which was relatively fresh, some leftovers. No takeout, no wrappers, no receipts. No paper record of the last week or so.

'Her online presence is relatively unremarkable,' Becky said without judgment. 'She has pics of herself out to eat or hiking, hanging out with friends. No steady boyfriends- er, or girlfriends- partners.'

'She dated a little,' Lennette said, sighing. 'But she was shy.'

'She hasn't posted anything in a few days, but if you look back through her history, that's not dissimilar to her normal activity.'

'Is there any indication she was planning a trip? Anything about buying new clothes or wishful thinking stuff- you know, 'I can't wait for the beach' kinds of posts?' I asked.

'Nothing.'

I sighed, and tidied the pile of papers I was looking through. 'You two stay here and keep at it, I'm going to go door-to-door to ask the neighbors if they saw anything. I'll be back in a bit.'

Based on the quality of the text responses in Lennette's phone, I was confident I could approximate the time when something in Janelle's life went amiss, which would be helpful in speaking with the neighbors.

I knocked on about fifteen doors that from what I could tell, potentially had a vantage point of sight or sound on activity from Janelle's apartment, the stairwell or the parking lot attached to her building. Only about half of the residents answered, and of those, only two were familiar with her at all.

One neighbor only knew her well enough to say hello, but hadn't seen her in weeks as they worked opposite schedules, and the other neighbor, Pat, had seen her the day before she (possibly) went missing, but knew nothing about any travel plans or romantic partners.

Pat told me she'd often have neighborly exchanges with Janelle, trading cookies or the odd cup of sugar, and that since she'd done so before, she felt sure that if Janelle was planning to go on a trip, she would have told Pat, so Pat could come in and water her plants.

'Do you have a key to her apartment?' I asked.

'No,' Pat replied. 'She leaves one with me when she's going to be away.'

'Okay, thanks for your time. If you remember anything... anything she might have said to you, or anyone you might have seen her with, can you give me a call?'

Pat's face went a bit pale as she nodded and accepted the business card I offered to her.

It was closing in on the time when we might be able to get some answers at the resort, and I wondered if I should try to find a quiet spot to make the calls away from Lennette. She was showing understandable signs of stress, and in these situations, creating a little distance to handle some aspects of the investigations was often best for the family of the potential victims.

I found a spot near the staircase that was shielded from the cold wind and the light flurries, and I pulled my coat tighter around myself. It was supposed to be secured with four toggles but one had come off and was currently rattling around in a drawer in my kitchen; I held the coat closed where the button was missing while I dialed the number.

The reception phone was answered after only one ring and I asked if Janelle Stevenson had arrived. The receptionist typed into her keyboard and confirmed that she had indeed checked in. I knew they couldn't give me her room number so I didn't ask, instead, I requested that I be put through. After several rings, the room phone was picked up, but then it was immediately slammed down again.

Okay, well, first of all, ouch, and secondly, now I knew that someone claiming to be Janelle had checked into a Mexican resort and had no interest in taking phone calls.

Well, shit. I guess I was going to Mexico.

Mexico

I relayed what had transpired when I came back into Janelle's apartment. We tidied up and locked the door as we left. Before the door shut, I secured a small string to the doorjam, which would fall down silently, and hopefully without attracting attention, if anyone else came in. Sometimes old school is the best.

Becky went home and promised to keep searching the internet about anything to do with Janelle, and get us as much information as she could on anyone who regularly interacted with her online.

Lennette not only insisted on accompanying me on the trip she also paid for my airfare up front. Was I going to complain? Certainly not. I wished all my clients had this kind of money to throw around. Maybe I wouldn't have a window in the front of my office that desperately needed a better paint job. The next flight to Puerto Vallarta was tomorrow, late morning, the same flight path that the person using Janelle's passport had taken.

I only packed a small carryon, and Lennette, since she had just flown in and hadn't even opened her suitcase yet, was already good to go.

She called her husband back home and after some hushed arguing which I did my best not to listen to, he arranged to

30

overnight her passport directly to my office. It arrived in the morning, within minutes of us needing to leave to make it to the airport on time.

During the evening that we were in my apartment preparing to travel, and while we were en route, we each tried repeatedly to contact the resort and the occupant of Janelle's suite. We were unsuccessful with every attempt, which I found unsurprising.

By the time we were on our first flight, the text messages to Lennette's phone had ceased entirely. The phone in the hotel room just rang and rang. The person didn't even bother picking it up to slam it back down again anymore.

We had to run, literally, throught the Charlotte airport to make our connection, and we arrived in Puerto Vallarta in the afternoon. A taxi took us to the resort, and when we arrived shortly thereafter, we had to walk past a police cruiser in the valet driveway on our way into the lobby.

'Don't panic,' I said to Lennette, who eyed the police car.

She took a deep breath and let it out slowly as we approached the reception desk.

I greeted the receptionist, whose name tag read 'Marie'. 'We are here to see a guest, a Janelle Stevenson. Can you phone her room and ask her to come down?'

All of the color ran from Marie's face and she began to apologize profusely.

'What's going on?' Lennette asked, clutching the edge of the countertop.

I glanced up as a man approached. He reached into his coat pocket and pulled out a leather wallet, which he flipped open to show his credentials.

'Sergeant Gomez,' he said, abruptly. 'Who are you, and why are you looking for Janelle Stevenson?'

'I'm her aunt, Lennette Golding, and this is my, uh, friend,' Lennette said, defiantly puffing out her chest. 'And someone better tell me *right now*, what has happened to my niece.'

'I'm very sorry,' the sergeant said, his eyebrows knitting together in a sympathetic frown. 'But it appears your niece has gone missing.'

'Oh, bloody hell,' I muttered.

'She requested room service, and when the server arrived, he found her door ajar, her room rifled through, and I'm very sorry, madam, but there are signs of a struggle.'

'Can I see the room?' I asked.

He levelled a gaze at me, and I didn't falter as I returned it. I held out my hand. 'D. Oshtrovsky, Private Investigator. Mrs. Golding hired me to find her niece. We tracked her here. And now, it seems, we've arrived too late.'

He waved a hand at an officer who was standing nearby. He gave the officer rapid instructions in Spanish, and then looked back at us. 'Officer Roman will take you to see the room, don't touch anything. Mrs. Golding, perhaps you will sit with me for a moment, and you can tell me what it is that brought your niece here, and why you had to follow her.'

He moved toward the lounge area in the lobby, and motioned for Lennette to join him.

She turned around and said to me, loudly, 'Let me take your bag.' Then she leaned close to my ear as she pulled my carry-on off of my shoulder. She whispered, 'He told his officer to watch you, note any movements you make, what you look at and what you say, and to make sure you don't touch anything- especially not the 'weapon'.'

I nodded once in reply.

I followed the uni to the elevators and we went together up to the fourth floor, and down a long corridor. Another officer stood outside the door to room 415, and he nodded at us as we approached.

They both accompanied me inside. The room was small, and had a nice view overlooking the pool and some hills receding into the distance. The sunshine was only blotted out for a moment here or there as a thick cloud quickly passed before it.

In contrast to the cheerful scene outside, the room was in chaos. There were lamps broken, furniture and bedclothes in disarray, and a suitcase opened on the floor, its contents spread out around the room.

I stepped forward, placed my foot very purposefully, and listened carefully as the bath towel sitting beside the broken ceramic lamp crunched beneath the toe of my boot.

'Don't touch anything,' Roman ordered and I nodded in reply. I paused for several moments to look at a broken chair leg, sitting on the carpet, with flecks of what was clearly drying blood splattered on the jagged end.

A passport sat open on the desk under the only unbroken lamp and the phone, the cord to which was unplugged from the wall.

Janelle Stevenson's face looked up at me.

A Theory

After a grueling two hours of questioning by the Sergeant, we were released (once he was able to confirm Stateside that we were indeed who we said we were, and he was satisfied that we were just as surprised as anyone else to find the resort room in such a state). He promised that he would keep us informed of any developments. Not that I expected any- but I didn't tell him that.

Lennette's face was red from crying, and her voice was hoarse from the hours of answering every question he lobbed at us, then re-worded and repeated. We had to find somewhere to go and wait for a while; the earliest flight home was a redeye. We gave up after a few minutes of a discussion about whether we should find a restaurant or cafe, and just decided to wait at the airport.

Sergeant Gomez's tone was much softer and maybe a bit sympathetic, as he kindly instructed an officer to drive us back to the terminal.

Once we'd arrived and both had a chance to wash up in the bathrooms, we found a quiet corner to wait out the next few hours. I relayed to Lennette what I'd seen in the room that was rented by whomever had used Janelle's passport- someone who I was now certain was an imposter.

'How can you be sure?' Lennette asked me, pacing in front of the window, watching planes taxiing and airport workers running to and fro across the tarmac.

'The room was staged- I'm sure of it,' I said. 'Whoever did it used a towel to mask the sound as they smashed the lamps. You wrap the item like so-' I took my jacket and wrapped it around my arm. 'Then, you put it on the floor and stomp on it. It breaks the glass, or lamp, but you can't get all the pieces out of the towel. Especially if you're in a hurry. They left the passport laying wide open on the table, under the unbroken lamp. The phone cord was simply unplugged, it wasn't ripped or torn out. The tables were all upright- and their surfaces were highly polished. Not a single one was scratched- which you would see quite a bit of if the lamps and other decor were hurled off of them. And the clothes from the suitcase? A mishmash of items from Janelle's closet at home. There was a turtleneck and wool pants for chrissake. Would she pack a turtleneck and wool pants for a trip here?'

'No, more like swimsuits and summer dresses I imagine,' Lennette said.

'Exactly. And the clothes were not thrown around, they were draped- after the room was destroyed.'

'How can you tell?'

'There were clothes *on top* of the broken shards from one lamp.'

'Wow, you saw a lot in just a few moments. What about the blood?'

'The chances of it being matched to your niece are slim to none. It would take weeks, if not months, for the Mexican authorities to coordinate with people back home to find and compare blood type, or DNA or whatever. In fact, I'm sure whoever planned all this was counting on just that- which is why they went through the trouble of sending the imposter all the way down here, instead of say, the south coast or Pacific northwest, or even just a state or two away.'

Lennette stopped pacing and looked at me. 'You think all of this is some part of a big plan?'

I shook my head from side to side in dismay. 'I've been going over it and over it. And the questions I keep asking myself are 'why go through all this trouble?' 'why more than one elaborate ruse?' You'd only do this if there was something to hide. Something big. And you were sure this plan would work.'

'Like... murder?' Lennette whispered.

'Let's not think the worst right now.' I tried to change the subject. 'So you speak perfect Spanish? I only have a little. Enough for a light conversation.'

'I taught Spanish levels three and four in community college for thirty years.'

'Oh, wow, that's great.'

'Yeah. Came in handy today, didn't it? The sergeant had no idea I was fluent, and I thought I'd keep it to myself while we were at the station. I learned he has very little hope of finding anything beyond what was at the resort. The woman who checked in looked just like my Janelle in all the ways that counted: height, hair color, and so on.'

'Of course she could have been wearing a wig,' I offered.

'Right. So they're just assuming it was her, and that she was kidnapped. To me, he implied very heavily that she might have been down here for illegal reasons, and that her criminal life just caught up to her.'

'So from what you gathered they're not terribly motivated to find out what happened?'

Lennette nodded. 'Unfortunately it appears that way. Apparently this mystery woman was blunt and quick with the workers, wore large sunglasses and a hat, and spoke no Spanish. She didn't tip the boy who carried her luggage upstairs and she ordered her room service in English. The kitchen said she seemed pissed when she called down for her meal, but that's about all I could get out of the conversations he was having with his officers.'

'That's a lot of information, and I must say for someone who isn't a detective you've certainly been very observant, all things considered.'

'I feel panicky. I'd say that I'm normally sharp but right now I feel like a bullet train.'

'You need to slow down, or you're going to collapse. Let's find a restaurant and eat some dinner. All this adrenaline coursing through you can't be healthy.'

Lennette nodded and grabbed her suitcase. By the time dinner was done, I could see she was crashing. We headed to our gate, making our way slowly, for we had loads of time.

'We know someone impersonating your niece went through the trouble of making themselves known, and then setting up a time where the room would be discovered then reported. But the biggest question is why? Are you absolutely certain Janelle wasn't mixed up in anything illegal? Drugs? Gambling?'

'I'll bet my life on it. She was too shy to order her own food at restaurants for most of her life. There's no way she's suddenly developed the balls to get involved in something illicit.'

'These things can start slowly, you know,' I said, quietly. 'A little loan here, a little bet there, someone coercing Janelle into storing a bag for them, or holding some money for them. Someone she thinks would never hurt her?'

Lennette shook her head, sadly. 'I guess anything's possible, but it just seems so unlikely. I'd say that Janelle could be very trusting, sure... I guess I only see the best in her. But when you put it that way, it's possible she might have listened to the wrong person. Especially if maybe, she cared for them.'

I nodded. I didn't know enough to hope for anything at this point, but if Janelle was as nice as Lennette made her out to be, there was a good chance she was easy to manipulate, or terrify, into doing something dangerous.

'I've been meaning to ask,' Lennette said, 'What does the D. stand for?'

I smirked a bit. It wasn't the first time I'd been asked that question and wouldn't be the last. 'Dea.'

'Yeah, the D. in your name?'

'Oh, I know. It stands for Dea. D-E-A. Dea.'

'Your name is Dea? Why don't you just use Dea- er, D-E-A instead of D- the letter D?'

'Yeeup. It's actually pronounced Day-uh. But everyone would say 'Dee'. And I got tired of correcting them. And then people ask me what Dea is short for. Eventually I just shortened it to the one letter.'

She let out a soft chuckle. 'Oh, so you just can't win, eh?'

'Exactly.'

We both slept a little on the plane, not soundly, but at least it was something.

Becky met us at the airport. I couldn't wait to get into my own shower. 'Lennette,' I said, 'I'm not sure how much more I can use your help currently. We have a lot of research to do, and I've got a lot of ground to cover. And things could get a little... well...'

'Dicey,' Becky offered.

'Right. So I think it's best for you to start planning to head home.'

'That's not happening.'

I sighed. 'Alright, but I can't bring you everywhere I might need to go. Are you sure you want to stay local?'

'I'm not leaving until I have answers. I've already made a reservation here at the airport hotel. I can't stand the idea of being in Janelle's apartment alone.'

I didn't say out loud what I was thinking- wondering if that was safe anyway- I left it alone.

'Are you sure?' Becky asked.

'Yes. I've been thinking about it since we were back in Mexico. I'm retired! I've got nothing else to do, nowhere else to be right now, not that I'd be able to focus on it if I did. My husband can look after himself, the house and the dogs just fine on his own. And that way if you need me, I'll be minutes away.'

'Okay,' I said. 'We'll drop you off. Call me if you think of anything, and I'll check in with you as much as possible about whatever I find.'

'Thanks, both of you,' she said as she climbed out of the car outside the hotel.

As we drove away, I asked Becky, 'Did you find out anything while we were gone?'

'Yeah. Janelle worked for a company called IEI-International Electrical Imports. They focus primarily on electrical engine parts for cars, but also service niche industries like marine and small recreational vehicles.'

'Sounds boring.'

'Yeah, even their website is dull. But they're a subsidiary of a larger corporation, and finding out info on that entity hasn't been as easy."

'Okay. What did she do there?'

'Well, she's not listed on their website under their 'team' but that only shows the principals, not the rest of the workers. So from what I can gather she did basic admin stuff. Filing, answering phones, filling orders.'

'Okay, well, that's shitty that they don't bother to include their support staff in their team bios but whatever. It's as good a place to start as any. Maybe she had some friends there.'

'She did- one girl I've been able to trace, named Abby Wilkins, had tagged Janelle in a few photos on social media last year. And *her* professional bio on *another* site lists IEI as a former employer.'

'That's great work Becky.'

'Thanks, you can buy me lunch.'

'I planned to anyway.'

Back at my apartment while we waited for the food to arrive, I showered and then did some careful, gentle exercises to relieve some of the tension that had built up in my left side from the stress of travelling, being awake so long, and the cramped seat on the plane.

I told Becky everything we'd learned from Sergeant Gomez and what I'd seen in the resort room.

'What could Janelle have possible gotten mixed up in that someone would go through so much trouble?' Becky wondered, digging her chopsticks around in a container of Szechuan chicken. 'I mean, was it really her in Mexico? Did she stage her own disappearance? Or was she running away and someone was coming after her, and they caught up to her there?'

'I'd also think something similar, if her apartment here wasn't so carefully cleaned and orderly,' I said, holding out my hand. She passed me the container.

'Right, right. So... what you're thinking is someone orchestrated both sites?'

'My theory,' I said, trying to not be overly rude as I spoke through a mouthful, 'which I haven't shared with Lennette, is that Janelle went missing, or was possibly killed, here- right here at home. And whoever was involved decided to cover it up with a spontaneous trip to Mexico; where she would conveniently 'go missing'. Never to be found of course.'

'Because she was never actually in Mexico.'

'Right. But the authorities would think she was, and then the trail would go cold and never lead anywhere.'

Becky nodded thoughtfully. 'And then all the bureaucratic red tape between the two countries would keep things nice and murky and slow for a long time-'

'If not forever.'

'Clever.'

'And insidious,' I added, shovelling rice into my mouth.

'That too.'

'No one who participated in the planning- and this had to involve several people- took Lennette or me into consideration. That tells me they must not have known Janelle that well, or else they might have known she was expecting her aunt, or she was terrified of flying. Hopefully it won't be their only mistake.'

'Right, oh shit, I have to go. I've forwarded everything I found to your email, so you can review it again later. Text me tomorrow and let me know if I can help with anything else.'

'Will do. Thanks, Becky.'

'No problem.'

I heard Becky and Chuck say hello to one another on the landing and I glanced at the clock. Chuck would just be heading out to cover the door at La Chatte. I smiled at the thought of him often coming home from there in the wee hours, covered in glitter. The girls would get it on the customers, the customers would get handsy with the girls, and then Chuck would throw out those customers. Third-hand glitter.

I packed up the leftover Chinese food to have again for a meal later, and spent the rest of the day going through everything that Becky had sent to my work email.

I fell asleep on my couch sometime in the evening, and then woke around two with a crick in my neck. I shuffled to the bedroom and didn't wake again until late the next morning.

Time to Hit the Pavement

I looked up the address of the company where Abby Wilkins currently worked, and entered it into my car's GPS.

Small, thin snowflakes drifted down around my car at every red light, and tried to settle on the windshield. I set the wipers on low, and by the time I'd arrived at the business complex, a soft layer of snow had settled in the corners of my car windows and along the sides of the roads.

The complex housed numerous businesses. Quite a few of them had names such 'Raymond Co.' or 'Howell Industries' and I had literally no idea what type of business they conducted. But the suite I was looking for was easy enough to find, and I parked and went inside.

At the front desk I asked for Abby Wilkins and gave my name. The office was done in a standard color palette of beiges and grays, with blocks of workstations in the middle of a large room, and private offices lining the sides. Quiet clerical work sounded all around me- phones ringing, clicking keyboards, softly spoken words. I felt out of place in my old coat, Docs, and worn out winter cap, and I guessed that after I left Abby would probably face plenty of questions from bored, curious colleagues about the nature of my visit.

She emerged from an office at the back, and was clearly

perplexed as she met me in the foyer. 'Hi, do we have an appointment?'

'No, I'm sorry, I'm D. Oshtrovsky. Can we speak privately?'

'What is this about?'

'Janelle Stevenson.'

Abby's brows knitted together in a frown, and she said, 'Uh, sure. This way, please.'

We went back into her office, and I sat down in the guest chair as she shut the door. 'Is Janelle okay? What is going on? Who are you?' she asked.

'That's what I'm trying to find out. I'm a private investigator.' I handed her a business card.

'Oh, my god, is she okay?'

'You're friends with Janelle?'

'Yes, we've been friends for a few years. We hang out, text.'

'When was the last time you saw, or spoke to her?'

'Um, let me see, it's been a few days. Actually, maybe a week. She sent me something funny.' She picked up her phone and scrolled through it for a moment. 'Here, this was the last time...'

She handed me the phone and I scanned through the text chain. Similar to Lennette's, I could see that Janelle- or Janey as Abby had her saved in the phone- wrote a lot, responded expeditiously, and shared a lot of funny images and videos.

'What about a boyfriend, or other romantic interests?'

'Nothing lately. Janey doesn't date much. The last person was someone I set her up with... it had to be more than six months ago. They went out for a while but... it sort of just... fizzled. Janey really was an introvert.'

'No one recently? Would she have told you about it?'

'Oh, yeah for sure. She always told me about her love life, even if it was just one stupid date.'

I nodded.

'Do you think...' she asked quietly, 'that she's been hurt? Or kidnapped?'

'At this point we don't know anything for sure. She hasn't been home and her passport was used on a flight-'

'That's crazy. She would never fly. Never ever ever.'

'Right.'

'Do you think someone stole her identity?'

'Like I said, I don't know anything for sure. I'm trying to find her. If you can tell me anything about her life, other friends, people she might confide in, or things that she may have said or shared with you, that maybe family wouldn't know about, do tell.'

Abby leaned back in her chair and looked up at the ceiling. 'She keeps in touch with some friends from college, but most of them have moved around the country. Angela is someone she's brought around to group hangouts.'

'Last name?'

She shook her head. 'I don't remember. But I'm sure she follows Janey on social media.'

I nodded. 'Can you identify her in Janelle's feed?'

'Of course.' Abby looked at her phone for several minutes, and I watched different colored screens flash as she quickly moved through various sites and posts. 'Here she is, the one in the green top.' She touched the screen to show the tags.

With her permission I took a picture with my phone. 'Anyone else? Favorite hangouts? Places she frequents, like parks or hiking?'

'She isn't very outdoorsy, but she sometimes goes for walks in the park near her apartment. I try to get her to go to the gym with me but she always says no. She works out at home, mostly, on her compact treadmill. Hangout spots? Um… she likes this one bar, near her apartment, it's nice, they have good apps… it's called… something dumb… oh- the Fox and Piston.'

'That *is* a dumb name.'

'Yeah. But they have like, really good five dollar app nights, and we've met up there a few times. She's friendly with one of the bartenders- his name is Brent.'

'Okay, that's good, thanks. Can you tell me about IEI?'

Abby blanched a bit when I mentioned the company name, then tried to play it off. 'Uh, it was just a boring gig. I got tired of it, sent out some resumes and started here last year.

Janelle still works there, that's how we met actually.'

'What does she do?'

'Admin. You know, orders, data entry, phones. She seemed to like it, when we worked together. She was never cranky at work; you know, sometimes people just walk in the door hating the place. She isn't like that.'

'What does IEI do?'

'Importer of engine parts. After-market copies of OEMs- er- *original equipment manufacturer* parts. Mostly electrical components.'

'Such as?'

'Starters, alternators, stuff like that.'

'Why did you leave?'

'Like I said, I just got tired of it.'

'Nothing else?'

Abby licked her lips and glanced upward.

'You can tell me,' I pushed.

'I'm sure it was nothing, in fact, I never even mentioned it to Janelle, but, I started to feel like they were doing something shady there.'

'Any idea what?'

'No, no idea. It was like, a bunch of little things.'

'Such as?'

Abby sighed. 'Nothing you know, obvious, or major. I'd been there for a while- almost five years. And my boss- he refused to give me a key to the building. Sometimes he'd run late in the mornings and I'd be sitting outside in my car, just waiting. It was annoying. I had a key to *this* place within a week of being hired. And, my desk was right outside his office, and sometimes I'd hear him taking these calls that were just like, I don't know how else to put it. Shady.'

'How so?'

'He used a different phone? He had his landline, his personal cell, and then another cell.'

'That's not unheard of.'

'No, but like, he only took certain calls on the third phone, and always shut the door. And- he kept it locked in the safe.'

'I see.'

'And there were other things too, like, sometimes trucks would come in and there would be guys with the driver.'

'What do you mean?'

'It wasn't all the time, and it was always different guys... but an empty truck would roll up, and get loaded from our warehouse, and it looked to me like they were, you know, guarding it. Most drivers would come on their own, or maybe have a buddy or a navigator. There was even a couple who long-haul truck together. A husband and wife team. But you know, it was obvious they were just truck drivers. As a whole, they're a little, well...'

'Scruffy?'

'Yeah. And they'd just wait in the office or the breakroom while the forklifts loaded the trailer. I got to know a few of the regular drivers, sometimes they'd come in and shoot the shit, you know? But the other guys who would come... the bodyguard types. They looked, well, harder. And they never waited inside. They'd always watch the loading.'

'I see. So you wondered, why would anyone need to guard a truckload of engine parts?'

'Exactly.'

'Why did you never mention any of this to Janelle?'

'I don't know. Once I left, I figured I was imagining things. Plus, she's just an admin. I was the boss' assistant. I thought if he was doing something illegal, I was probably unknowingly helping him do it. And then, well, eventually I thought I was just being paranoid. You know, watching too many action movies.' She shrugged. 'Janelle had a hard time finding work. She would get so nervous when she went to job interviews that she'd throw up in the parking lot.'

'So you didn't want to cause her any undue stress?'

'Yeah, I guess.'

'Alright, that's all I need for now. If you think of anything else, anything at all, please get in touch with me.'

'Thanks. And, will you keep me posted?'

'Sure.'

'I'll send you the contact info for some of our other friends.'

'That would be very helpful. Thank you for your time.'

The Fox and Piston

The bar with the dumb name was only a few minutes drive away from Janelle's apartment. The parking lot was empty save a few cars, which I correctly assumed belonged to the first shift workers who'd come in to open.

The place was comprised of two rooms, a smaller one in front which handled sit down meals, then a larger room in the back which was more for drinks and socializing. The bar was an enormous oval in the middle of the space.

The decor was trendy- lots of exposed light bulbs and words made with rough-cut steel letters, distressed wood and metal stools.

The place smelled of stale liquor and industrial cleaning fluids. The kitchen hadn't started cooking so the aromas of food hadn't yet begun to warm the place.

A loud radio was playing rock music from the kitchen. I followed the sound, and in a moment recognized the din of prep work: knives chopping, trays slamming, dishwasher doors rattling then the whoosh of the water, and the opening and closing of ovens and refrigerators. Following this cacophony to the double swinging doors, I was nearly run over by someone carrying two large crates ladened with glassware.

'Yo! We are closed!' he yelled at me, as he spun to the side to avoid what would have been a noisy and most likely very painful collision.

'Sorry,' I said, 'I'm looking for Brent?'

'Oh, uh, that's me. Who are you?'

'D. Oshtrovsky, private investigator.'

'Aw, fuck me man, I knew she was married!'

'Excuse me?'

'You're here about Kate? Look, I've only been seeing her for a few weeks, she told me her husband had left, but his shit was still in the house. I should have known she was lyin'.'

'Uh, that's not why I'm here but it sounds like maybe you should cool things off with her until that all gets sorted.'

'Wait, why are you here then?'

'It's about Janelle Stevenson.'

He looked confused for a moment then I was pretty sure I actually heard the click of the lightbulb go off inside his adorable himbo head.

'Oh, right, Little J! Man, she's cute as shit. Took her a good year before she said a word to me besides 'mojito, please'.' He laughed out loud.

'So you were friendly?'

'Aw, man, not like that. She didn't try to flirt or sleep with me for free drinks. We were just friends. She actually let me crash a few months back when a pipe broke in my apartment.'

'That's really nice of her.'

'Yeah it was cool to walk to work for a few days and not have to take the bus or hitch a ride.' He was unloading the crates as he spoke, stocking the glasses behind the bar where they belonged.

I followed him into the kitchen when he went back to collect the next two crates. 'How close were you? Did she confide in you? Tell you anything about her life?'

'Sometimes. Hey, why are you asking? Is she in trouble?'

'We're not sure. I'm trying to find her.'

He finished the second two crates and leaned against the bar. 'That's whack. She was like, you know, like a clock. Always the same schedule.' He untied the apron which had gotten damp from the crates, hung it up on a hook behind the bar and tied on a dry one.

'She kept a strict routine?'

'I knew what day and time it was by when Janelle walked in the door.'

You could tell that by looking at your phone too but I appreciated the sentiment. 'What did you two talk about?'

'Her work mostly, she didn't have much else goin' for her in her life. We only got a chance to talk at all cuz she usually only comes here when we aren't busy. We have a few nights a week where we run specials, so it's packed, and it gets pretty bumpin' in here on the weekends. But she usually came when it was quiet, which is funny. Sometimes she'd come in with friends for the specials nights, but only a few times.'

'What did she say about work?'

'She liked it. She said they sell car parts or some shit? I don't know. Sounds boring to me, sitting in an office, at a desk, you know, nine to five and shit.'

I nodded. I doubted I was going to get much more out of this guy. 'Well, thanks for your time...'

'Oh, wait, she just got promoted, though, last time I saw her. She was celebrating. I gave her free drinks that time. Can you believe she tried to tell me no? Crazy. Only person I ever met who tried to turn down free drinks.' He laughed again, good naturedly. I could see why Janelle had felt comfortable becoming friendly with him.

'Promoted to what?'

'Like, assistant to the owner. She was pretty stoked. Nice pay raise.'

'Okay, thanks for your help.'

The Car is Found

Lennette called me, her voice hoarse. I assumed she'd been

crying. 'They found Janelle's car,' she said. I said in my head as she said out loud 'at the airport.'

'Where is it now?'

'Police impound lot.'

'Will they let you see it?'

'They said I can come anytime 'til four thirty.'

'I'll pick you up, I know where it is.'

Shortly thereafter, Lennette and I stood at the gate to the impound lot waiting for the guard, who I knew, to open up. Gary was nearly retired, and moved a little slower these days, his paunch grown considerably since the last time I saw him. His bushy white mustache lifted up in a wide smile when I waved to him through the guard house window.

'You're a sight!' he said, giving me a hug and a thump on the back. 'What can I do for you today OshyKosh?'

I shook my head at the well-remembered nickname, and nodded toward Lennette. 'I'm working on a case, this is my client. We're here to see a car that was brought in today.'

His smile dropped and his face went serious; he knew the reasons that brought a car to his lot. I appreciated his respectful treatment toward Lennette. 'It's a blue sedan, brought in-'

'From the airport earlier. Yeah, I know which one. Come on, I'll take you to it.'

Gary led us to the vehicle, sitting off to one side of the property. It had frost on the windows and the doorhandles creaked from the cold when I opened them.

The interior of the car smelled crisp and fresh, and not just from the winter air. There was the sharp smell of disinfectant, and everything was clean. Cleaner than my car.

I popped the trunk and found it to be empty and recently, rather thoroughly, vacuumed.

Gary and Lennette were having a quiet conversation a few paces away, and I heard Janelle's name, and Gary offer his sympathies and well-wishes for a positive outcome.

I pulled a small box out of my coat pocket and sprinkled the soft dust all over the steering wheel, gear shifter and dashboard. No prints. Or, at least, only tiny, incomplete ones that weren't usable.

I took a deep breath. Okay, well, it's winter. Janelle might wear gloves. Every single day. All the time. Forever.

Back at the Office

I emptied the pockets, then threw my coat and hat on one of the guest chairs and shivered. The thermostat said fifty-nine and I wondered what idiot left it down so low. Oh yeah, me.

I cranked it up to seventy and listened to the ancient furnace in the bowels of the basement chug alive, sending hot air up through the vents. I had updated the utilities to the second floor when I bought the building, so there were two newer, small furnaces in the basement that heated my and Chuck's apartments, but I'd left the downstairs utilities alone. I guessed I only had another year or two of life in the old furnace and crossed my fingers it would hold on a little longer.

I sorted through the objects from my pockets, my mood dropping as I put them away. The last item sat untouched, shining in the light from the lamp, dead center of my desk.

I had asked Lennette to provide a DNA sample, in case we needed to make a familial match. Through her tears, she agreed. The sample kit glared up at me and I sighed heavily, then filed it away.

The leather on my desk chair was hard and cold when I sat down, and I shivered again. I could always go upstairs for a sweater or a banket or something but laziness was overruling my good sense and I just decided to deal with being cold for a few.

When I opened my laptop and email I found some new information from Becky, as well as something from Abby. Abby had sent me the contact information for some friends in their group. From Becky, it was more stuff she'd mined online, which I could see showed some of the same names as the list from Abby.

I wasn't in the mood to talk to people, so I decided to put off the calls 'til later, and do some digging into IEI instead.

I started simply, with the company's website. There was all the run-of-the-mill stuff to be learned, generic public info, stock photos of people doing office tasks and images of what I guessed were the automotive parts they sold.

I glanced through the information that Becky had found, and like her, I was unable to find much of anything on the parent company other than a public record on some random info search site, which asked for a membership to continue viewing the document. I glanced at the clock. The public records office was still open for a few hours.

Fred, the desk clerk, rolled his eyes when I walked in the door.

'Hey Fred,' I said, leaning against the desk.

'Yeah, what is it today?' he asked, not bothering to hide his irritation. He tucked the paperback he'd been reading into a nook under his desk. I'll never understand why he doesn't like helping me, his *entire job* is fetching records when people request them, and he had to do it for people all day. Who cares who it was doing the asking?

I gave him the two company names and told him I'd wait.

'It's going to take me a while,' Fred said, glancing at the door.

There was no one else in the office.

'I can wait,' I said, smiling. *Like your paperback,* I thought. I sat down on a bench to the side of the room, and pulled out my phone. I scrolled while he plunked his fingers across his keyboard, searching up the records for any and all properties associated with the names I'd given him.

A while later (and I had a nagging suspicion that he. took. his. time.) he printed me out a page showing the registered businesses and associated addresses, and I was surprised to see a longer list than I had anticipated. IEI's parent company, Global Manufacturers and Logistics, had a slew of other ancillary companies in addition to IEI.

'Anything else?' he asked, haughtily.

'Not today,' I said in an overly friendly voice. 'Thanks for your help, this is a good start.'

Back in my now warm office, I spent a few hours searching for anything I could find on the list Fred gave me, including the addresses of the properties, and then looking at maps and satellite footage whenever available.

From what I could tell, the companies mostly dealt with shipping, and had a variety of storage locations and warehouses, which I guessed all served specialized purposes, or maybe handled different aspects of the company. Perhaps some were for dry goods, some for refrigerated items, others maybe had to be built with different standards for food handling. I didn't finish going down the list; when my eyes began to strain and the buildings and addresses run together, I took a break to start making calls to the friends of Janelle that Abby sent me.

Most of them said the same things about her as Abby had- she was painfully shy and introverted, but pleasant and easy-going. No one knew about her promotion, much less had celebrated with her.

I wondered who'd joined her at the bar then, as I got the impression from Brent that she hadn't been alone. It was late at night, but I knew the Fox and Piston would still be open.

Back at the bar, Brent had quite a bit of difficulty hearing me over the music as I asked him who Janelle had been celebrating with when she was promoted.

He didn't know any names, but he was able, however, to tell me it was a man, and that Janelle seemed pretty cozy in his presence.

The Investigation Continues

Most of what I do, unfortunately, is usually internet research (hey, Becky doesn't do it *all*) and stakeouts. Before I plan a stakeout, I first check out the area- mostly so I can locate the nearest bathroom. But also because I need to try to not be spotted- which is pretty hard if I'm watching someone's house or place of business. People tend to notice a weird car or the same person standing outside for hours or days.

Some places are easier- bustling city centers for example; I can hide in the comings and goings of a lot of individuals, and people tend not to notice one person who, like me, doesn't stand out much. It helps that my face and hair are nothing to write home about. I'm not being down on myself, I like me, it's just that no one's writing epic poems or invading Troy on my behalf and that's alright. It's not like I wear a lot of lime green leopard print. But, for suburbs or - yikes, rural- areas, it's a huge challenge to surveil without being noticed.

There isn't much that's glamorous or exciting about private investigating- I'm usually sitting outside hotels or houses sometimes for days, waiting for philandering spouses to emerge looking a little tired, dishevelled and flushed. You'd be amazed at how many of them give one last smooch on the front steps, or outside the door, or when they get to their cars. Like, dudes, haven't you ever seen a detective movie? Someone's gonna see you. Oh well, thanks for making my job easier- now I've got it on camera. Dumbasses.

Anyway, this case was proving to be a little more

challenging. So far, I wasn't seeing anything that would make Janelle seem like a target. But with the deliberate way the scenes were set, I had no doubt in my mind that she wasn't a random victim of kidnap or assault.

There was too much premeditation here, and I like to think all of my years of being a detective gave me some decent instincts. While I am a big proponent of listening to one's gut or inner voice, good old fashioned facts and evidence are good too. Sometimes feelings can complicate judgement; but you can't argue with facts.

Even if Janelle was the victim of a crime of passion, or a romantic partner, there was too much clean-up afterwards. Too much covering up to make it something as simple as an argument or a tiff that went south. Something bigger seemed to be brewing here and I needed to figure out a path to follow. I needed to pick someone to surveil and go where they took me.

I was struggling to build an accurate picture of the most recent days of Janelle's life. It's possible it was because nothing interesting happened, at least, until she disappeared. She could very well have just gone about her normal business, quietly and without making a fuss or documenting anything.

I made a few calls to some of the restaurants that her old bank statements had shown she frequented, and got a hit

on one who had delivered to her address the night before...
what? the night before *something* went sideways.

It took an hour for me to get in touch with the delivery
driver who had brought her food, but apparently, Janelle
hadn't been alone.

Now I had two people who say Janelle was cozying up
to someone- but she hadn't told any of her friends. And
Abby said that would have been very odd, for her to keep
something like that to herself. I needed to go back to
Janelle's apartment.

I rang Lennette and told her what I'd discovered, and she
told me she'd like to meet me at Janelle's place. A little while
later, I found her waiting at the bottom of the stairs that
lead to Janelle's front door.

'I didn't want to go up alone,' she said, sighing.

'It's alright. Let's go,' I said.

'What are we looking for?'

'Evidence that someone else has been here- and not just
once.'

When I opened the door, the string I'd secured to the
doorframe fell silently. That was a relief. At least I knew no
one had been here in the interim.

The interior of the apartment smelled stale; that
claustrophobic stillness of a place that has been shut up
for a while- no air circulating, no food cooking, no laundry

spinning in the dryer.

'Check the dishwasher and tell me exactly what is inside it,' I said. 'I'm going to start in the bedroom.'

Lennette went into the galley kitchen and I went down the narrow hallway to the bedroom.

I knew from when I'd been in earlier which side of the bed Janelle preferred. The nightstand had a pile of books, a box of tissues, a variety of items in the drawers, and easy access to a trash can and an outlet which I'm sure usually had a phone charger plugged into it. The other nightstand contained only an herbal sachet in the drawer, and a few bits and bobs, like some costume jewelry and lip balm.

I clicked on my flashlight and leaned down close to the pillow on the lesser-used side of the bed. It took me a few minutes, but I eventually found what I'd been looking for- tiny, cut brown hairs, from someone with a short hair style. Since Janelle had been seen in a man's company recently, my guess was they were from him.

I used clear tape to collect them, and tucked them into an evidence bag.

I heard Lennette saying something from the kitchen, so I rejoined her there. 'What was that?'

'Four plates, a handful of silverware, two mugs, two wine glasses, three water glasses, two pots, a frying pan, one or two other little things and some containers- those are probably from her lunch bag.' She held up the insulated bag from where she'd found it in the cupboard.

I nodded. 'So, she got home from work, had someone here for dinner, then they had breakfast together.'

'Could be.'

'Is Janelle very good with doing her dishes?'

'Nope. She says she doesnt like to waste water, so she normally *packs* the dishwasher before she turns it on, she'd never run it with all this empty space.' Lennette closed the dishwasher carefully. 'Do you think... this boyfriend may have gotten... rough?'

'Don't let your mind go to the worst possible thing,' I cautioned. 'Let's focus on what we know.'

She crossed the dining room and grabbed her purse from the couch. 'I want to leave.'

'That's fine, I have one more thing to do, and I'll be right out. I'll check in with you later.' She nodded and left.

I watched from the open doorway until she was down the stairs and heading for the parking lot, and I pulled a small spray bottle and a second flashlight from my coat pocket. These massive pockets are the best. They hold everything.

I shut the door and then the blinds as tightly as they'd go and pulled the curtains closed. With only a few windows exposed to direct sunlight, this darkened the apartment quite a bit. I studied the room, and tried to ascertain where a struggle could have occurred. The home was so tidy, it was difficult to find any one place that stood out from the rest. No unexplained carpet divots, no whiff of recent bleach.

I started with the standard places: the corners of the coffee and dining tables, the edges of the kitchen counter, bathroom sink, and shower. I spritzed the fluid from the bottle- luminol- and then shined the black light over it.

All I found were a few faded drops of blood around the bathroom toilet and sink, easily explained by a cut during shaving, a menstrual cycle or tending to a small injury on a finger for example. Nothing conclusive, particularly telling or worrying. If Janelle met a violent end, it didn't appear that it happened here at the apartment.

Slightly relieved but still hoping for some result, I got ready to leave. I set the string in the door jam again, hurried down the staircase and climbed into my car.

I wondered if my contact at the cellular carrier would help me out again, for old time's sake.

'No, no, no, no, no,' Trent said, when I finally arrived at his extension, after navigating the mobile service's intricate customer service system. 'Absolutely not, I told you last time was the- uh, the last time.'

'I know, I know, but I need to know who this person has been calling. She could be hurt, or in danger.'

'They're always 'possibly hurt or in danger' with you!'

'Well, Trent? C'mon! What do you expect!'

'I could lose my job. And then what? You'll have no one to help you.'

'You're currently not actually helping me.'

'That's right, and I'm not going to.'

'Don't you want to possibly save someone's life?'

'That line won't work on me *again*.'

'Why do you hate saving lives?'

'Stop! That's not it!'

'Sounds like it!'

'Fine! Whatever! Fine!' he hissed into the phone. 'What is the phone number?'

I relayed Janelle's phone number, and I cold hear him angrily punching it into his keyboard. 'I'm emailing you her records now,' he fumed, 'Don't call me again.'

'Thanks Trent, talk soon!'

'No!'

He disconnected the call and I smirked. I made a mental note to buy him some nice gloves or a cashmere scarf or something for the holidays.

After a few moments, I checked my email and there it was, Janelle's phone records from the last few months. Now, to start a few hours of cross-referencing with the info I already had from Abby and Becky, and then internet research to identify the unknown numbers. (Ugh.)

If I get no results online, then I'll call them from one of the burners I kept for this specific reason, and hope they use their names in the voice mails (almost no one answers calls from unknown numbers anymore) or finally if they do answer, maybe they'll identify themselves when asked (this almost never went well).

Not to make it sound too exciting but the reality of investigative work is that a lot of it is tedious research and internet searches. Snore.

IEI

The main office for International Electric Imports was a low, brown brick and concrete building with tall, thin floor-to-ceiling glass windows set at regular intervals, a slanted roof and heavy glass doors that opened into a small foyer.

On the rear of the building loomed a large warehouse, made of the same brown brick and concrete, but it was windowless.

Well, it hadn't always been windowless- at some point in the years since it had been built the windows that had been back there had been bricked up, resulting in large rectangles comprising slightly different color tones in the brick.

The architecture was mid-century modern bordering on brutalist; tidy and sharp, no nonsense, but holding up nicely, with only small spots of rust stains on the bricks from decades of rain coming down the facade.

The interior had been redone sometime in the early aughts; maple chairs with gray upholstery, and chrome with frosted glass light fixtures on the walls.

I waited where the receptionist told me to, and took stock of my surroundings.

There were no open workstations or blocks of cubicles; the receptionist's desk stood apart, in front of a wall that showed a simple, clean applique with the company's logo in navy blue.

After a while, she told me he was ready for me, and stood to escort me to the boss's office. We went through a door to the right of her desk, and down a long hall.

His office was in the back of the building, where it connected to the warehouse. A staircase led up to a mezzanine level, and I followed her through a door at the top.

An assistance was seated at a desk on the other side of the door, and when we came in, she relieved the receptionist of her guide duties and accompanied me through the next door, into the private office of the owner, manager, boss, whatever.

He was younger than me but not by much, and he smiled without showing his teeth when I came in the door. He stood and offered his hand. 'Miles Stanhope, have a seat.' He motioned toward the guest chairs and took his seat again. 'Renee tells me you are a private investigator? How can we help you?'

'I'm looking into the disappearance of Janelle Stevenson.'

'The disappearance - ?' He looked at me with wide eyes, and his eyebrows raised.

'You didn't know she is missing?'

'No- uh,' he stammered, 'I mean, since when?'

'You weren't concerned when she didn't show up for work?'

'She just took a few days off...'

'Can I see a copy of the time off request?'

'Uh, yeah, sure. Whatever you need.' He picked up his phone, and pressed a button. 'Hey Renee, can you pull up Janelle's time-off request for this week and print a copy for me? Thanks.' He let go of the button and looked at me expectantly.

'When was the last time she came into work?'

'Last week, like normal.'

'What did she do here?'

'Admin stuff, you know, answering phones, customer service. And recently I promoted her to my assistant. Renee's filling in for her while she's uh- on vacation.'

The door opened and Renee came in carrying a sheet of paper. She handed it to Stanhope, who glanced over it before he held it out to me.

It was a typed form, showing Janelle's name and employee ID number and the dates she was requesting off. There was nothing handwritten.

'How is this type of form sent?'

'It's done online, you can use a laptop, or your phone. It's an app.'

'I see. Can I keep this?'

'I don't see why not.'

'When was the last time you spoke to Janelle?'

He paused for a moment before he replied. 'The last day she was here, at work.'

'You didn't speak to her after she left the office the last time?'

'N-no.'

'So all the calls and texts I have on her phone records between you two until a few days ago were... entirely work related?'

His face fell. It's a satisfying moment; one of my favorites.

'Well, yeah, of course.'

'What did you talk about?'

'Oh, it was just, well, some paperwork I needed, uh, to know where she put it.'

'Okay. What about?'

'That's proprietary.'

'Fair enough. Did anything seem strange to you, before

Janelle went on vacation? Was she stressed, or upset about anything? At work or in her personal life?'

Stanhope glanced away for a moment. 'Not that I noticed,' he said. 'She was always very pleasant, nice to be around.'

I carefully pulled my phone out of my pocket while keeping my hands below the desktop and out of his line of vision.

'What is it you do here?' I asked.

When Stanhope predictably looked up and to his left preparing his spiel, I lifted my phone the tiniest bit and snapped a couple quick photos of his face.

'We import electrical parts for engines. Starters, alternators, harnesses, et cetera. Some are sourced directly from the manufacturers, some are designed by third parties based on manufacturers' specifications.'

'Any manufacturers in particular? Specific makes and models?'

'A wide variety. Dozens- spanning automotive, marine and recreational.'

'How did you get into this?'

'I started the business with a friend from college.'

'And where is he now? Still partners?'

'He moved on a few years ago.'

'I see.'

'Look, if there's nothing else, I have a conference call in a few minutes, and uh, well, I'm sorry but I don't think there's anything else I can tell you, I didn't know what Janelle's plans were for her days off.' He stood up and raised one hand, indicating the exit. I stepped ahead of him and went to the door, which he opened. 'Let me know if we can help with anything else.'

'Thank you, I will.'

I moved through the assistant's office toward the staircase, taking a step or two down until I heard the click of the door as it shut.

I turned around and smiled at the receptionist who was standing behind me, and she gave me a half smile back. 'Thanks, have a great day. I'll see myself out.'

'It's policy. I have to see you to the door.'

'Has that policy been in effect long?'

'Uh-'

'It's okay. I know Stanhope told you to see me out.'

'Wha-'

'I heard your messaging program chime, and you shoved your chair pretty hard.'

We were nearly at the front of the office now, and she seemed embarrassed.

'It's alright, I'm not offended. Investigations make people uncomfortable.'

'Sorry, um, have a nice day.'

'You too.'

Back at the Bar (I'm Starting to Like This Place)

The Fox and Piston was hopping, well, hopping for a suburban bar on the side of a highway.

Music pumped from the speakers overhead and groups of sequined women stood at tables and danced together in groups like ornate birds. Smiling faces sipped colorful drinks, leaned close to one another to speak in ears, laughed and tossed their hair. I envied their easy movements and seeming carefree natures, the endless possibilities that lay out before them, most of them only in their twenties. *Enjoy it while it lasts!* I thought, then got annoyed for thinking that. I liked my life.

Men in flashy or tight shirts flitted in and out, carried multiple glasses from the bars, were welcomed or rebuffed, almost in waves. The night was still young and the drinks hadn't begun to take effect, hands were still being kept to themselves, glances were still coy.

There was a crowd a few people deep at the bar, and I saw the barback, his shirt-front damp, come out to haul away a crate of empties. I noted the apron tied around his waist and wondered why he didn't secure it higher, and stop his shirt from being splattered with spilled liquids. I flagged him down. 'When you come back up, please tell Brent I need to see him.'

'Look lady, I'm not his secretary, tell him yourself.'

'Woah! I'm not his latest girl, kid, he's helping with my work- I'm an investigator.'

'Oh, uh, alright, sorry. Give me a couple minutes.'

'No problem.'

I waited at the end of the bar, watching Brent moving swiftly from one customer to another, his hands glistening with runoff or condensation from the drinks he whipped up with expert speed. The barback returned and spoke to him, and Brent looked up from the shaker in his hands, and when he saw me, he flashed me his wide, friendly grin.

He brought me a water with lemon when he had a moment to come talk to me. 'Hey little lady, what's up?'

I smiled back and held up my phone as I spoke loudly over the music. 'Was this the guy having celebratory drinks with Janelle?'

He frowned and squinted, so I used two fingers to zoom in on the picture of Stanhope. 'Yeah,' he said after a few seconds. I appreciated him taking the time to concentrate. 'That looks like him. Real dork.'

'Did they leave together?'

'Yeah, after the other guy left.'

'What other guy?'

'He came in after they were already here for a while, like I said, she was celebrating. I assumed it was a coworker, they all seemed to know each other. Well, the guys did at least. She didn't talk to the other guy much.'

'Did you get a name?'

'Ha ha no way! It was busy and I never left my bar. They were at a table-over there. I just made the drinks she ordered. Only reason I knew what was going on at all is that she ordered special drinks, different from her usuals. But,' he nodded toward my glass, 'the other guy only wanted water with lemon, same thing all the cops order when they're on duty.'

I walked into my dark office and clicked on the desk lamp as I sat down in my hard, cold chair. I jammed my hands into my pockets and hugged my coat closer around me.

I felt it was pretty obvious that Janelle was seeing Stanhope outside of work, and he clearly wanted to conceal that fact from me. Even if he'd done nothing wrong, it was still understandable to be discreet since they were involved in a personal relationship.

But Brent's last comment had left me with a sense of foreboding I didn't normally deal with when it came to investigating taudry relationships or the odd missing person (all of whom had so far, in the history of my Private Investigations business, been wayward spouses on getaways with their affair partners). One question that was rattling around in my brain; who was the cop?

Back to Abby

The next morning I visited Abby Wilkins again. She looked sad, and tired. 'I'm sorry,' she said, 'I've not been sleeping well, and I'm worried about Janey. I called out the day after you came here, I couldn't bear to sit here all day, running reports and answering phones.'

'I understand. I just have a few more questions if you don't mind.'

'It's fine, but, do you think we could go outside?' She held up a vape pen.

'Of course.'

Her vape smoke smelled sweet, it reminded me of the pipe tobacco my Granpop smoked- not exactly the same, but it invoked a memory I hadn't thought of in years.

I gave her a minute to take a few draws before I began. 'Did you know Janelle was dating Miles Stanhope?'

Her eyes expressed what I interpreted as genuine surprise, and I watched as she did some quick calculations, or ran through a series of memories, hunting for things she might have missed.

'Honestly, no,' she said, eventually. She took another draw on the pen. 'I must have missed it entirely. We hadn't spoken much the past month or so, and we hadn't been able to make plans work, you know? We kept missing each other. I just figured it was one of those times... when you can't make your schedules line up. She must have just been seeing him instead. I feel like she would have told me though- I keep going over it and over it in my mind. I know we were good enough friends that she would have eventually told me.'

'Maybe she was worried about what you might have thought, it's kind of cliche, you know, sleeping with the boss.'

Abby sighed. 'Also, I bitched about him a bit too, to Janey, now that I think about it. He was Ivy League, Mr. Privileged White Guy. One of those people who don't have to pay for their first rusty, broke ass car out of their money from a job in fast food. He was not someone that people like us- I mean, Janey and me-'

I gestured to my own personal appearance. 'Ha! Don't worry. Me too.'

'Right. He wasn't someone who'd normally give people like us the time, much less, you know, be serious about. He'd had other girlfriends, I'd been working with him long enough to see them come and go for lunch dates or see their pics on his phone in passing; women who came from his world.'

'Maybe Janelle was worried you wouldn't approve.'

Abby's eyes filled with tears. 'I'm sure you're right. I

probably wouldn't have. I'd have told her to back off him, that he was probably just using her-slumming for a thrill. It's what those people do.'

I had a feeling Abby had first-hand experience with that, and I didn't push it. 'I'm sorry to upset you,' I said, quietly. 'I just have one more question. Do you know anyone who was a cop, present or former, who hung around with Janelle or Miles? He was seen in their company at the bar she liked.'

Abby took a deep breath and thought for a moment before answering. 'It's hard to say,' she replied. 'Some of those guys who'd come by the warehouse, you know, with the late shift trucks, looked, well, cop-ish. The haircuts, the shoes. But I don't know anyone who would have been friendly with Janey. The guy must have been at the bar to see Miles.'

I nodded. 'Okay, thank you. I think that's all I need for now. I'll be in touch.' I left Abby outside, standing next to the side door of the building, a fresh puff of vape smoke floating overhead, in front of a gray metal door in a brick wall; uninspired design, black, patched asphalt of the parking lot sliding away toward the edge of the property and the road beyond. A random building in the middle of a random town, but here was a person crying over a missing friend, and that had to mean something.

Shanks

At the start of my investigation, I'd set up news alerts for keywords that included Janelle's name, the company she worked for, some that had to do with the kind of case it was, and a slew of others that I knew might be more annoying than helpful, such as 'warehouse' 'imports' 'exports.' So far all of the results had been unrelated to my case, and I was considering narrowing down the search parameters to limit the results I was getting, but I hadn't gotten around to it yet.

I was working down the spreadsheet of phone numbers from Janelle's records, filling out the names of the people and companies I'd been able to identify thus far, and the frequency of calls, dates, times, et cetera, to nail down who she spoke to in the last few days, and why. I was hoping someone besides Stanhope might stand out, but I wasn't getting very much.

I was annoyedly hanging up with yet another person who didn't answer or have identifying info in their voice mail message, when I got an alert that there was a news blurb about a warehouse worker who was missing.

Assuming it was about Janelle, I opened the article and scanned it, but was surprised to see a name I hadn't heard of yet. One Robert, a.k.a. Bob, Shanks- forklift operator. The photo that accompanied the article was terrible, it might have been from a driver's license.

The surprising thing about the article was the fact that his last known place of employment was IEI, and I immediately wondered why Stanhope hadn't mentioned he had *two* missing employees.

It wasn't hard to find Shanks' last known address, and I bundled up and headed over there.

Shanks' apartment was listed as a 'B' and when I pulled up to what looked like a single-family home, I checked my GPS to make sure I'd come to the right spot.

The house was ramshackle at best, a shithole at worst; at first glance I couldn't figure out where a 'B' would even fit.

I shrugged and climbed the front steps onto a wooden porch that had no safety railing around it, and knocked on the door. It was a steel door with a small window at the top, and was the color of faded primer; it had been installed right from the store, but was meant to be painted first. Now, though, it was colored with all the dings and scratches that come from years of neglectful ownership.

Two metal chairs and a full coffee can of cigarette butts were all the decor that rested upon the porch, and I heard the bark of a big dog from inside.

The door was opened by a woman who apparently, didn't

only smoke outside.

'Yeah?'

'Good morning, I'm a private investigator-'

'Who hired ya? I didn't think Bob's family had any money.'

'I've been hired to find another missing person and -'

'Oh yeah, who's 'at?'

'I'm sorry. What's your name? Are you Bob Shanks' partner, or-'

She burst out laughing and I could see that she wasn't big on dental care. 'That drunk? Not on my worst day. He was my tenant.'

'Oh, can I see his apartment?'

She looked me up and down and drew one long pull on her cigarette, finishing it off, then she flicked the butt past me- I stepped aside just in case her aim wasn't true- and shrugged. 'Sure, what the fuck ever.'

She pulled the door shut behind her and led the way down the porch steps and around the building. Our shoes- well, my boots and her house slippers, crunched in the light frost that was settled on the old, thinned out gravel of the driveway that ran down the length of the house. Instead of ending in a defined line, it simply merged with the patchy dead grass of the backyard.

We arrived at a back door, and she felt around on top of the lintel and produced a key. 'He's always losing his keys late at night, and he'd come knocking on my door, drunk and stupid, so I started keeping a spare up here,' she said in a way of explanation.

She stepped inside a tiny kitchenette, which I suspected was once a laundry room that was converted, and not recently. There was a small bed to one side, a narrow doorway which showed a bathroom with a shower stall on the other side, and that was the extent of it. I had a feeling this was not exactly a legal, properly up-to-code rental unit; the space heater standing near the bed- unplugged and as cold as the ambient air - told me I was right.

I could traverse the entire space in less than ten steps. A small folding tray held a tv, one of those old ones from the late nineties that had a VCR in the bottom, and there were some plates and glasses- clean ones- lined up neatly on the countertop. The trash was full, a quick glance showed me it was a lot of beer cans, takeout containers and the like, and I was struck by how tiny and sad the life lived in this room must have been. The air was stagnant from the old garbage and the smoke that emanated through the thin wall that separated his room from the main house, and Shanks was not much of a cleaner. The bathroom was deeply stained and the floor throughout the apartment was in desparate need of a mopping. The place was tidy- the bed was sort of made, the sink was empty. But it certainly wasn't clean.

'Do you know who his family was, do you have information on how I can get in contact with them?'

'Far as I know they ain't talked to him in years,' she said, patting the pockets of her oversized hoodie and pulling out the lighter she'd been looking for. She lit a fresh cigarette, and didn't bother to blow the smoke outside.

'How long had he lived here?'

'On and off for a couple years.'

'Did he pay his rent on time?' I had a feeling she was the kind of landlady that changed the locks if your rent was late, tenants rights be damned.

'Well enough, I let him stay, didn't I?'

He didn't seem to be a person who had a lot of choices, I thought, but kept it to myself. 'Do you know how I can get in touch with whomever filed the missing persons report?' I asked. I had assumed it was a friend, or perhaps a family member.

She laughed again, a mirthless, mean-spirited laugh. 'It was me, man you ain't too bright are ya? He ain't been around for a couple days, I thought he was avoiding me cuz he blew his rent money again. Then, I went looking for him down at the station to see if he was locked up, cuz I needed the rent money. And the cop down there asks me if I wanted to file a missing persons. Can you believe that? And all these people were looking at me so I did. Cuz I figured, then, I can put the room in the paper again, can't I, cuz if he shows back up I can say he was missing, and can't have the room no more.' She chuckled at her own ingenuity, and my skin crawled. What did life do to this woman, to shape her thus?

'Alright,' I said, stepping outside again. The cigarette smoke was making me nauseous, although it might have been the company also. 'Do you happen to know what kind of car he drives, maybe the license plate number?'

'I do have that, actually. I had to help him get it out of impound. I got the receipt still.'

We walked back up the driveway, and she stepped inside the house, but left me standing on the porch. No complaints.

A few minutes later, long enough for me to wonder if she was just fucking with me and was just planning on leaving me standing out there empty handed, the door jerked back open, and she shoved a wrinkled yellow receipt at me. I recognized the form, I'd seen a few of them over the years, and the make, model and tag of Shanks' car was visible in some officer's scratchy handwriting.

I handed her my card. 'Can you call me if he shows up? I'd appreciate it.'

She pushed the card deep into her hoodie pocket, and I suspected it would be in the trash before my car was even away from the curb.

I Really Need to Hire More Help

The conundrum facing me now was how to surveil Stanhope. The IEI facility was located in an industrial area, surrounded by parking lots, sparsely occupied roads and convenient on- or off-ramps to the interstate. There was nowhere I could park and be unseen by the small amount of workers coming and going from the building.

An easy internet search gave me his home address, and when I knew he was at the office, I took a ride past his house. It was a newer build on a two lane road, set back from the curb far enough that it couldn't easily be watched from the street, which didn't have much of a shoulder anyway, and a car parked on the side would draw plenty of eyes.

There were no businesses near enough to give me a view of the property while also letting me hide among the customers coming and going, and there were no places along the street, say, like a library, where I could park and spend time in the car without attracting much attention.

(Rich people with their nice, tucked-away homes in quiet neighborhoods, am I right?)

I figured my only course of action was to find somewhere to stash some cameras, and set about making a plan to do just that.

At the office, I unlocked my storage cabinet, and pulled out a heavy metal box contained within.

I dug through every camera I had inside, and sorted them, choosing two which I could power with small solar cells.

The power cells were a little bigger than a credit card, and the camera was the size of a large button. With luck, no one would notice them. Over the years I've been an investigator, one thing that has stood out to me is how often people don't notice small changes in their environment. I definitely used this to my advantage for sure, but it also made eyewitnesses particularly unreliable.

The glen of trees growing between the road and the house made it easy enough to mount a small camera aimed at Stanhope's house, which also covered a patch of the driveway. I would be able to see the driver of every vehicle which left the property.

The office was a different story, and proved a little more challenging. I could easily see several security cameras aimed all around the building, which I didn't want to be caught on while placing my own device. The parking lot was large and empty, and completely surrounded the building. Anywhere I tried to plant a camera I would be seen. The only option was the traffic signage located not far from their driveway.

I got bundled up in jogging clothes, including a balaclava.

I had several; Chuck and I ran together in all weather. I wore my perkiest clothes to appear as innocent as possible. Purple coat, blue hat. Nothing too bright, no flourescents. All very forgettable. I am just a cute suburban lady going for a nice run in the cold.

I parked my car at another business about a mile down the road from IEI, double-checked the camera was operational, stuffed it into my coat pocket and set off. In front of IEI, I had to tie my shoe and do some stretching, like any jogger might have to. There just happened to be a nice little camera stuck to the side of the sign post when I was done. Hopefully, no one would notice it before my case was over.

They were designed to activate when they detected movement, and the camera near his house was activated by deer more than the movements of humans coming and going.

I soon regretted my choice of location for the camera covering the office, the damn thing was recording all frigging day. Hours of cars and trucks during the daytime hours. However, it was the night deliveries that were probably more pertinent to my case; the ones Abby was suspicious of.

But before I could look into them further, I needed to find a girl- Stanhope had a new one (that was fast; seriously dude, I tell you your girlfriend is missing and you've already moved on? Or were you seeing both women simultaneously? Dog.)

The first night she stayed over, I caught a break; she had on a work shirt when she was leaving in the morning. There was a logo on the left side of her chest, and my camera caught it clear as day, as she waited for a car to pass so she could exit his drive.

It was for a popular chain coffee shop, and if she was wearing that shirt in the morning, chances were she was heading straight there for a shift.

Becky agreed to come along to the coffee shop to help me check out the girl, and listen in on any conversations she had with coworkers.

We found her at the second location we tried. We spent the better part of the morning with our noses in our laptops and made multiple coffee and food orders (we were really hungry, and the food was quite good, and we did actually get some work done) before I finally had a chance to talk to the girl- er, woman, whose name I now knew was Siobhan, and that I also knew was older than she appeared from a distance. She was the manager of the store, and I even had an opening- we were wearing the same Docs.

Finally, a late morning lull set in, and Siobhan told her coworkers she was taking her break. Becky and I exchanged a knowing glance. She was going to stay at the table, and

I would follow Siobhan wherever she went. But, I was grateful to see Siobhan pulled off her apron and left it by the cash register, then grabbed a sandwich and a drink and sat down at a table against the far wall, where she pulled out her phone and scrolled while she ate.

I gave her a few minutes to make some progress on her sandwich because I'm not a total psycho, and then I stood up, and casually browsed the shelves of goods for sale that were near her table.

After a few minutes of sniffing scented candles and admiring ceramic mugs, I glanced over at her and then said, in my friendliest voice, 'Oh, cute, look, we are wearing the same boots.'

She looked up at me and gave me her customer service smile, and said 'Nice. you have good taste!' Then looked back down at her phone.

I waited another few seconds and said, 'Do you know if these mugs are made locally?'

'I'm sorry, I don't. I'm on break, so if you have any questions about the mugs you can ask Sean, behind the counter.'

I nodded and then, 'Are they supplied by IEI Imports?'

Siobhan frowned and looked at me, then asked, 'What?' in a quiet voice.

I moved over and sat down in the chair across from her, leaning back to give her some space. She sat up straight, her face showing caution and worry, but also a little bit of curiosity.

'I know you're seeing Miles Stanhope. Would you mind if I asked you a few questions about him?'

'Yeah I would mind, who the fuck are you? And why do you know who I'm dating?'

I decided to slam dunk on her, to shake some of her confidence that she was the one in charge here. 'I'm investigating him as a suspect in the disappearance of a young woman. He was dating her, and she is missing, presumed dead. She looked a little like you.'

At this, all of the color ran out of her face, and her mouth hung open a bit, but she didn't make any noise.

'So, would you mind if I asked you a few questions?'

Her voice only came out in a bit of a whisper. 'Uh, I guess… not.'

'Great.'

I glanced over at Becky and gave her a nod. She returned it. 'How did you two meet?'

She cleared her throat. 'Here. He uh, last week, he asked me out.'

'And you've only been on, what, a few dates?'

'Yeah that's about right.'

'Has he mentioned his exes? Is he a talker, oversharer, anything like that?'

'I wouldn't say so, no.'

'Has he ever mentioned anyone named Janelle?'

'Is that the woman?'

I didn't reply.

'Um, he said he was concerned about someone by that name, that she'd taken vacation and not come back. He said... he said he was worried about her.'

'So he didn't mention that he had been seeing her?' She shook her head, and I could see that she was struggling to process what I was saying. I felt a little bad, but I needed to keep her off-balance, so she would be more likely to be honest. 'Does he talk about work much?'

'Not much. He's answered my questions about it, but, um, he doesn't really volunteer anything.'

'So this is the only coworker he has mentioned?'

'Yeah... actually, now that you ask... she's the only one he's talked about.'

Interesting. Is he playing a long game, giving himself a character witness? Or is he genuinely concerned, because he really doesn't know anything about what's happened to Janelle?

'Has anyone come to the house while you've been there? Any strange phone calls?'

'...strange phone calls? Like, people hanging up, or breathing heavy? I don't answer his phone.'

'No, as in, really late at night, ones where he gets angry at the caller, arguments, that sort of thing.'

'He did have an argument with someone, early this morning actually. I was coming down from the shower, and he was out on the deck. His back was to me but I could tell he was speaking angrily, he was waving his arm around, you know, gesturing a lot, he was tense. And he tried to turn it off when he realized I was there, you know, like, smile and act like he was fine? But I could tell he was pissed.'

'Any idea who he was talking to?'

'No, he just laughed it off and apologized, like 'work',' she said, imitating his reply and shrugging.

'Has anyone else come to the house, or come around when you've been with him?'

She shook her head. 'It's... it's early days, yet, we haven't introduced each other to friends or family or anything. And I have no reason to go to his work.'

'Alri-'

'Wait, there was one guy who drove up when I was leaving, the first night we hung out at his place. He was driving a big suv, and pulled into the driveway just as I was getting in my car.'

'Did you see his face?'

'No, I don't know what he looked like, it was dark and he didn't get out. I had a feeling he was waiting... you know, for me to leave.'

'You're sure it was a guy, and not a woman?'

'I could see his torso, kind of muscular. He was wearing a dark colored shirt, with a logo, right here,' she pointed to the left side of her chest, where the logo was on her own shirt. 'That's the only reason I remember it, cuz, at first I thought he was wearing, you know, one of our uniforms.'

'Could you tell what the logo was?'

'No, but it reminded me of a cop badge.'

'Okay. I'm sorry for startling you. Thanks for your help.'

Becky was watching us carefully, and when she noticed I was preparing to leave the table, she collected our things swiftly and was standing in a moment.

'Uh, you're welcome I guess.' I took two steps away from Siobhan, then she said, 'Hey, wait, who are you? Are you a cop?'

I gave her a half smile and hurried to Becky, who was waiting for me at the door, and we were in the car and gone in seconds.

Golden Girl

I still had one or two friends who were on the force, even though we weren't really in touch anymore. I knew how hard it was for them to see me, to know what I'd been through, and I didn't want platitudes.

Of the few officers on the job who I'd call a friend, one was Doris, and she'd been supervising the traffic department for longer than, well, anyone. Most cops find traffic to be a boring, shit beat, but for Doris, it was a chance to chill, do some good work for the community, and work toward a pension that was going to make for a half-decent retirement. She wasn't trying to be a detective or commissioner, she was a career desk jockey, and felt that it was A-OK.

She was, also, super happy to hear from me and we spent a good twenty minutes catching up before she finally asked, 'Hon, I know you didn't call just to hear the melodious sound of my voice. What can I do for ya?'

'You got me,' I said, laughing. 'I was hoping you could check out a plate for me, tell me whatever you can about it's movements or violations lately? It might be related to a missing woman I've been hired to find.'

'Lay it on me,' she said.

I gave her Shanks' plate number, as well as the vehicle's make and model. I heard her typing and then 'Hm,' she said. 'This guy's not out here making great choices.'

'What do you got?'

'He's got traffic tickets, parking tickets, he's been impounded, DUI's out the wazoo. This guy's a menace.'

Doris hated people who violated traffic laws.

'What's the most recent?'

'Last thing I've got is, let's see, he was caught speeding on a traffic cam, going east on Valmer Boulevard. Unpaid ticket might I add, auto-mailed to his address. He was really flying.' She gave me the dates and times, and my stomach fluttered. That was right in my window for something going awry with Janelle.

'Okay, Doris, you're a dream. Kiss Petey for me.' Petey was her prize-winning bloodhound. Prizes at dog shows, not for police work.

'You got it, and listen, me and you need to catch up, for real. Okay?'

'That would be great, thanks, friend.'

I looked up Valmer Boulevard and the approximate location of the traffic cam where Doris said the car was pinged. It was in the middle of nowhere; all interstate and highway changes; some roads leading off into the city, some heading down to the coast. He could have been heading literally anywhere.

Becky Finds Some Bullshit

Back at the office, Becky and I sat down for some good ol'

fashioned internet sleuthing. This is so much easier than what we had to go through to gather information in the '90's. Damn I'm old.

A quick search told me which ivy league college Stanhope had graduated from, and I set Becky on a quest to gather any information she could about his time there, particularly, who he'd made connections with, who his professors were and his subsequent journey to his current career position.

I busied myself cataloging my notes about my meeting with Siobhan, and I did experience the teeniest pang of guilt over blind-siding her about our investigation into her boyfriend. I hoped she was too rattled to keep it to herself, that she blabbed to her coworkers immediately and was met with a round of advice to leave him, ghost him, ditch him, whatever the kids are calling it nowadays.

I mean, that's a pretty specific hope I know, but she looked like Janelle. The guy had a type, and I didn't even want to let my mind wander anywhere near that for now.

'Oh that's just fucking great,' Becky's voice cut through the murky thoughts that were steadily gaining steam in my mind.

'What is it?'

In response, Becky rotated her laptop around to show me the screen. It was a photo of Stanhope, smiling, standing beside a friend of similar age and description, with their arms around one another's shoulders. They were wearing matching uniforms, clearly they'd been on the same team, doing, I don't know, something sporty. 'What sport is that? And who's that guy?'

'Are you serious?'

'About the sport or the guy?'

'It's crew.'

'Okay, so our boy can row a boat. And?'

'That *guy* is none other than George Harrison Hackerman.'

'Why's his name sound familiar?'

'Oh dear lord, don't you vote? He's our current representative in *Congress*.'

'Oh bloody hell.'

'Yep. Bloody *motherfucking* hell. This guy's really connected.'

'We don't know that they're still in touch with each other, much less an integral part of one another's lives.'

Becky did her 'oh really?' face at me, spun her laptop around, typed furiously, and then turned it back toward me once again. 'This is Hackerman's wedding photo from last year. A style magazine- called Abundant Life- covered it. Look at groomsman number three.'

'Great. Great. Great great great great great,' I sighed and pulled up a different program, to start combing through video footage of Stanhope's movements from the past two days. 'Great great just great,' I muttered periodically, almost without realizing.

'In case you're wondering,' Becky said, thirty minutes later, 'Hackerman's wedding was covered in a full spread because his new father-in-law owns Forten Media. And I don't mean he's the CEO. I mean he *owns* it. So when I say your boy is connected, I mean he doesn't have to go on a waiting list to join a country club.'

'I get it, I get it,' I grumbled.

Becky closed her laptop. 'Robbie's not gonna be happy about this. It's bad enough when you're investigating some jerkoff who owns a big contracting business or a string of bars. And he's got enough money to slime his way out of whatever you get on him. But this is big, like *real* big, like, *you'll* be the one who goes to jail or disappears, big. Even if we're wrong and he's not the guy, he still has enough pull in these circles to make things very hard for you.'

'Well I guess we better be extra careful then.'

Becky made her 'okay smartass' face at me and turned back to her screen.

'We need to find out who Stanhope is connected to in law enforcement,' I said.

Becky sighed and it was her turn to mutter, 'Great. This is getting better and better.'

An hour or so later, the sun had set thoroughly and a heavy darkness had long since settled outside. I stood and stretched my aching legs and bent backward a little to flex my lumbar. I walked around the office and clicked on a few lamps. I didn't want to beam our eyeballs so I picked a few small lamps that weren't strong enough to eliminate the darkness that had filled the room. Just enough so that Becky, who was going to head home soon, could see to gather her things before I locked up and went upstairs.

Who's Watching the Watcher?

I stood for a few moments in the dark vestibule right inside my office door, and I watched some cars drive by in the distance. On a clear night in winter, a night like tonight, through the skeletons of the trees that lined the roadway, I could see the lights of the vehicles moving along the interstate. Red and white lights streaked by, interspersed with the amber running lights of the trucks mixed in the bevy.

The land across the street from mine was owned by the county and had been for sale for a while. But ours was a quiet road, and it probably didn't help that the property ran alongside the buffer zone for the interstate, with no exits close by, so there hadn't been any buyers as yet. No complaints here; buyers meant buildings, and buildings meant more people and more money, and that would mean my taxes and assessments would go up.

There was no moon, and the stars were crisp against the black sky. The passing cars zipped through my view, and I wondered where the occupants were going, what they were doing, knowing that their lives were just as complex and busy as my own. There's a word for that... what was it? Sonder. Was that a real thing- I mean, in the dictionary? I made a mental note to look that up online later.

I had floodlights in the front lot but I hadn't turned them on yet; it was an old building and they weren't on an automatic timer or sensor.

A light flashed outside and I was immediately alert. It was by the edge of the road, about fifty feet away. A spark and a small yellow flame; someone was lighting a cigarette. The cherry glowed, a warm orange ember floating alone in the darkness. Then it disappeared; the person must have been hiding the butt in their hand. I flipped the switch for the floodlights and in the second after they came on, while I blinked to adjust my eyes to the bright lights that now lit the entire property like it was noon, the person was gone.

I told Becky about it; we both wanted to believe it was just someone walking by, along the road. A random stranger just getting where he needed to go. But we were too anxious about the case that was in front of us to believe our own words.

Becky had parked right in front of my door, not two feet away from the glass. She tried to insist on sleeping over, but I told her not to be paranoid, plus, Chuck would be home soon. She watched from inside while I checked over her entire vehicle for GPS trackers, anything that looked touched or out of place. I tried to blame it on the cold that my hands were a bit shaky. Then I put Becky in her car, and she immediately locked the doors. I stepped back inside the building, the thunk of the lock engaging in the door jam was a comforting sound. I watched for several moments to make sure no car followed behind her after she turned onto the road, and then I turned to click off the office lamps once again.

Two doors opened onto the staircase that led to my and Chuck's apartments; one was in my office, and the other was on the back of the building. Chuck used the rear door to come and go; he usually parked his van out back so as not to take up space in my parking lot, not that I usually had customers fighting over the three parking spots or clamoring to get inside.

There were uncovered windows that lit the staircase during the day, which overlooked the front and rear parking areas. I did install motion sensor lights in the back of the building and in the stairwell for Chuck when he moved in; his late hours meant he was almost always coming home in the dark, and I wanted there to never be a time when there wasn't a light on for him. I made a mental note to have Chuck help me install motion sensor lights out front, ASAP. I had security cameras but they were pointed down at my doors, and didn't cover more than a few feet of the parking lot. I didn't want them picking up traffic all day coming and going from the neighboring business which was bustling for most of the daytime hours. I added to my mental note, to have Chuck help me aim their viewfinders up a little higher. I double-checked the rear door, and content that all was secure, I went up.

Too Creeped out to Sleep

Later, after (maybe obsessively) following Becky home via our tracking software, I sat on my couch mulling over what I'd found out so far. It was alarming, sometimes, at the quantity of information I was able to glean about people's lives from the internet.

I'd ruled Siobhan out completely; based on what I'd found out about her I decided there was little to no opportunity or reason for her to be involved in Janelle's disappearance at all, or even know anything about it.

She had plenty of socials that showed me a pretty clear picture of her normal, fun-loving life. She seemed to enjoy her job, had a lot of friends, and I could follow a pretty clear time line of what her life looked like for the last year or so, and then up to a few days ago, which was her most recent post. Most importantly, there were multiple videos of her enjoying herself at a music festival two states over in the days surrounding Janelle's disappearance.

It was a relief to remove someone of interest in my case even though the person ranked pretty low on the list. Progress is progress.

I absentmindedly clicked on the tv; I needed something to distract me from the frustration that was mounting. I had a dead weight in my gut; I knew this case was building in front of me, that it wasn't simple, but there was so much to do, I was struggling with where to go next. So frequently, the cases I handle are cut and dry. 'I think my husband is cheating' and then within a week or so, 'Here's proof your husband is cheating'. No big deal (to me anyway, not to sound crass). But this one was different. I felt like every time I peeked at something, like a crack in a cave, a larger room appeared behind it.

It was like having to do literally every house chore, in a messy, smelly house, and being frozen from not being able to decide which place to start cleaning first.

A sitcom danced across the screen; well-known actors hamming it for laughs. It was a welcome reprieve for a few minutes, and I was able to let go of a small amount of the anxiety that had been brewing.

I took a deep breath and pulled out my small pocket notebook, to try to organize my thoughts.

I had no luck in coming up with someone who was connected to law enforcement through Stanhope's professional pages online, and he didn't have any social media, that we could find anyway, and that was significant. Almost everyone had some reflection of their lives online, and he did not appear to do so, at all. It was diffucult, therefore, to get an accurate picture of how he spent his free time, and the places and people he regularly interacted with.

Becky and I had scoured everything we'd been able to find on him, searched every name that came up in the articles and images, and none of the people he'd been photographed with or who were part of his company appeared to have anything to do with the police, security or the feds.

But despite the fact that the easy to smile Brent only had two brain cells floating around behind his gorgeous face, I trusted his instincts that a 'cop' had been with Janelle and Stanhope when she was celebrating.

There had to be someone, and perhaps the surveillance equipment would tell me who.

Just Tidying the Flowerbeds, Pay No Attention

In the morning, I stood on the landing of my staircase for a good while, off to the side of the window. I scanned the area near where I'd seen the person light the cigarette. I knew it well enough from living in this building for years, but I'd never looked at it from this point of view before- as in, using it to surveil *my own* building. There were a few objects: a mini electrical substation, a few measly shrubs and small trees, that could provide a bit of cover.

My neighbor was a deli and convenience store, privately owned and operated and open until around eight pm, and six on Sundays. Their property was surrounded by a tall privacy fence, which did a good job of blocking light from their building or the headlights of customers' cars from coming in my office windows. Chuck's apartment was on that side, and I knew some of the light kept his bedroom windows illuminated at night, but since he mostly slept during the days, it wasn't an issue.

There were also a few trees along my side of the property line, so they offered a bit more cover from the lights and traffic.

Someone could, theoretically, enter their lot from the far

driveway and park against the fence, hiding their vehicle from any view out of my building at all. And then, stand behind the electrical boxes and plants even though they were bare, and observe my office relatively unnoticed. I never had a reason to be wary of being watched before.

Some thought rattled around in my mind about the irony of being the one under surveillance but I let that go.

I know the deli had a camera at the front entrance but I doubted the person who'd been standing and watching my building last night got caught on it.

Confident that no one was there currently, I went outside and hurried across my lot. It was frickin cold out, and I'd neglected to put on my coat. Under the pretense of buying a sandwich, drink and chips, I carefully looked around and ascertained that I was not currently being surveiled. No cars lingered in the deli's lot, no one glanced at me, or was loitering.

Carrying my lunch home again, I walked much slower, and paused to examine the area where the person had been standing the night before.

The deli owner, a good neighbor and kindly man named Nasir, took a lot of pride in ownership, and kept his property very tidy. It would annoy him that there were multiple cigarette butts left on the ground in his flower beds. I collected them in a small clear plastic bag I'd brought with me.

I looked around again while unlocking my front door and sighed. I needed to follow Nasir's example better.

Beyond the small parking area in the rear of my building was a little patch of land with some trees and underbrush, nothing substantial, but nice all the same. It led into another area owned by the county which bordered the neighborhood beyond.

On the opposite side of my building from the deli was an open space, usually overgrown and messy, part of my property but the previous owner had never paved it. I think he'd tried to sell it as a subdivision once, but didn't get any buyers so he included it in the sale to me. During the summer I hired landscapers to keep the greenery under control but now it sat quietly hibernating and relatively empty, save for a few bits of litter flapping depressingly in the winter wind.

Someone parked or sitting there would stand out; there was no cover. Beyond the edge of the lot was a small side street that led to a neighborhood, which had much better highway and shopping access several miles away from a different direction.

All of this made the fact that someone was standing out front, when the deli was closed and there was no where really to walk to, for long enough to smoke three cigarettes, especially unnerving.

I put my lunch in the fridge, grabbed my coat, hat and gloves and headed back out again, not before finding myself double-checking my locks. I did not like feeling jumpy.

I started off into the patch of woods behind my building, knowing the way well. Straight for a bit, head a little this way, then a little that way. A few minutes of walking brought me to Alfredo's.

Calling it 'Alfredo's' was a little inaccurate; it was technically still my property. But (as he had informed me when I was the new owner, and had taken a walk to follow my property lines and look for the surveyors' stakes) he had lived there longer than me.

He knew I was coming before I arrived; I didn't try to decrease the noise I made or surprise him. He was standing outside his lean-to, holding a cup of something hot. I noticed his setup had gotten a bit busier, he'd added a second solar panel and a few more layers of roofing.

'Hey Alfredo,' I said, holding up a hand in a wave. 'How are you?'

'Good, good. Living the dream. Want some?'

I didn't know what 'some' was, and I already had three cups of coffee, so I politely declined. He nodded and sat down on his chair beside a cold chimea, which was held up on a stand he'd fashioned himself out of the remains of a broken metal patio chair. It appeared that he'd just woken up, his eyes were puffy from sleep. 'Some' turned out to be soup.

'What brings you out here?' he asked. I knew Alfredo didn't mind me visiting, as long as I kept my visits short and infrequent. He rather bluntly told me as much when we first met.

'I was just wondering if you'd seen anyone hanging around? Anyone new, not kids.'

'Nobody out here.'

'What about at the deli?'

Alfredo looked at me like I was stupid, I think he was sure I was, sometimes. 'How'm I supposed to know somebody new's been coming there?'

'I don't mean shopping. I mean standing around and watching.' As long as he didn't panhandle by the front doors, Nasir didn't mind Alfredo using the deli's restrooms which had separate access on the back of his building. And there were a few people who lived around town who frequented the deli for their daily coffee or lunch, who knew Alfredo and looked out for him.

'Oh, somebody's got their eye on you, eh? Like you been doing to other people? How's that feel huh? Probably not great.' I gave him the 'that's enough' look, and he chuckled. 'No, Dea, I haven't seen nobody. But I'll start paying more attention.'

'I'd appreciate it,' I said. 'You need anything?'

Alfredo poked the ashes in the mouth of the chimea with a stick. 'Some water, and thermals. Next few weeks are s'posed to be rough.'

'Okay. Me or Chuck will be back, as soon as we can. Alright?'

'Yeah.'

'Thanks man.'

'Yeah. Later.'

I turned and went back the way I'd come, and just so he didn't have to wait long, I went straight to the deli, bought two gallon jugs of spring water and delivered them immediately. I sent Chuck to see him the next day, with two packs of thermals, a twelve-pack of warm socks, and some canned foods for good measure.

Oh, Somebody's Pissed Off

Scanning through video footage is mind-numbingly boring. I had a system, a graph I used on paper, to keep myself alert. (I learned years ago that if you vary the tools you use, you can retain information easier- for example, write things down with pen and paper instead of using a phone or laptop all the time, and alternate between reading things on paper or in a book and on a screen and it helps the way your brain stores the information. Is it bullshit? I don't know, but I do know it works for me.)

So instead of cataloguing data on one laptop while the videos ran on another, I used a paper graph: makes, models, license plates, times, directions, visible occupants, all recorded by hand.

My morning espresso was barely making a dent in the fatigue from watching three hours of cars driving by on video, and I was considering taking a break to stretch and eat when a car sped into my real parking lot.

I knew the car, the driver, and suspected the reason he was visiting. I was out of my chair so fast it spun, and I beat him to the door, locking it just as he got to it.

That didn't stop Stanhope from screaming at me through the glass. 'What fucking right do you have, harassing people I date?'

I shrugged.

'I didn't hurt Janelle, asshole! She left me, you got that? *She* left *me*! I don't know where she is, and I had nothing to do with her- her- whatever happened to her. So fuck off, and stay out of my life!'

I shrugged again. What made him so sure she'd left him? A note? A text he forgot to mention to me? Or something else? Furious, Stanhope stamped back to his car and slammed the door hard, then he peeled wheels out of my lot. I was a little shaky, I'll admit, so I left the door locked.

Guess I was getting somewhere, but I did feel a little bad about cornering Siobhan. I'd be a monster if I didn't. I hoped he was mad because Siobhan dumped him, and that she was well out of his life now.

I sat down and took a deep breath. I leaned back in my chair and stared at the ceiling for a while, watching the reflections of light from passing cars flash across the tiles. Then, I resumed my work.

Two or more (who watches a clock when they don't have to?) hours later, I was seriously considering packing it in for the day, or the week or the month or the rest of my life, when something caught my eye.

A vehicle had come into the IEI parking lot after hours, pulling close to the rear of the building and parking. A standard issue Tough Guy™ got out and strode toward the back of the building, disappearing around a corner.

I could see why Brent had used the word 'cop'; this guy was fit and had the hairdo and body carriage to match; legally he couldn't be a current law enforcement officer and also be a security officer but there have been plenty of cases of cops moonlighting in security roles so it wouldn't surprise me in the least if that's what I was looking at here.

But that wasn't the interesting thing- what had caught my eye was the emblem on his jacket which was clearly visible on the left side of his chest. He'd had to wait while for a car ahead of his to move a bit so he could inch into the driveway, so he was moving slower than he might have if he'd had a clear path. I rewound the video repeatedly until I could pause it on a frame that gave me the best image, which I then screen-shot it and filed immediately.

Siobhan was right- it was a badge that looked like one that might be police issue. But I could read the company name, clear as day.

What is With the Dumb Names?

'The Solution Security Services? What a dumbass name,' said Becky, making a face like she'd just smelled something awful. 'Who thinks of this crap?'

'I know. But at least now we're getting somewhere with who might have been partying with Stanhope and Janelle.'

Becky nodded and sipped her coffee. She was wearing two sweaters, a scarf and had her hands wrapped in knitted rainbow handwarmers, just the tips of her fingers peeking out of all that yarn.

'Is it that cold out today?' I asked, 'I haven't been outside yet.'

'It cold as a - what's the phrase?'

'A witch's tit?'

'No, it's cold as a, a, ugh, I don't know. It's fucking freezing.'

I chuckled and walked across the room to the thermostat,

which I turned up a few more degrees. 'I've done some preliminary work on the security company- they don't have a website-'

'Really?' Becky asked, her voice tinged with disbelief. 'Who doesn't have a website nowadays?'

'Maybe they're a new organization, or -'

'Or maybe they're just shady as fuck.'

'Or maybe they're just 'shady as fuck',' I agreed. 'In any case, they're local, and I found the name of the person listed as the owner of record- one Carter Linhurst.'

Becky frowned. 'Linhurst?'

'Yeah, why?'

'That name is ringing a bell. I'm not sure from where though, give me a few minutes for my coffee to kick in and my blood to start flowing.'

'Take all the time you need. I'm gonna order breakfast delivery. You want pancakes or a bagel? Bacon? Potatoes?'

'Yes,' Becky replied.

Later, over takeout containers that were empty save for some leftover syrup and various crumbs, Becky cried out 'Ha! I found him.'

I'd been working to organize as much information as possible on all the entities listed as holdings under the umbrella of Global Manufacturers and Logistics, and I'd come up with a list of their addresses and images of their locations, but it was all starting to run together.

'He's the owner of a consultant company- CL Consultants.'

'Clever name,' I rolled my eyes.

'Right. So many of those. *But,* he's also listed as the owner of the security company, and his consultancy firm has their *own* holdings. The firm has been hired by several of the other companies we've been linking to IEI, under Global.'
'Really? That all sounds incredibly intermingled.'

'Yeah- they've got some probably fake testimonials, but they also have names of these companies listed, among other businesses, in their 'About Us' section.'

'That's some legitimacy,' I mused.

'Right. Some of these other companies are big names too; there's a pharmaceutical company, a carmaker, a law firm.'

'You know, I've always considered hiring a business consultant. Who is the youngest employee?'

'Uh... that looks like... probably this guy- Pete Elliston. He was made a consultant last year.'

'Give him a call and make an appointment- pretend you're my oh, let's say Executive Assistant. We'll make a lunch appointment. Let's dress fancy.'

'I can't wait.'

'I'll print up a couple of bogus business cards and call a guy I know-Georgio- who is a manager at La Polpetta, and let him know I'll need a table on short notice. He'll help me out;

I found a bunch of money and property his brother was hiding from him when their father died.'

'Damn.'

'Yep.'

The following day, (this is one reason why you reach out to the junior employee-they're not as busy yet and they're eager for new business to build their clientele!) Becky and I were sitting in our finest business attire (we clean up pretty good) at a fully set table covered in white linens with maroon napkins folded expertly, edges sharp enough to cut paper.

Georgio was looped in that we were going to be at the restaurant under false pretenses; I ate there regularly and well, I tend to have a certain look. So I didn't want to get any (good natured) comments from the staff on my appearance today.

Ever hospitable, Georgio gave our server instructions to give us as much space as possible, but to tend to us as speedily as could be managed, and make no small talk.

Becky looked amazing but was a bit fidgety; she had been letting her hair stay wild and free for so long that keeping it tucked up tight in a bun was uncomfortable. She'd complained the whole ride over here, but I totally understood because these worsted wool trousers and sensible heels were making me want to jump off a bridge.

But it was important to look the part, so we sat waiting for Pete, suffering in silence like every other business person who was here at the restaurant engaging in a working lunch.

Thankfully he was punctual, and I did feel a bit bad about the subterfuge because he seemed like a nice kid.

We exchanged business cards and pleasantries, ordered lunch and got right into it. Becky and I had rehearsed ahead of time about the nature of our 'business'. We spoke about our interest in growing, expanding, entering new markets, diversifying our product and other meaningless jargon. When Pete asked more in-depth questions about our business we answered by re-directing and asking him about CL Consultants, and in that way over the course of an hour, we managed to mine him for information about his firm without him realizing it.

We carefully navigated the conversation until we learned that the consultancy for the companies that we were interested in was handled exclusively by Carter Linhurst himself.

We ended the lunch with the excuse that we had to get back to the office for another meeting, thanked him for his time and after insisting that he let us get the bill with *our* expense account, we let him convince us to allow him to pay with *his* expense account.

THE GIRL WHO DIDN'T GO

Georgio gave me a wink and a smile as we left, which I returned.

In the car, Becky pulled the pins out of her hair and fluffed it until it stood up almost maniacally.

'Better?' I asked.

'Better.'

What The Consulting Meeting Tell Us

I spent an hour on the phone with Lennette, giving her, admittedly, a heavily edited version of what we'd uncovered so far.

'I'm getting somewhere, Lennette, and you're not going to like it.'

'I can take it.'

'You say that, but maybe you should go home.'

She sighed. 'I don't want to. But I'm starting to think that I should.'

'I'm sorry. I don't have a very good feeling about where this investigation is taking me.'

'I can hear that in your voice.'

'Yeah, I've never been a good liar.' I took a deep breath. 'I want you to begin to prepare for the worst. Obviously I want to tell you to remain hopeful-'

'I'm not an idiot,' Lennette interrupted, 'If Janelle was still alive, she would have contacted me. And the more you find out, the less likely it seems that she's going to just come walking into her life again.' Her voice cracked, and she started crying.

I gave her a few minutes, there was no rush. 'I'm sorry, I wish I had evidence that bore better tidings.'

She took a deep breath, and her words were shaky when they finally came. 'I already booked my flight home. I leave tomorrow. I just need you to promise me, that you're not going to let this go until we have a resolution.'

'I promise.'

'I mean it.'

'So do I.' I wasn't sure how helpful it would be to her, in her present state, to be informed of the entire scope of my investigation. The amount I was billing her was not even close to the quantity of hours I'd been working; this was rapidly growing outside the scope of a missing persons case, and I felt it wasn't Lennette's responsibility to pay for this much work; call me a softy but this was shaping up to be bigger than finding Janelle, and I couldn't justify charging Lennette for how much I was doing.

The web of people and companies on my white board was growing. I'd taken to storing the board out of sight in a storage closet in the back of my office, and wheeling it out when necessary. For added security and because I was feeling especially paranoid, I even made sure to keep it facing backward toward the rear wall of my office, and not allow anything on it to be seen from the front window. I considered that it was probably long past time to get some shades installed. Why had I never thought of that before you ask? Oh yeah, because I never had an investigation lead me into international imports and exports and multi-national corporations, run by shady people who I wasn't even sure actually existed and also who were having me watched.

People who hide money or infidelity are usually too wrapped up in their own lives to notice a relatively uninteresting woman following them a bit here and there, and tend to give up the goods in a matter of days or weeks. This was more, oh what's the word... substantial.

Becky and I stared at the board for a while. 'It's just too convoluted,' I moaned. 'Too many people, too many moving parts. I can't see the reason why any of them might need to get rid of someone as- and I know this sounds shitty when I say it out loud- unimportant as Janelle.' I (we) had started like many investigations- with a timeline and who we spoke to when. But the info was building faster than we were used to, and a pattern remained elusive.

'Let's rearrange the board,' Becky said, frowning. 'Look at it with fresh eyes.'

'That's a good idea. Let's put everyone at the top, and run connections to the companies. I think I have a chalkboard in the storage closet- we can use the to rewrite our timeline.'

'Perfect,' Becky replied, and she stood up and started pulling the pictures and papers down off the board, and piling them neatly on the coffee table.

I dug around in the closet and pulled out a dusty old chalkboard, and was struck by the notion that I couldn't remember where it came from, or why I had it.

'Do you even have any chalk?' Becky asked, mockingly.

'For your information, I think I actually do,' I replied, with a chuckle. 'I'm pretty sure I have some in a drawer over here- ha! Yes, here it is.' I pulled out one old stub of chalk, but it was enough.

When we were done, Becky and I sat back and looked at what we'd put together. A neat timeline of Janelle's recent movements, calls and messages, until she went 'missing' in Mexico.

Then on the whiteboard, faces, company names, corporate logos, all with brightly colored dry-erase marker lines connecting them in various ways. This CEO, this business manager, this company hired that company, this firm hired that firm, this person was hired to consult for these businesses, this guy went to school with that guy, this person co-owned a company with that guy.

'I think I'm starting to get an idea,' I said, quietly. 'The major players here are the imports and exports companies. Well, they're probably smuggling- or trafficking. That would be a good reason to get rid of Janelle- if she saw something she shouldn't have. But... why hire a consultant? And why does he work for all of these companies?' Then, a lightbulb went off in my mind. 'Oh fuck me,' I said, and Becky raised her eyebrows in response. 'The consulting business - I bet it's how they launder their money.'

'Consultancy firms don't take cash. It would be pinged immediately. You need a cash business to launder money.' Becky frowned. 'All these companies, legit on paper, paying each other for services. Just shuffling money back and forth. But where does the money come from, and where does it eventually land?'

'Hm, did we identify the companies that are listed as holdings under the consultancy firm?' I asked.

'Not yet,' Becky said.

Less than ten minutes of quick internet searches later, and we had located the last of the businesses that Becky had found while hunting down info on Linhurst and his consulting agency. We had a nice shiny list of five motels. 'Gotcha,' I said, smiling.

The Bird Show

'I'll never understand why he likes to meet us here,' Becky said, paying for our tickets at the counter with the bills I handed her. It had only taken an hour to get in touch with the person we'd come here to meet.

'Because he's paranoid, but also, given the circumstances, his paranoia is valid. Someone who isn't supposed to be *here* will stick out like a sore thumb.'

'You're telling me,' Becky said, taking a seat. 'How many times have we seen this show now?'

'At least three times.'

'I hope they bring out the macaw, he's my favorite.'

'I'm partial to the cockatoo,' Grassy said, sitting down on my left.

The keeper for the petting zoo's large bird population emerged a few moments later, and greeted the modest crowd, comprised entirely, with the exception of our party, of parents or teachers with young children.

The trainer had a blue macaw on her arm, and she introduced herself and the bird, and proceeded with her planned dialogue, which we knew well.

'What can I help you with?' Grassy asked quietly.

Becky and I did our best to keep our voices as low as possible while we brought him up to speed on our investigation, omitting unnecessary details.

'Okay,' he said, 'The corporations should not be too difficult but obviously security firms are, by nature, super difficult to gain access to. I appreciate the compliment of you thinking I'll be successful there.'

'I understand it might be beyond your capabilities but anything you can do to give it a go. We need to know all the locations that they provide security for…. If you can't access their client list, or locations served, maybe you can-'

'Look through the list of companies you've compiled and get proof they're paying security invoices-'

'Right. We've got a web of connections between these companies, so anything that you can find that connects them will be good- it might be what we've found already but I'm sure you'll find more than we've already got.'

'Ok. I can probably manage that. I'll keep you posted.'

'Thanks Grassy.'

'My pleasure. Oh, good, here comes the cockatoo.'

So as not to seem rude, the three of us remained seated until the show was over, and I have to say, I think it actually keeps getting better the more times I've seen it.

So Many Properties, So Little Gas in My Tank

Twenty years ago I would have had to drive to all the

properties and addresses (to look at them with my eyeballs or take photos with a film camera which I'd then have to get processed. And wait more than a day to review) that Grassy was able to locate when he began to dig into all the companies on the list we gave him. But with the internet, I was able to comfortably check them out online, and see, for many of them, street view images, satellite maps showing their surroundings, and real estate transactions. More warehouses, more loading docks, more parking lots.

Information from Grassy trickled in here and there, over the days following our meeting at the zoo, providing even more data points, logos and names to add to our collection. The biggest mystery, he admitted, was one name that appeared to be a shell company called Seaside Optics, which he said was regularly paid for 'logistics' but it was taking longer than usual to get into- and that he was determined to crack it.

Becky and I sat looking at the whiteboard, our heads spinning.

'One thing I've realized,' I said, 'is that if Janelle did see something that put her in danger, the people involved in this organization definitely have the means to craft her fake vacation to Mexico, stage her apartment to look like she'd left willingly, and then access her phone to continue communicating like she was still alive.'

'You're right. One person, a bad boyfriend, a fight. He might have just fled, or dumped the body, or something like that. But this? These people would be able-'

'And willing-'

'-to pull that off.' Becky finished.

'But that begs the question, who is the fake Janelle? They would have had to hire someone. And her face has been on the news and in the papers. If it was an actor, a legit employee who wasn't aware of the scope of the task, what they were being asked to do; they'd know by now it was serious.'

'But if they had a personal stake- if Janelle's silence benefited her in some way, maybe...' Becky wondered.

'Yeah, but none of the people we've discovered so far match Janelle's frame, or description. Even the wives of these men who are running these businesses.'

'It's always possible that one of them has a mistress, and had her be the doppelganger.'

'True. But there is literally no way we can investigate each of these dudes individually and find that out.' I shook my head and sighed.

'I know. I think we need to be prepared that the identity of the doppelganger might be something that we never discover.'

'That's a good point...' I replied, my voice trailing off. My mind was running and I needed a second to formulate my thoughts. 'Who would you hire if you were doing something illegal, and needed a woman who would never go to the cops, but might imitate someone for money?'

Becky's face fell. 'No.'

'Yes.'

'Those women have it hard enough. They don't need grief from us.'

'I know- but think of it this way- if a working girl carried out this job, she'd be a loose end now. And potentially be in danger, if she's even still alive.'

'Fuck.'

'Exactly. You stick with research. I'm going to start following Stanhope. It's the weekend- if he's hiring girls, or frequents places where they're working, I might be able to get a lead on who he might have hired.'

'If it even was him.'

'Yes, but right now, he's the only one we know for sure who's slept in Janelle's bed, and lied to me about it.'

Lots of the Backs of Cars and Heads

Every job has it's tedium or irritations and the one I had the hardest time with was following targets. People in general are pretty boring and predictable, everyone has to go to stores to buy clothes and toiletries, everyone has to pick up pet food or home improvement supplies.

I'd love for every person I follow to drive straight to a place where they commit their crimes or adultery in a wide open field so I can easily photograph them and then be on my way, however I spent more time waiting off to the side of a lot or road for someone to pump gas, put air in their tires, grab a coffee in a drive-thru, and so on than I'd like to. Of course, I usually bill for those hours so I try not to get cranky about it.

When surveilling and following someone, it's obviously important to not be seen, which is tricky when you're pulling in and out of parking lots, getting through intersections and having to sit and wait while someone is in a bank for example.

You see a lot of their rear bumper, the back of their head, the side of their face; the trick is to make sure they don't spot *you*.

This particular evening, Stanhope stayed late at the office. The sun had long ago gone down and I was glad of the darkness, and the cover it provided.

When he finally came outside, there were only a few cars left in the parking lot; I had to wait until he was out on the road before I put on my headlights and followed.

He stopped for gas and then continued on his way; after

a short time we merged onto a main thoroughfare where more and more businesses and traffic converged. With this it became increasingly difficult to keep an eye on him.

I kept my distance as well as I could but when he turned into the parking lot of La Chatte, I groaned audibly.

Chuck

I met my tenant Chuck when I almost had to maim him. He was a retired wrestler, and had had a few years of success, nearly making it big with a contract in one of those professional wrestling organizations. He currently works as a bouncer at a couple different bars and nightclubs around town- including, you guessed it, La Chatte.

Once, when I was on a case, an unfaithful, general louse of a husband found out his wife had hired me and paid Chuck to rough me up. I knew exactly what he'd come to do as soon as I laid eyes on him, and the golf club I was aiming at his kneecaps told him I wasn't going to make it easy. (When your opponent is exponentially bigger than you, *always* go straight for the tender bits- the knees, the arch of the foot, the groin, the soft tissues. Always.)

I didn't know it in that moment, but the fear of fresh agony in his bum knee was enough to shake him out of it, and give him a reason to think twice about what he'd set out to do. I realized later, in addition to him generally preferring to be a good and decent human, that that was the hesitation I saw in his eyes, and his movements.

So we called a truce, shook hands and ended up talking it over, and that's when I learned he needed a new apartment. In the subsequent years, I've learned that Chuck, or Charles Shetland III, as the IRS knew him- 'if they could find' him, he'd laugh- was the son of - you guessed it- Charles Shetland II. Charles the Second played pro football in the sixties and did well, by all accounts. Which meant for the rest of his life after retirement, his brain matter degraded into paste, leaving him quick to anger, unpredictable and violent.

So when Chuck the Third expressed interest in following in his father's footsteps (at twelve he already had the frame for it) his mother promptly put the kibosh on that idea and enrolled him in track and field instead- against the begging and pleading of every football coach in a twenty mile radius- where he became incredibly talented at shotput. In high school she permitted him to try wrestling, at which he also excelled.

Fending off the football coaches became increasingly difficult for Chuck's mother, as they resorted to manipulative, underhanded tactics when he was alone at school. He came home many a day, convinced she was trying to stifle his potential, seeing her as the obstacle to his guaranteed success.

That is, until his father suicided, which Chuck told me was the worst wake-up call a frustrated teenager could be subjected to, and put an end to his aspirations to play pro football once and for all.

During college, Chuck's talents in the wrestling ring came to the attention of the pro circuit, and he got a little taste of the attention, money and fame that such a career could bring him, until a bad hit took him out for good. The damage that was done to his knee was catastrophic, and he said, the doctors worried that he might even lose the ability to use the leg completely- given his size and weight. But he worked as hard as he could in physical therapy, and got use of it back, although it was never the same again and pained him quite a bit on rainy days and in the deepest part of the winter.

He had never taken a job as a bruiser or a leg breaker before we 'met'. He was reluctant and hesitant, and I had seen that in his eyes. He had been sleeping in his van and feeling pretty desparate. He was having trouble finding somewhere to live; his Black skin and towering size makes people nervous. Making morons nervous is a good thing in his current line of work, but it makes it hard for him to navigate the normal, quiet spaces, and he's gotten more than his share of toxic reactions and vile behavior from people over the course of his life.

He's spent years trying to make himself seem friendly and approachable to people who were absolute shits and don't deserve to know him, and he's exhausted. So he mostly keeps to himself, and has a small group of close friends, one of which I am grateful to call myself. He deserves to occupy the space he is in without grief, and that's that.

My size makes people think I'm delicate like a toothpick, and I never hear the end of how small I am. I'm *not* saying I have an inkling of what it's like to be anyone else, I'm not comparing our experiences. But like, yeah, I get it. I'm short. And skinny. You think I don't know what I look like?

Chuck and I make quite the pair when we go for our weekend runs around the resevoir. Basically he could easily pick me up and hurl me like a javelin. But I share my kale smoothies, and he changes the lightbulbs in my ceiling fixtures, and always knows which wine to pair with our food- it's a gift. And if it takes getting to know him, and learning about all the things that make him the intelligent, caring and affectionate person that he is, for someone to look at him and unironically, tone-deafly, say 'oh, he's one of the good ones' then they don't deserve to share his space anyway. The pain in his eyes told me everything I needed to know about him the minute I saw his face for the first time. Oh yeah- and that cheating husband who hired Chuck?

Well, he got his- I gave all my evidence to his wife, but withheld a few things for my own personal use. She raked him across the coals in court and got everything- the dog, the house, the cars. Then, after he was drained clean of personal assets, his company (basically the only thing he had left after the divorce) was 'anonymously' reported for some substantial fraud a year later, and he's sitting in jail now. Sometimes things work out okay.

La Chatte

I hated involving people I knew personally in my work life without their knowledge or consent- thankfully it's almost never an issue. It was one thing if they wanted to help, another thing entirely if my investigation took me trotting through their life without warning.

As fast as I could, I shot Chuck a text message that I was following a lead who was heading into his club. I added a photo, and hoped Chuck had a minute to see the messages. I waited in my car, watching Stanhope walk in the front door. Chuck got up from his stool, and took a few minutes longer than he probably would normally have, checking his ID. I saw Stanhope become agitated and I blessed Chuck for existing.

He allowed Stanhope to go into the club, and then sent me a

message to tell me what door he'd gone through.

I took off my hat and my coat - my sweater was cute and presentable enough- and I fluffed my hair, grabbed my phone, wallet and keys, then hurried across the icy parking lot to the front door.

Chuck nodded at me and opened the door when he saw me coming, and gave my shoulder a small affectionate squeeze as I hurried by.

Inside, there was a dimly lit foyer, with dark purple curtains draped along the walls. To the left, a large black door had the silhouette of a curvaceous woman kicking her legs in purple neon flashing above. To the right, a duplicate door had a neon green shape of a muscular man flexing like an Olympian. I went through the left, and waited for a second along the wall, to give myself time to adjust. The inside was nearly as dark as it was outside, and the light and music were pumping.

Almost naked women danced on the stage, and milled around with customers, serving drinks and enticing patrons into the private booths. In the adjacent room, nearly naked men were doing the exact same thing with their customers. It was a one-stop shop.

A dancer approached me and smiled. She leaned close and asked if I wanted a dance. I told her yes, and hid behind her as she led me into a private booth toward the back. I got a clear look at the patrons at the tables, and spotted Stanhope easily. The dancer was a good deal taller than me, even without her vertiginous heels, and her giant boobs hid my face as we made our way across the room, so even if he had been looking around, he most likely wouldn't have seen me anyway.

'What's your name, honey?' the dancer asked me, as she closed the curtain. I gave it a tug to keep it open a few inches, giving me an eyeline straight to Stanhope's table. She pushed my shoulders gently until I sat down on the tufted red pleather bench, and I told her my name. She straddled my lap and bobbed up and down a few times, bringing her bosom so close I felt a ribbon from her skimpy top tickle my nose, as she majestically flipped her hair back and forth.

'What's yours?' I asked, leaning close to her so I could look over her shoulder or around her ribcage, depending on how much she bounced.

'I'm Jasmine. What do you want baby?' She stood up again and began to dance in front of me, rocking her hips back and forth in a way that made me envious of her youth and agility. She must do a lot of yoga. Or pilates. She spun around and bent over at the waist, rolling her bottom around in circles near my face, then whipped her hair up as she snapped back to standing. It was all so fast and impressive I found myself momentarily distracted from my stakeout.

'Uh, Jasmine? How much is this dance?'

'It's fifty bucks for fifteen minutes.'

'I'll give you a hundred bucks just to sit here with me for a bit.'

She stopped gyrating and looked down at me, frowning. 'What is this? You a cop? Is this like, a raid or something?'

I shook my head.

'Oh. You just looking for someone to talk to or what?' She held out a hand.

I put a pile of tens and twenties into her palm. 'Actually, I'm a P.I. and I'm on a stakeout.'

She plopped down onto the sofa beside me, crossing her long, muscular legs. 'No shit?!' She said, thumbing through the bills. She separated fifty to pay the house for the dance, and then tucked her own fifty deep into her bra with her right boob. 'Who's the mark?'

I laughed out loud.

'What?' she said, winking. 'I watch a lot of cop shows and listen to true crime podcasts.'

I nodded toward the curtain. 'You ever seen him in here before?'

She leaned over me (she smelled like flowers and vanilla cookies, and got glitter on my pants) and looked out at Stanhope. 'No, he doesn't look familiar. If he's been in here before he hasn't bought a dance from me. What did he do? He cheating on his wife?'

'Nothing like that.'

'Listen, what kind of cases do you take, cuz I got this problem- my ex stole my car when he skipped out on me- left me with the whole ass lease too- and the cops won't do shit. I had to get one of the other girls to move in with me to help with rent for a while. Do you track people down?'

'Yeah,' I said. I pulled a wrinkled business card out of my pocket and handed it to her. 'Give me a call and I'll see what I can do.'

'Thanks, D,' she said, tucking the card in with her money.

We sat together for a bit; whoever Stanhope was waiting for, either the person was late or Stanhope had come to the club early. He was fidgety, and didn't really make any progress on the drink that was left in front of him.

Jasmine busied herself by examining her manicure and adjusting the buckles on her shoes.

'Tell me about yourself,' I said, sensing she was getting bored.

She laughed, and it was genuine and made me smile. 'Do you want to hear the story about how I'm just doing this to put myself through school?' she asked. 'Well, it's nothing like that. I just make a shit ton of money, so I like it. Decent clientele too. Business guys who like to hear how handsome and successful they are, you know? Sometimes I can get them to give stock tips, and I can tell how the market is doing by how often a few of them- the higher rollers- show up, and how much they spend. So... I communicate with my broker accordingly.' I must have looked surprised because she laughed again, heartily. 'Oh honey, nobody's gonna hand you a piece of the pie. You gotta take it.'

'Yeah, you're right there.'

'Damn straight.' She twirled a lock of hair between two fingers. 'I'm looking to retire comfortably, not broke.'

'Tell me more about this place,' I said; I liked her voice.

'Well, let's see. The bouncers here are actually nice guys who don't let the customers pull any stunts. The last place I worked wasn't so good. Real shithole. The manager would make you blow him before he paid out your tips. Not every night, but often enough. And don't even get me started on what they'd expect you to do for the high rollers, a term I use for them loosely. They weren't even big time guys. Just big time for that place, I guess.'

I grimaced.

'Yeah. It was hard to leave too. I quit once and the next morning there were two dudes bangin' at my door, tellin' me if I didn't get my ass to work the cops'd find my body down by the river.'

'Fucking hell,' I said, looking at her in horror. 'What did you do?'

'What *could* I do?' she shrugged with a nonchalance that made me instantly sad. No one should shrug at that kind of treatment. 'I took my ass to work. But I started skimming money, cuz I had to get out of there. Girl, never was there a minute I wasn't scared as shit.'

'I bet,' I said, wondering if I could ever be as brave as Jasmine.

She went on, 'I managed without them noticing- took me a few weeks- to get enough so I could take off, move out of my apartment. I found a new place but I could only go so far, you know? I got friends, and family 'round here. Thankfully, the club shut down after- I think the feds came in or something. Man I was relieved when I got that news, I could sleep again, not afraid anymore about them finding me. You wanna hear the funniest thing? Turns out the manager was skimming too. The owners were real shady, some of the girls said they were mob. He was just gone one day. Nobody knew where. No big loss though.' She shrugged again. 'This place is a lot nicer.'

'I'm glad for you.'

'Thanks. How did you become a P.I.?'

'I was a cop. I got shot. Kind of forced me to retire.'

'Damn.'

'Yeah, it sucked too.'

She shook her head slowly, and sighed. Then she smiled again. 'Hey, you want a shoulder rub or something? I give really good ones.'

'Actually, that sounds great-' I said, shifting in my seat so my back was to her. Then I ducked as her long leg, made eight inches longer with the height of the heel strapped to her foot, whipped over my head with a speed that was incredible, and settled down on my right side, nestling me comfortably in front of her. But then someone approached Stanhope's table and sat down. 'Wait a sec, something's happening,' I said.

She scooted in close to me, which flattered me that she felt safe enough to embrace me in such a way (how often do you get held tight by an amazon of a woman by both her arms *and* her legs?). She rested her chin on my shoulder, peering through the curtain as well. Man, it's been so long since I was the little spoon, I could have cried.

'Oh, that guy,' she said, '*He's* here all the time. Huge asshole. Has definitely gotten handsy with lots of girls, but he's some local bigshot, so they haven't banned him. I don't know his real name but everyone calls him Sarge.'

'I know his name,' I replied, sullenly. Kevin Werth, a.k.a. Sarge a.k.a. Kev when we were friends. My old boss at the precinct. We worked together for years, sometimes closely, on task forces and a variety of cases. Before I was injured I reported directly to him along with a dozen other officers. He came to the hospital to visit me- once. Called me when I was home- once. And then I never heard from him again.

I could see by the way he held his shoulders, and glanced around every few seconds, that he was already agitated before they even began talking.

We watched as they spoke in rapid conversation, and it became quickly apparent that it was escalating into a heated argument.

'Damn, what do you think they're fighting about?' Jasmine asked.

'I'm not sure, but it can't be good,' I replied.

We were both surprised when Kevin took hold of Stanhope's shirt and gripped it tightly, pulling Stanhope's face close to his own.

'Woah,' Jasmine whispered.

A group of young men were seated at the table beside them, and Stanhope pulled his shirt out of Kevin's grip and motioned toward them. I partially heard Kevin remark that he didn't give a fuck about those idiots, and Stanhope told him to keep his voice down. That was all I could make out.

They resumed their discussion and I really wished I'd learned how to read lips, because I couldn't hear what they were saying, but I didn't dare get any closer.

Next thing I knew, Stanhope had his finger in Kevin's face,

and when Kevin smacked it away, Stanhope's arm flew backwards and hit one of the drunk patrons at the next table, right in the back of the head.

'Oh, no,' Jasmine groaned. 'That guy's a brawler.'

True to her word, the man stood up, and drunkenly leaned over Kevin and Stanhope's table. *His* voice, I could hear clearly. 'Th' fuck's your problem man?'

Stanhope attempted to apologize, and Kevin also tried to calm him down but it wasn't working. The man's friends tried to intervene, unsuccessfully.

Then, Stanhope made it worse by shouting insults at the drunk customer, telling him to go fuck himself.

'Oh, here we go,' Jasmine said. Within a few seconds, all hell had broken loose, and fists were flying. The nearest girls scattered like sparkly birds flitting in multiple directions, and I saw Kevin duck out, weaving between tables and exiting just as Chuck and the other bouncers came together and moved swiftly toward the fight, which had absorbed another table of drunk dudes. I could no longer see Stanhope, and I wondered if he was even still in the middle of the melee, or if he'd also managed to wiggle out.

'I need an exit,' I said, and Jasmine nodded.

'C'mon,' she replied, and took my hand. She pulled me through the curtain and we hurried past the writhing mob who probably didn't even know why they were fighting, and the large bouncers who were pulling people apart and tossing them out to the parking lot one or two at a time.

Jasmine took me through a door hidden behind a heavy curtain at the back of the stage and down a long, dimly lit hallway. She brought me to a rear exit, and held the door open for me. 'Good luck,' she said.

'Thanks, you too,' I replied, jogging off through the parking lot, and around the side of the building. The temperature had dropped considerably, and I hurried to my car and jumped inside. I was cold, and I didn't take enough time to ensure there was no one in the parking lot who would recognize me, unfortunately.

These are My Jams

Troubled by what I'd witnessed, I missed my main turn heading home and ended up along a stretch of highway which housed a lot of big box stores, most of which were now closed but still bathed the entire area in an unnatural amount of light.

I had a variety of different routes that could take me home, but I needed to focus and decide which way to go. I sighed, considered turning around, then changed my mind. My fridge at home was empty and my stomach was too. I pulled in toward a grocery mart and drove across the parking lines.

The nearly empty lot was illuminated in red and white and orange from the light of the store's signage, which glowed with a gentle hum. I parked in the first space nearest the door.

Due to the late hour, the cart returns were all empty, and the wind whistled across the open space, making my ears smart.

Late nights are the only time I can handle going to the grocery store. There's a surreal technicolor to the food labels under the glare of the fluorescent lights, that seems enhanced when there's no sunlight from the outside to soften it. I find that I don't get as frustrated at the amount of time it might take me to choose an item, or feel as weird about standing and staring at the options for probably longer than it takes other people. The aisles are usually close to empty and typically there are no lines at the one or two open registers.

The best part is I can hear the music, which- I don't know why- seems to be a lot of bangers lately.

I was bopping to the music, nudging my handbasket along the floor with the toe of my boot, and trying to decide if I wanted vermicelli or linguine when someone said my name.

I looked up, and knew immediately I was unsuccessful at hiding my initial facial expression- which was fear. I did my best to set my face to a neutral expression, even feign warmth or enthusiasm; but the glint in his eyes told me I was caught. 'Uh, hey, Kevin,' I said, my stomach doing flip flops.

'Oshtrovsky, good to see you. How have you been?'

'Oh, you know, same shit. I hear you were promoted a while back?'

He half-smiled and nodded. His hair was grayer, and his midsection was wider than the last time I'd seen him this close. 'Yeah, to lieu.'

'That's great. How's Linda, and the kids?' *Remind him of how well you know him. Try to rock him off balance.*

'All good, all good. How 'bout you?'

'Fine. We're all fine.'

'You still got that tenant? Charles-'

'Yeah. He's great.'

'Heard there was a call out at his club tonight, seems things got a little rough.'

'Oh?'

He looked at me for a moment, expecting me to elaborate. I did not. 'Well, seems like there might have been a misunderstanding. These things happen when there is drinking involved.'

'Yeah. Probably,' I said.

'Listen-'

I quickly interrupted him. 'So what are your plans? You ready to retire soon?'

He nodded. 'I did already, actually.'

'Wow, good for you, what do with all your free time? You were never a golfer.'

'Security. A couple of the guys from the department came over with me to the private sector. We got a good crew.'

'Security? Is there much need for that around here?'

'We've got some contracts with local warehouses, stuff like that.'

'IEI?'

He was silent for a moment, and I saw the tiniest muscle twitch in the side of his mouth. 'We've got a handful of clients all around the state.'

'What do you want, Kevin?'

'I can't just say hi to an old friend?'

'First time for everything.'

'That's not fair.'

'Lots of things aren't fair,' I said, waving my shrivelled left hand at him. 'Look, I gotta go. It was nice catching up. Good luck with... everything.'

I grabbed the vermicelli and scooped up my basket, hurrying to the cash register, and the safety of the one or two people waiting to ring out, before he had a chance to try to keep the conversation going.

'Take care of yourself Oshtrovsky!' he said loudly after me, and I knew that was a threat.

I (overly) cheerfully engaged in conversation with the single man who was checking out ahead of me, and he seemed grateful for the exchange, pausing to wait for me to pay for my items as we continued conversing. From the corner of my eye I saw Kevin exit the store; I could see he was watching me, and I acted like I didn't notice. I'm sure I didn't act that well though; I felt like my fear and tension could probably be seen from space.

The man with whom I was chatting walked into the parking lot with me, and I was grateful to see Kevin was already leaving. However, instead of exiting the lot, he drove past us as we walked across the pedestrian zone. The man I was with cursed him out for driving so close and fast past us, and I felt badly for him- he obviously didn't realize Kevin was doing it on purpose, why would he? When Kevin turned right onto the road, I hurriedly ended the conversation with my new friend as politely as I could and sped out of the lot, making a left of course, and it took a few miles until my pulse slowed down, but my mind raced for hours.

I didn't know Kevin's role in any of this. But a couple things I was sure of, as sure as there was a nose on my face, that spring follows winter, that we are floating on a rock in an infinite universe that is expanding and that eventually the sun will burn out and die, was that our meeting hadn't been by accident, and I finally knew who the 'cop' was.

Chuck Has Great Ideas

Chuck knocked on my door in the wee hours. This wasn't unusual. I sometimes dealt with bouts of insomnia, and the walls were thin. He could tell when I was awake at night, as I often paced. With his late hours, sometimes he'd come over and we'd watch a movie or have a few drinks while we talked through what was keeping us awake, 'til one of us nodded off.

I opened the door and immediately felt terrible. Chuck had a massive bandage covering the left side of his face.

'What happened?' I asked, already sort of knowing the answer.

'I don't know who that clown was you followed into the Cat tonight, but he took a cheap shot at me before I got him out.'

'I'm sorry, Chuck, does it hurt much?'

'It's okay for now, got some stitches. This bandage is a lot bigger than it needs to be. But I'm out of work for a few days 'til the cut is healed, so, you want some help?'

Over the years, Chuck had assisted me once or twice, for pay or for a break in the rent, whichever he requested, and much like it was with Becky, I was always happy to have his insight.

'Sure, come on in.'

'So who were you following?'

'He was the missing girl's boss- and the person she was dating.'

'Cliche. You think he's got something to do with her going missing?'

'Yeah- well, sort of. But I can't figure out if he's directly responsible, or if he is just a small part of something bigger. Or if he's not even involved at all.'

'You want me to sit on him?'

I resisted the urge to giggle at the thought of Chuck actually seated upon Stanhope. 'No, he seems more... sketchy than our normal clientele. He knows something's up, and he's on alert. I think he'd spot you right away. But thanks all the same. I've got something else you can help me with, though.'

'Lay it on me, but can you make me one of those smoothies first?'

'You got it.'

While I made the smoothies, I sent Chuck downstairs to pull the whiteboard out of the closet. After I poured the drinks into two tall glasses, I left the messy blender on the counter and joined him downstairs.

He moved to turn on more lights and I told him not

to. I relayed about the night someone had stood outside watching my office, and showed him the cigarette butts I'd collected.

'Lots of people smoke,' he said, handing the bag back to me.

'Yeah, but they don't stand in an empty parking lot staring at my building while they do so,' I replied.

'Good point.' Chuck took a long draw on the straw sticking out of his glass. 'So, walk me through what you have so far.'

Thirty minutes later I'd caught Chuck up to speed on Janelle's movements, and the names and information Becky and I had collected, and the reason I was following Stanhope tonight.

'If he's getting squirrely I bet you're right that he'll notice he's being followed,' Chuck said. 'Doubtful you'll get anywhere with him now.'

'I agree,' I said. 'Never in a million years would I have guessed that someone I used to know, much less worked with at the precinct, might be wrapped up in all this. But now...'

'What?' Chuck asked, loudly finishing his smoothie. I hadn't even touched mine yet. He pointed to it.

'Go ahead,' I said, my voice barely above a whisper. 'I've just lost my appetite.'

'What's up?'

'The apartment, the plan to have Janelle become a missing

person in Mexico. The messed up hotel room... It's all breadcrumbs.'

Chuck frowned at me in confusion.

'Investigative breadcrumbs,' I continued. 'Designed- by someone who knows police procedure- to lead us in a specific direction.'

Chuck stopped sipping and looked up at me. 'Goddamn.'

'Yeah. Thats an understatement.'

'So when are we leaving?' He asked, stirring his drink with the straw.

'What?'

'When are we getting *the fuck* outta here and this town and state and country?'

Need a Full Tank Now, Don't I?

Internet searches are great but there always comes a point where they can't offer any more that what you've already found, and I'd arrived at that point.

I'd spent nearly an entire day going from anonymous warehouse to anonymous warehouse, from non-descript office buildings to non-descript business parks all day, trying to get an idea of what any of them actually did.

I drove for hours, and took dozens of photographs of trucks, warehouse workers and admin employees heading out for their lunch breaks.

Once the sun began to go down, frustrated and exhausted, and wondering if I was way *way* off track and just snapping pics of literally nothing except boring old commerce and the shitty backside of capitalism, when I saw a basic silver sedan pull into the parking lot of the building I was currently surveilling- a facility called Cornwall Imports. Moments later, a tractor with an empty trailer pulled in, and backed up to the loading dock.

I knew the office employees had all left- I'd photographed them exiting the front doors shortly after five o'clock. There were two cars still parked in the rear lot, cleaners or warehouse workers were my guesses.

Two standard issue tough guys got out of the sedan, and I wondered why they all wore the same smooth leather jackets. Like, do they go to 'The Tough Guy Warehouse' and pick out the same coat, pants and haircuts? A one stop shop to look like the door guy at a back room poker parlor?

When one of them lit a cigarette, it meant nothing until he carefully cupped the cherry into the palm of his hand, hiding it from the wind. And from being seen.

I took several deep breaths to calm my nerves (lots of people probably smoke that way) and zoomed in as tight as my camera lens would allow, and took as many pictures as I could until the men were out of sight behind the building.

I was parked across the street, my car nestled in among several others- the vehicles for the cleaning crew for the multi-story building on this lot, which housed a multitude of random companies (and the sign out front offered office space for lease, so I knew some of it was empty too).

I took my camera and a few self-defense items just in case and scurried across the road, using a large hedge at the border of the parking lot for cover, and grateful for the early darkness that winter brought. I followed the edge of the property until I could duck behind the dumpsters, then I peered out around the side.

I had an okay view of the interior of the warehouse; two of the four loading dock doors were wide open and all the lights were still on inside, casting a bright fluorescent glow down into the dark parking lot. The dock where the truck had pulled up was blocked by the trailer but I could see, through the other bay door, the forklifts moving swiftly back and forth. I could only see the one Tough Guy- the one who had been driving. I could see everything only for a few minutes though, for the smoking guy (who appeared to be in charge) emerged from a human door in the back of the warehouse, shouted at his driver, and that guy quickly pulled the door down to close the open bay.

I'd photographed as much as I could, but without being able to crack open one of those crates, there was no way to prove they didn't in fact, contain exactly what was stamped on the sides of them.

Guess I was gonna have to come back later.

I ran back to the car, well, ran as well as I could hunched over to stay below the line of the hedges, and then across the road to my car. I left the lot and drove a few miles away, then decided I may as well get some dinner while I waited, and headed to a chain restaurant that I remembered passing on my way up earlier.

After I paid my check, I called Becky to let her know what I was planning.

'I'm not crazy about this,' she said.

'You think I am?' I replied. 'I just wanted to let you know, I'm not expecting to be back until late. I'll keep you posted but right now I gotta go.'

'Are you alright?'

'Yeah, I've just got to see a man about a horse.'

'What?'

'Nevermind.'

The Guard

The cleaning crew, whose cars had given mine some cover earlier, were done and gone by the time I returned. I could also see that the tough guys, truck driver and the warehouse workers who had loaded the crates on the trucks at Cornwall Imports had also left.

The industrial park didn't allow a lot of place to hide a car. Mostly empty roads and few trees-the ones that were there were ornamental plums, short and skinny. I parked in the lot to the side of Cornwall, so I could leave my car behind the hedge I used for cover earlier. However, I'd still have to cross the wide expanse of empty parking lot.

The warehouse looked like every other warehouse on the planet. Basic cinderblock walls, flat roof, everything painted gray, weeds popping up thorough the cracks in the parking lot and striped yellow lines in the fire zones where you weren't allowed to park.

The unspoilt snow lay evenly across the ground in the spaces between buildings and warehouses, where no one had a reason to walk or drive. Barely touched save for a few animal tracks. It must be lovely at night; all that perfect white snow glowing in the moonlight.

Now that I was at the back of the building, I could see that one car was left in the lot; a different one than had been there earlier. I hazarded a guess there was a night security guard.

I moved to the human door on the back of the building, and placed one hand on the handle and tried it; unsurprisingly it was locked. Not to worry. I made quick work of it.

I knew it would be alarmed; the sticker with the name and logo of the security company was featured prominently in the front window of the office. I knew what their devices looked like, and more importantly, how to trick them. From surveillance earlier, I'd seen that whoever had installed the system had put the boxes in the same corner on several of the doors- I deduced the warehouse human door would be the same. If I was wrong, well, I could run fast.

I pulled a flat piece of metal out of my pocket, and as I slid the door open (as slowly as the main character in Poe's Telltale Heart opened the bedchamber door to look upon the old man sleeping in his bed, and cast light from his lantern upon the Evil Eye) I moved the bit of metal into the jam and covered the sensor to the alarm box, so it registered the door was still closed. Then, holding the metal in place, I stepped inside, shut the door slowly, holding it steady so it didn't make a noise as it closed. I left the metal piece wedged in the doorjam, and waited for my eyes to adjust to the darkness of the warehouse.

There were two emergency lights on up by the front of the space, near the doors which I assumed led to the office.

I moved along the wall, watching carefully for security cameras, but seeing none. There had been two outside, pointed at the driveway and front door. I guess if you're involved in illegal activities, you might not want much video documenting it.

I eventually located, with some difficulty, several crates which looked identical to the ones that were loaded onto the truck earlier. From the material to the stamps on the side, they appeared to have arrived in the same shipment as the crates which were taken away.

I didn't know what any of the markings meant, but with gloved hands, I carefully removed the shipping labels from the plastic pouches attached to the sides, and photographed the documents before replacing them.

It would have been noisy to try to open some of the crates; they were all still nailed shut. But I found several that were open, with different markings on their sides, the contents appeared to have been removed a little at a time, for sales I imagined.

They seemed to contain nothing more than metal parts, which I could not readily identify. They were, most likely, real items for legitimate sale.

I heaved a deep sigh and crept along the wall again, until I reached the office door and looked through the window. My heart pounded when I saw the silhouette of the security guard, and it took me a few seconds to ascertain the distance between us. Then he disappeared around the corner which led to the front of the building and the reception area, and I took hold of the doorhandle and opened it slowly. I was at the end of a long hallway lined only with more closed doors. The slender glass windows in all of them showed darkened rooms. Within a few seconds I was inside the one that looked the most like a manager's office, and I pushed the door shut swiftly and quietly. Then I pressed my back against the wall. I needed to get an idea of the security guard's route so I could plan accordingly. After what felt like a million years, he finally walked by the door. I saw his profile as he peered into the room, but he moved on after a moment.

I heard the squeak of his rubber soles against the floor down at the end of the hall, and the click of what I assumed to be the warehouse door I'd just come through. Give him five or ten minutes to walk the perimeter of that space, I guessed.

I braved the chance to rifle through the filing cabinets (filing cabinet locks are a joke) and the documents littered across the very messy desk.

I saw a few items that seemed like they might be helpful- invoices, carbon copies, some pages showing lists of names and phone numbers. I took a picture of the desk as found it, heavy packets of pages held together with extra heavy duty staples, binders with company names and logos, trucking contracts. There were no photographs, no personal items, no duffle bags of gym clothes or a change of shoes in the cupboards along the wall. Just office supplies, previous years' inventory checklists in binders, old dusty phonebooks, coffee pods stored beneath a counter that held a one cup at a time machine like the one I had at home.

I flipped through the papers, took as many pictures as I could, then did my best to put the desk back the way I found it.

I heard the door down the hall open and shut again. I squeezed myself against the wall beside the door to the office, and watched the shadow go by. Then, another squeak of his soles, and I perhaps had another five minutes.

I clicked the computer on, and waited for it to boot up. Once the password request box popped up, I inserted a very special USB drive that Grassy had given me, and waited for it to upload and begin.

Within a moment, more dialog boxes began to pop up, and I instructed them to do their work.

Several of the longest seconds later, and the password was cracked. The program showed me what it had discovered, and hurriedly, I scrolled through recent documents, checked the search history and email contacts.

I produced an external hard drive from my coat pocket and plugged it in, then began moving over as much as I could grab.

My heart leapt into my throat when I heard a sneeze, followed by a second one. The silence was so heavy that the slightest noise sounded sharp and almost felt like it hurt my ears. I was afraid he was right outside the door, but then the echo of his subsequent sniffs and a cough told me he was still down the hall.

I tossed my coat over the laptop to hide the light from the screen and crouched once again by the door. My heart was pounding, and I was working hard to control my breathing as I listened to his quiet footfalls as he moved along the corridor.

He didn't stop to look in the window of the office door this time; I heard him sneeze once more, then mutter some curse words. A moment or two later, I heard an overhead fan come on, and him blowing his nose several times, the noise echoing- he must be in the bathroom.

I lifted my coat and was relieved to see that the files had finished transferring. I unplugged my devices and turned the computer off.

I snapped a few more photos of the desktop, and then I moved back over to the wall beside the door.

My still pounding heartbeat was thundering in my ears, and I was sweating. I needed to get out of there, I was pushing it. What I could see outside the door was severely limited since the window was so narrow, and I knew that whenever I moved, I was taking a chance at being seen. I cracked the door open ever so slightly, and listened carefully. I could still hear the fan from the bathroom, and hoped this was my chance. I hadn't heard the toilet flush, or water run yet. I opened the door wider.

I tried to control the door again as it shut, but I let go a second too soon, and it clicked. It wasn't very loud, but in that silent hallway, I may as well have been ringing the bells of Notre Dame.

Two doors down, the guard burst out of the bathroom.

'Hey! What are you doing?' he called out. He was bigger than me, and was blocking my exit. Swell.

'Hi, I was looking for the manager?'

'Wha-?'

'Oh, I uh, have a delivery.' Good one.

'You're not carrying anything.'

'Right, well, it's outside in my vehicle, it's heavy, uh, I need someone big and strong to carry it.'

He had a sidearm which he made a point to rest his hand upon, (on closer examination I realized it was a taser) and he came nearer to me, until he was close enough that I could smell he used a bunch of cologne instead of washing his clothes. 'Do I look stupid?'

I smiled and shrugged in reply, grateful that he was close enough.

'Let's go,' he said, reaching one huge ham hand toward my good arm.

In the split second before he could grab me, I hammered two solid jabs right into his diaphragm, then I pulled back swiftly and with an open hand I chopped him in his windpipe (which he'd helpfully brought into my reach when he doubled over).

He crumpled into a ball, coughing and spluttering on the floor. I gave him a solid kick in the stomach for added spice and he threw up all over the shiny white linoleum floor. (I felt a little bad about that later).

I could see well enough in the low light; running through the warehouse wasn't an issue. I caught my metal shard as it dropped out of the back door frame, and I staggered a bit because I almost lost it. Seconds later I was back in my car and out of the lot, and as far as I could tell, the guard hadn't made it off the floor in time to follow me.

More Questions Than Answers

My pulse didn't settle until I was at least a mile or two away from the warehouse. I could faintly smell vomit, and confirmed later that some had splashed on my boots. Gross. Once I was finally back in my office, I took a few minutes to center myself and clear my head. No use going through the papers I grabbed or pics I'd taken with my mind in a muddle. I made a cup of coffee and put an embarrassing amount of sugar and cream in it. It was basically a dessert. It was late, but after that encounter there was no way I was going to sleep for a while.

(I also took a solid amount of time carefully cleaning my boots. The only thing worse than someone else's vomit on your belongings is someone else's dried up crusty old vomit.)

I started with the wrinkled documents I pulled from my coat pockets. Most of them appeared to be run-of-the-mill paperwork for shipments coming in and going out, weights, times, illegible signatures of recipients. I tried to make sense of what I was reading. Was there anything amiss in the times? The weights of the trucks? The origin of the shipments? I could see today's date on one of them, and the name of the carrier that had picked up the late night shipment. Finally, something relevant. It called for ten crates, listing the part numbers that should be contained within, but I knew I had seen the forklifts loading at least twice that many.

I air-dropped the pics from my phone to my laptop to view them on a larger screen. The manager's desk at Cornwall was messy but I could read more company names, many with which I was already familiar, and text on the documents that I hadn't grabbed. I scrolled around, taking screen shots, and zooming in and out, until one stood out to me- a shipping form where a list of crates was to be transported to none other than Seaside Optics. We still didn't know who they were, or where they were located. Sigh.

I focused initially on the documents that were piled to one side, zooming in to try to read anything legible. I jotted down the parts of the names I could see, the logos, the acronyms. I even zoomed in on the pens, and recorded the company names I could see on the cheap, plastic writing utensils sticking out of the metal wire cup. More potential business partners that warranted further investigation.

I pulled a laptop out of my file cabinet and unscrewed the casing, just like Grassy taught me.

I removed the wifi board and placed it on the table, then I replaced the case and flipped it back over. I booted it up and logged in and gave it a minute to finish warming up.

The external hard drive I'd copied from the warehouse office was still in my coat pocket, and I plugged it into the disconnected laptop. I spent two hours or more, combing through the treasure trove of insanely boring paperwork. I read more files, shipping notices, and emails about incoming and outgoing items, questions and answers regarding products, their usage, their warranties and components. Tons of advertisements and coupons for some hunting and fishing company- the manager clearly spent his time doing outdoorsy stuff, or at least shopped like he did.

I scanned the entire hard drive for conversations or paperwork regarding the shipment I watched being loaded tonight, and found only a digital copy of the shipping label I currently had sitting on my desk. Any conversation about tonight's activities that were in addition to the legit paperwork I'd stolen-*ahem, acquired*- probably took place via a shared email account or a burner phone, and not the official company computer. The manager must have scanned the shipping label to send it to someone, but I couldn't find out who.

After a while, exhausted and frustrated, I leaned back in my chair and gazed up at the ceiling.

Is this where the investigation was going? Was I anywhere closer to finding a reason for Janelle going missing? What did any of this matter? An endless loop of faceless corporations, all exchanging money and goods with one another, infinitely, like hippies in a park playing hacky sack? The problem was that I had all these names of businesses owners, DBAs, subsidiaries, all connected and inter-connected and partnered with places like Cornwall Imports and IEI. But every single place appeared to be operating a legit business.

I was hoping for something, *anything* at Cornwall Imports

to give me some idea that it was just a front: an empty office, bare warehouse shelves, shabby, unused furniture. But it looked tidy, well-used and they even employed a guard! Who does that?

The companies were clients of CL Consultants; did that mean that CL was the ringleader? Or was it The Solution Security? So many of the companies in question were paying for their services. Was IEI just some arm of the company, doing whatever they were told? What could Janelle have possibly uncovered? This has all taken me hours, days of searching. As far as I could tell, Janelle just went into work and did her job every day. I doubted she'd look twice at a shady invoice or a late night truck and decide to become a whistleblower.

One thing I knew for sure, is this was getting too big for my britches.

The Feds Get in My Face

Late the next morning, I was at my desk, trying to work while I waited for ibuprofen to kick in and clear up my headache. I looked up when sunlight flashed off the window of a car that pulled into the parking spot in front of my building.

Before the car's doors were even open I had my baton in my

hand and extended under the desk, and I was frantically trying to calculate if I had enough time to make the run up to my apartment and get my revolver, as pale Yale male and female partners climbed out of the standard issue, unmarked, black SUV. They both had dark hair, and wore serious government agent shoes. The woman had her hair pulled back into a tight military-style bun. The guy, I kid you not, even had on aviator sunglasses.

Neither of them had a logo on their chests, so I relaxed slightly. I felt confident they weren't Kevin's troops, but it still begged the question: What fuckery is this now?

Keeping my office door locked was becoming habit, so I stood in the vestibule as they arrived, but I waited to unlock the bolt.

'Dea Oshtrovsky?'

'It's pronounced Day-ah.'

'*Ms.* Oshtrovsky?'

'Yes?'

They both whipped out their badges and showed them to me. The driver spoke. 'I'm Special Agent Bowman and this is Special Agent Grant, we'd like a word.' He eyed me up and down slowly, making little effort to hide his opinion. If that's what passes for a poker face in the FBI, we're all screwed. So maybe old overalls and Doc Martens isnt the best, most professional look, but who cares? I was comfortable and I liked my outfit. Also, fuck this guy.

I unlocked the door and moved aside a bit to let them pass. 'Have a seat.' I raised my arm and set the baton upon the desktop.

Bowman glanced at it, and his eyebrows flicked up a tiny bit, then he cleared his throat. 'We have come to learn that you are investigating a company that has been on our radar recently, and we'd like to know why?'

'Why?'

'Yes.'

'No, I'm asking you. Why do you want to know?'

He was clearly not prepared for me to give him any sass. A quick flash of confusion played across his face and then was gone. He walked in here assuming I'd immediately start shaking in my wee boots, and not dare to give any pushback. What a douchebag. 'We're not here to exchange information. We need to know why you broke into Cornwall Imports.'

Oh, so that's the company you're interested in, I thought. *Not the dozens of others I've been looking into?* I remembered how the building across the street had had empty office space for lease. I guessed the FBI was borrowing that space to do its surveillance. I replied, 'Just for fun. You know, my lock picking skills get rusty so I like to practice.'

'Ms. Oshtrovsky, we can have you brought up on charges

related to the B & E.'

'Why do you think it was *me* who broke in?'

'We have you in pictures and on video. You can't deny it.'

'Oh, so you're surveilling them?' God, this was too easy. It was hilarious.

His mouth set in a terse line. 'Obviously.'

'What does the federal government care about some obscure import company? They just bring in electrical parts.'

'So they say.'

'I'm not sure how I can help you, the company name came up in the course of my investigation into a missing young woman. They're partnered with the company where she worked. So I was just wondering if there was something there.'

'I can assure you, there isn't.'

That means there is. 'If you say so.'

'I'm telling you, there's nothing there. Direct your inquiries elsewhere. This visit is a… *professional* courtesy.' (I noted a thick layer of sarcasm in the way he said 'professional'.) 'If we catch you poking around again, you will be arrested. I strongly suggest you get back to snapping dirty pics of cheating husbands.'

'10-4 roger roger, sir.'

Agent Grant, who'd been standing, silent and stoic, against

the wall next to the door, snorted a small laugh out of her nose. That was the only noise she'd made since they'd walked into my office.

Bowman stood and gestured to my window. 'Get your sign fixed,' he said contempuously as they walked out the door.

'Get your sign fixed,' I mimicked, like a twelve year old. 'Get fucked!' I said louder, smiling and waving as they backed out of my parking lot.

So! The feds were sure that Cornwall Imports was involved in some shady business, and I had in front of me, a potential web of companies that all had a hand or a finger or some other appendage in this pie, which meant they'd probably also made the same connections. The question was now, who was the one holding the umbrella?

Funny How Time Flies

Grassy had sent me a final collection of data, with a missive about how he wasn't sure he was going to get any further. He'd hit wall after wall trying to get a name on Seaside Optics. He said he wasn't giving up, just taking a break to handle some other business and would get back to us as soon as he could.

I replied with my undying appreciation, wired him his fee

and got started sorting through what he had found. Soon, the whiteboard was looking like it was going to cave under the weight of the crap that was had pinned to it by magnets, and I was feeling incredibly tired.

I checked the doors were locked again, and dragged myself upstairs. I shut the blinds in my bedroom, turned on some music and unrolled my yoga mat. I laid on it, intending to do some stretches and try to get the blood flowing and the aching in my joints to chill.

I must have fallen asleep, because I woke up several hours later. I thought I heard something through the music pounding out of the stereo but I didn't bother to get up and check, as I quickly recognized Becky's voice. 'Helloooooo? D?'

'In here,' I called.

'Stop sulking,' she said, standing in the doorway of my bedroom, arms crossed over her chest. She grabbed the remote from on top of the dresser and paused the music.

'Hey,' I said, twisting my head around to look up at her. 'I'm not *sulking*.'

'Yes you are. You're laying on the floor in your bedroom, *blasting* Tears for Fears. What is this? Dea circa 1985?'

'Yeah, and this noise has been annoying the hell out of me,' Chuck added, standing behind her. 'Get your ass up, I got Thai food,' he ordered.

'Fine.'

'Don't you say 'fine' to me like I didn't just bring all this food for your ungrateful ass.'

'Sorry, Chuck. Thanks for the food. What time is it anyway?'

'That's more like it. It's almost dinnertime, you lazy sack. Why you sleeping on the floor anyway?'

'I didn't sleep at all last night. I came up to stretch and must have dozed off.'

'I've been calling and texting you for hours,' Becky said. 'I got worried and came over, and Chuck said you'd had the music going for forever.'

'I slept right through it,' I said, sighing. 'I guess I was more tired than I realized. The food smells amazing. You guys are the best.'

'Yeah, we know,' Chuck replied. 'And I brought an off-dry Riesling to go with it.'

'I'm not going to pretend I have any idea what that means but I'm sure it will be good.'

'Damn right it will be. Now, why you moping?'

'I wasn't.'

'Ha!' Becky exclaimed from the kitchen, where she'd been digging around looking for the corkscrew. She held up the missing button from my coat. 'I'm mending this right now,' she said, handing the wine key to Chuck and grabbing my coat from where I'd draped it over the back of a chair. She went over to the side table in the living room and pulled out my tiny sewing kit.

'You really don't have to do that,' I said.

'Too late, already started,' she replied. She tucked the kit into her jeans pocket and collected the plates, utensils and wine glasses from the kitchen.

'Okay, okay, I get it, I get it,' I said, 'apparently I'm very readable. I've hit a dead end. I've got nothing new to go on, and I'm extraordinarily frustrated.'

'Let's see what you got,' Chuck said, walking out the door with the food and wine still in their paper bags. Becky followed him without a word, my coat draped over her arm, leaving me standing alone in my apartment, hair askew, clothes wrinkled, stomach growling. I huffed a sigh and followed them down into the office.

Becky opened the wine to let it breathe, and then sat down on the old leather couch against the wall and started measuring thread for the button repair.

I waited until Chuck gave me the okay, then I poured, and helped Chuck bring the plates and glasses to the coffee table.

'Lay it all out,' he said, taking a seat beside Becky on the sofa.

A New and Improved Knot in My Guts

'Well if you're going to hide a lot of money, that's a way to do it,' Chuck said, finishing off what was left in one of the containers. 'Who is really going to sit down and go through invoices if one company says they shipped something and another company says they received it? I mean, the paper trails are probably pretty solid.'

'I know. I'm so mixed up I don't even know what I'm looking at anymore,' I said. 'I could be looking at a massive spiderweb of illicit activity, or I could be looking at boring, above-board international commerce. I have no idea anymore.'

'Did you finish with the last of Grassy's finds?' Becky asked.

'Almost. There are a few companies I haven't looked up yet; some properties that have had deliveries or are otherwise part of the logistics data. There are names but I don't have addresses yet.'

'Give them to me and I'll finish it.'

'Thanks.' I showed here where the file was in my laptop.

Chuck munched his last few bites thoughtfully. 'Who would have thought that a case of a missing woman would have led to all this?' he asked.

'I know. Certainly not me, that's for sure.'

Becky stood and made some notes on the whiteboard. One of them sent a cold shock wave through my body, making me nearly lose everything I'd only just finished eating.

'Why are you writing that?' I asked, my voice much louder than I meant it to be.

'It's one of the addresses,' she said, her eyes wide. 'Why are you yelling?'

'What address? Where did you get it?'

'It's for someplace called, uh, Blue Wave International. They're a warehouse-'

'That's not, that wasn't the name- the same name-'

'Dea! What are you talking about?' Chuck asked, his voice louder than mine.

'That's where I got shot- the call - I responded to!' I cried. I was standing and pointing at the whiteboard like it was a some poor innocent woman I was accusing of witchcraft. But I couldn't stop the tears, the memory of my partner laying on the ground, the searing pain ripping through my skin, my muscles, my face as I stammered- 'That's the call!'

Well That Sucked

My partner Perkins (Caleb Perkins, or Cale or Perkins or Yo, Asshole!) and I had had a relatively quiet morning. We'd wrapped up our most recent case- a human leg that had washed up on the side of a small creek behind a private residence.

DNA confirmed our suspicions- the person who previously owned the leg had been a victim in a motorcycle collision a county over. The leg had come off during the wreck, landed in the water, and travelled with the current. There had been a state-wide all-points to be on the lookout for a leg, so we weren't too surprised when it turned up, but obviously we had to confirm who it had belonged to before we closed the case.

Eventually when the river slowed down it had washed ashore, was nibbled on by some nocturnal animals, and then was discovered by a homeowner who was clearing out the underbrush along the water's edge. He'd previously been in the army and had seen some shit; he was calm when we arrived, and didn't vomit.

On this particular day, Perkins and I finished our paperwork and went out to eat, enjoying the few moments after closing a case before we got started on the next thing. We decided to drive around a bit after lunch, run an errand on the way back to the station, windows down, and enjoy the nice weather. It was then that we got *the* call.

Dispatch reported suspicious activity, not far from our location. Perkins was driving, and I asked for clarification. We were told it was an anonymous tip, that something was happening at a warehouse, possible B&E, or loitering. Someone was there who wasn't supposed to be.

But Perkins had said something on the way there, and it has never made sense to me. 'That place?' he'd muttered.

We parked and let dispatch know we'd arrived. The business appeared deserted. The multi-story brick building was surrounded by an overgrown parking lot and had old, paned windows, which were once painted white, but had long ago lost the paint to wind and weather. It appeared to be an out-of-commission mill, but showed signs of recent activity; someone was cleaning it out to repurpose it. There was a new dumpster that was filled to the top, and some decades-old office furniture piled up beside it. It looked like squatters had been removed, as well. Stained mattresses, ripped tarps and evidence of cooking fires, food waste, et cetera indicated people had been sheltering here. I had a vague recollection of reports of drug activity, or vagrants in the area, but we hadn't been the responders, or had reason to follow up on the reports, so I didn't know the specifics.

I asked Perkins if we should call some uni's to help; as detectives, we didn't normally respond to these types of calls, but we were the closest car.

He shook his head. 'It doesn't look like anyone's here now, maybe it was just some kids fucking around. Let's check the doors are still locked then get out of here.'

I nodded and we exited the car. I walked ahead of him, making for the front door, which was relatively new. I could see signs of it being previously boarded up; screw holes in the wooden door frame all around the new steel door. There was a window on the second floor that was cracked open, and something glinted in the sunlight. I frowned and tried to focus on it, as my partner said 'You'll never believe who owns this place-'

But he didnt finish because the roar of gunfire sounded from the floor above us, from behind and below us, I couldn't even figure out where it was coming from.

I felt my skin, my body, my hair, yanked and hurled in multiple directions, my brain couldn't process the sensations fast enough, couldn't identify what to do or how to react. I was spun around and landed on the ground, hard. I understood why Robbie had been resistant to me picking up private investigative work, getting mixed up in people's messy lives. The incident, which left my arm permanently damaged nearly cost me my life. A 'hail of bullets' puts it mildly, and the doctors- hell even I- could never figure out why I was still alive. My shoulder, chest, arm and stomach had been hit multiple times, the most damage sustained by my arm. One bullet grazed my scalp. But amazingly, all of my major organs and arteries were missed. I don't remember doing it, but apparently before I lost consciousness I'd been able to press the button on my radio and ask for help.

When the EMT's found us minutes later, my thumb was, apparently still pressing the radio call button, and my partner was dead.

What The Actual F

'Jesuschristmaschrist, Dea,' Becky said, wiping away tears-unsuccessfully. She was rapidly adding to the pile of tissues building on the coffee table before her. 'What the *fuck* is this investigation about?' She finished her sentence with difficulty, then fresh tears started.

'Gimme that,' Chuck said, holding out a hand. Becky handed him her laptop, then blew her nose loudly.

I was shaking, and while my tears had stopped, my eyes were swollen and achey. I felt cold, angry, frustrated and afraid. None of those were fun.

'The current owner bought the place years ago,' Chuck said, scrolling through real estate listings. 'Looks like, not long after you got wrecked. Let me see if I can find the previous owner. Gimme a minute.'

'No fucking problem,' I said, 'I can barely think straight right now anyway.'

Becky had stopped crying and was hiccuping quietly. I just stared at the floor. Was it always this shitty looking? The old linoleum tiles, the same ones installed in countless early- to mid-century school buildings and hospitals, were worn and some were chipped on their corners, and could use a serious, professional cleaning. My furniture was a mis-match of stuff from my old house; some of it, like the sofa Becky and Chuck currently were sitting on, was super old, like from my ex's college apartment. My desk was trashpicked. My chairs didn't match. I was getting angrier. So nothing matched, so what? What P.I. needs a curated office space? Have you ever seen a noir film? I noticed dust that had gathered against the legs of the sofa, the bottom of the filing cabinets, that I hadn't cared about before.

Was this my life? A sad collection of horrible memories, second or third hand furniture and dust in the corners? What was the point of it-

'Fucking hell on a hellfucking stick,' Chuck said, and I was momentarily impressed by what must have been the first time those words were ever grouped together in such a fashion.

'What is it?' I asked.

'Blue Wave Imports bought the building from a company called Grayhawk, which was co-owned by Linhurst and none other than your boy Kevin. Grayhawk was shut down shortly after your bad day. Looks like, a few months later. Now you know, drumroll please, that this Linhurst guy owns The Solution Security. Who wants to take bets that

Kevin is a silent partner, or they have some other kind of arrangement?'

Nope

Less than two hours later- one whole hour of which I spent in the hottest shower in human history- I rejoined Becky and Chuck, now in my living room.

We'd shoved everything to do with the case back into the closet and locked up the office, and I needed alone time to think, but didn't want to be alone. Funny combo, that.

So we compromised: they hung out in the living room, and I took a shower. Robbie called to let Becky know he was going to dinner with his colleagues, and would be home late.

When I came out of the bathroom, smelling a lot better and flushed from the heat of the water, I felt reinvigorated- not with peace of mind, but with the fury of a thousand burning suns.

'My partner knew who owned the building,' I said. Becky muted the tv. 'He knew the place- that's the only reason he would have said what he did when we got there.' I took a deep breath. I was finding it harder than I thought it would be to say what I wanted to say next. 'To that end, it seems obvious it was a hit. He knew that Kevin owned the building- and we were outgunned, outmanned, unprepared. I think Perkins might have known Kevin was up to something, knew about the location-'

'I was thinking that too. *Why* would they take him out? Try to take you out? Maybe Kevin wanted to recruit him,' Chuck suggested. 'Maybe he brought him in on some of what he was building- the connections, the security work; it was a fledging enterprise then. And your partner turned him down.'

'That would be a viable motive,' I said. 'And partners share a lot. Kevin might have been worried what *I'd* been told. But why take us out on your own property? You'd be questioned.'

'You said there had been reports of drug activity in the area, and that the spot had previously been abandoned, right? And his company was fixing it up?' Becky offered.

'And it was desolate, and there were no neighbors,' I said.

She continued. 'Maybe he figured he'd be able to skirt that- claim it must have been the people he'd been trying to clear out, you know, in his efforts to clean up the place. He was a well-respected officer. People would believe him. The benefit of taking you out of sight of anybody, minimal collateral damage, a place he knew and could control. Plus, you guys were nearby anyway.'

'That's true. He might have been having us tailed, and they took an opportunity. We could sit here and speculate all we want, but we're not gonna know for sure 'til the bastard tells us himself. So let's focus.'

'But also!' Becky blurted out. 'Also, why did he let you live?'

'Well I was a *hero* wasn't I?' I said, sarcastically. 'What happened to us was in all the papers, was all over the news- even a few national outlets covered it for a day. If I died after that, it would have looked a million times worse than what they've always said it was- that we must have interrupted some drug deal.'

'I always thought that story was fishy,' Chuck said shaking his head. 'It was weak as hell.'

'I know, but the amount of time it took for me to recover, get out of the hospital, I was useless by then. I couldn't investigate my own case- I was forced to retire, I was cut off from the whole system. And I was absolutely good for exactly nothing. I could barely walk, feed myself or comb my hair, much less be involved in a vigorous investigation. Thinking back on it now, it never even occurred to me to ask who owned the property. Everyone worked so hard to convince me it was a dead case, there were no leads, no real idea who the perps were. Which is the opposite reaction of what you get in the movies and tv shows when cops get shot. They make it look like the whole army is coming in hot to track down the bad guys. But I guess when you're the one spinning the story, you can make everyone believe what you want, and Kevin must have done that. He had plenty of time to lay the groundwork while I was recovering. And I guess even if I knew something, they figured I'd keep my mouth shut out of fear. Then, when nothing happened, they must have decided I wasn't a threat after all, and let me be.'

'Til now,' Chuck said.

'Til now,' I agreed.

'So what do we do about it?' Becky asked, her voice not so shaky anymore. 'How do we fuck up these guys?'

'We build an iron-clad case, and hand it over to the feds,' I said. 'That's the only way.'

'What could we possibly do that the feds can't do themselves?'

'Break into places.' At this, Becky and Chuck each gave a surprised laugh, which I shared. It felt good to relieve a little tension. 'I can gather info without a warrant. If I took the temperature right, the feds are in a surveillance phase. Which means something pinged but they might not know yet who the players are, and how they're connected. And they didn't indicate to me that they had any bodies. Right now, their case might just be fraud or illicit financial activity. So we have to figure out what Janelle saw, when she saw it, and who found out. Not necessarily in that order.'

Back to IEI

Based on what I learned from my camera that was still going strong at the driveway of IEI, the business kept a relatively regular schedule, with the exception of the late night shipments.

The admin staff came and went between eight am and six pm, and there were two shifts for warehouse staff which came a little earlier, and left a little later than the admins.

Stanhope, who I'd come to believe was just a sad pawn in all of this, or maybe, being used for his connections, seemed to keep an orderly schedule, and, I gleaned from the footage outside his house, hadn't seen his girlfriend Siobhan since before the day he'd screamed at me through my door. I guess she did dump him. Good for her.

I picked an evening directly after one of the late night trucks. Up to now, just from what I could surmise from the time I'd been surveilling them, they didn't do late nights two days in a row.

There were no cars in the lot, front or back. I was able to break in without any trouble, once again this was a warehouse that only had security cameras in a few of the exterior areas. Thank goodness for shady characters and their reluctance to be recorded.

I moved quietly through the warehouse, searching for any

crates or boxes that resembled the ones I'd seen at Cornwall Imports. There were several similar ones, but they were nailed shut, and there was no way I was getting them open.

I was miffed that even though I was sure their business dealings were illegal, I hadn't been able to confirm it with actual hard evidence. But I needed to focus less on a reason *why* Janelle was missing, and more on *how* she became that way.

Logic dictated that it was in the warehouse where she might have witnessed something, especially because of the fact that Shanks was still missing as well. If nothing turned up there, I planned to get into Stanhope's office, and go through his computer and files (a scenario I was dreading).

I moved over to the wall that led to the office suite, and looked around, as if I were a normal office worker carrying out my business. Where would I walk? Who would I speak to if I was innocently coming out onto the floor?

I pulled a large spray bottle out of my pocket and began to coat the floor with the contents. I walked low, moving toward the warehouse manager's desk, a nearby wall phone, and the human door in the side wall.

Then I turned and clicked on the mini black light, and backtracked where I'd sprayed the luminol.

After a few minutes- I could have cheered- I finally had it. 'Bingo,' I whispered to myself. Then I smelled something new- I sniffed the air; what was that? Stale cigarette smoke?

'What ya got there?' a man's voice said, right next to my ear.

The Pummeling

Like I was saying, it's funny that nobody ever mentions how annoying it is to get the shit kicked out of you.

If your opponent is a trained fighter, you barely have enough time to process the individual blows before another one comes. All you can do is try to block, deflect, maneuver away. I was outmatched, despite the hundreds of hours I spent boxing at the gym. I know I put up more of a fight than he was expecting; he pulled a piece and seemed shocked when I struck him so fast in the wrist that it went flying; I heard it clatter and slide, then collide with something metal- probably a support leg for the shelving. But by the time I heard the clang of metal against metal, he was already coming at me. At first, the attack was measured, calculated. But when I didn't go down right away, it became more aggressive, animalistic, frantic.

I blocked and countered, threw punches from my hips, protected my face. I used low counters; he had too much meat on top for me to keep up a fight above the belt. Also, I fight dirty. Who follows rules when someone's trying to kill you? To make it even more terrifying, dude was wearing a ski mask- yeah- one of those masks that only psychos wear? So I couldn't get any kind of look at his face, much less a good one.

In seconds which felt like an eternity, every blow the guy landed was agony, and it was all I could do to deflect the worst of them. It didn't take long for him, who had expert use of both arms and at least a hundred pounds on me, to wear me down.

One solid blow to my left temple sent me sideways, then he pushed me, hard. I didn't have any grip or stance, and I went flying. The floor, while concrete and dirty was smooth enough that I slid a few feet, but my head stopped me by colliding with something hard - my bell was officially rung.

Dazed, I quickly glanced back. I had enough time for one option- he pulled back a kick, and just before he made contact with my ribs I clenched my abs, tucked to absorb his leg, and then I held on for dear life.

'Fuckin' fuck! Let go! Stupid bitch!' he ranted, as I clung to him like a psychotic monkey made of glue. He stumbled but stayed upright for a few seconds, and just before he leaned down to try to punch me off him, I just barely, so so barely, managed to get my hand into my pocket, and pulled out a heavy rectangle. I slipped my hand up under the cuff off his jeans, and pressed the button.

For a few more agonizing seconds, I feared the stun gun was

not working, for he was still upright, but then, thankfully, he fell over, not unlike a tall tree, and crumpled into a wimpering heap.

I unrolled my aching croissant-shaped body and sucked in a few deep breaths, coughing and retching violently. Even though I'd caught his leg, the impact had still really hurt, knocked my wind out, and I was afraid might have cracked a rib. I attempted to sit up but my body was like 'Ha, no, fuck that.' I lay there for a few seconds, heaving breaths in and out. I heard him moan, and in a second of panic I threw myself toward the sound. Terrified he was coming around already, I pulled his shirt up and shocked him again right on the stomach.

When I was sure he was absolutely not getting up, I laid back down and I closed my eyes. My brain tried to soothe me to sleep. It was legit like 'Okay we had a good run, let's have a nice permanent nap'. I heard a tiny noise and opened my eyes again, confused when two cheerful rainbows came toward me.

I thought maybe I was finally being lifted off to heaven! But then they started smacking me in the face.

'C'mon, get up! Get up! We have to run!' Becky was yelling, she leaned down, took hold of my good arm and pulled me upward. I knew I should have been in pain but adrenaline and dopamine were still coursing through me.

She yanked on my arm but I made her stop. 'Wait, wait,' I coughed. I ran back to where the fight had started. My blacklight was on the ground, still on, glowing purplish blue in the dark. I found the spot where the luminol had shown a pool and a smattering of bodily fluids. It was hard to focus, I felt confused and was probably concussed. But I made it, and I dropped to my knees on the floor.

'What is it? Oh my god, hurry,' Becky pleaded, glancing back toward the man lying prone on the ground. He moaned again.

I used a penknife and scraped as much of the paint off the floor as I could, keeping the blacklight surprisingly steady. I dropped the flakes into a plastic baggie, and sealed it as Becky pulled me up again.

Becky Drives Like a Demon

We hurried across the warehouse floor and out of the doors. She threw me into the passenger side of the car, where I landed in a heap in the front seat. The car was running, and she hit the accelerator hard. The tires squealed as she peeled out of the lot.

'I told you... I told you to stay in the car...' I coughed, my voice wheezy and hoarse.

'Well we all know I'm no good at that!' she shrieked at me,

taking a turn hard and blowing a stop sign. 'Who was that guy?'

'I'm not totally sure,' I whispered, 'But I have some ideas.'

Becky drove frantically for several miles before I told her to please calm down, to take it slower. We'd left the industrial complex safely, there was no one following us. We were approaching busier intersections, open businesses, crosswalks.

I told her to take me to the hospital; I needed to get checked out. I knew the head nurse in the ER: Beth Thompson- her husband had cheated on her with their nanny and then tried to move their life savings without Beth noticing, you know, so he could start a nice new life without his wife and kids. Welp, he's paying a load of alimony now and oh yeah, the nanny dumped him pretty quickly, before the divorce papers were even signed.

Beth jumped up from behind the nurses' station when I shuffled in through the sliding doors, with Becky holding my elbow.

'Oh hell, what did you do now?' she lamented, shoving me down into a wheelchair and whisking me through the hospital's halls, with Becky jogging close behind.

'Just a few bumps and bruises,' I coughed.

'Don't listen to her,' Becky said. 'She totally got her ass kicked.'

'I can see that!' Beth said, pulling up to a bed. 'Hop out, now. Tell me where it hurts the worst.'

I pointed to a few spots as Becky told Beth what she'd seen of the fight right before I zapped the guy. She left out what she told me later- that from where she was sitting (waiting in the car, out of sight behind some old trailers that were empty, parked at the rear of the property) she saw, through a small window, the rapid movement of my black light as it went flying, landed, then spun around on the floor.

She came inside to check on me, worried I'd fallen down from some high place. By that point, the man that neither of us knew was even in the building had already knocked me down. She'd been hunting for a pipe or a piece of wood to try to hit him, when I managed to stun him. She was definitely more shaken up than I was, and I knew I was going to get my ass handed to me again when Robbie found out about all this, and I definitely deserved it.

'Well at least you got him. I'll need a description in case he comes wandering in here later,' Beth said, as she took my vitals and used a tiny flashlight to check my pupils. 'I'm going to do some scans,' she added, 'get comfortable.'

A couple hours, some stitches, cold packs, gauze and tape and heavy-duty ibuprofen later, Beth was sending me out the door with a smile and a wave, and instructions to not get into any more fights.

STEPHANIE ELLIOTT

Thankfully the beating I'd taken didn't appear to have left any damage that wouldn't clear up in a few days with rest. The rib wasn't cracked, merely bruised, which still hurt like a motherfucker.

'I'm going to stay at your place tonight,' Becky said as we pulled into my parking spot to the side of my building. 'Robbie won't be back from St. Louis until tomorrow night anyway.'

'Thanks Becky, you're the best.'

'True.'

'Are you gonna tell Robbie...'

'Oh, yeah. For sure. I'm not keeping this from him! You *must* be crazy.'

I sighed. He was really going to let me have it.

But then, Becky continued. 'Buuuut, I guess it can wait until, I don't know, 'til after we've solved the case?' We looked at one another and smiled. Poor Robbie. I do believe he thought he was marrying a nice, quiet, gentle granola lady. 'He's going to be so mad,' she said. 'But, he'd be more upset if you were dead, so, you know, there's that.'

'What would I do without you?'

'Nothing, obviously. You'd be dead. Now, go to bed, you need to sleep. I'm not tired yet so I'm going to watch tv for a while.'

I shuffled to my bedroom and only managed to kick off my

boots before collapsing onto the mattress. I rolled myself into my comforter like a burrito and was out in a matter of seconds.

Ouch

I woke up sometime in the wee hours. There were sounds coming from the tv, but the rest of the apartment was dark. Light from the streetlamps outside made pale yellow lines across the rumpled folds of the comforter that I'd apparently unrolled from and then kicked off in my sleep. My jeans were twisted around my legs and everything hurt. Every. Thing.

I hoisted myself up and couldn't stop a groan from escaping my throat. My hair was matted to my head and all I wanted in the whole world was a nice, long, hot shower. And pizza.

Becky was asleep on the couch, and the television sent multi-colored light flickering through the room. The volume was on very low, so I did my best to make as little noise as possible as I crept into the bathroom and started the shower. After twenty minutes or so of me just standing still under the blazing hot water, I heard a quiet tapping on the door. 'Yeah?'

'Can I come in?'

'Sure.'

Becky shuffled in and while I couldn't see her through the shower curtain, I heard her yawn as she asked me how I was feeling.

'Alright, sore all over, but okay. I'm hungry,' I replied.

'Me too.'

'Is that twenty-four-hour pizza place on Route 140 still in business?'

'Yeah- great idea. I'll order.'

'Get whatever you want, my wallet is on the dining room table. I will literally eat anything right now.'

'You got it.'

When I was done showering I dug out some loose-fitting pajamas for Becky to wear and she washed up also. My pajamas were so small on her she looked like a kid who'd grown comically large overnight and could no longer fit their clothes. On me they were long sleeves and pants, on her they were three-quarter sleeves and capris.

Minutes later we were shoveling pizza, appetizers, and milkshakes into our gobs like we hadn't eaten in weeks.

My phone beeped from somewhere in the apartment; I hadn't checked it since we'd been home. I dug it out of my coat pocket and checked the screen.

The message was from Beth at the hospital, to tell me that as of the end of her shift no one matching my assailant's description, or bearing the injuries he would have sustained, had arrived in her emergency room. My mind clocked that as 'he knows how to get healed up from a fight without alerting authorities'.

I leaned back against the couch and clicked through the tv channels. Becky stood up and moved to tidy, and I waved my hand at the mess. 'Just leave it, just leave it,' I said. Dawn was beginning to break, a line of gentle pink forming at the horizon. The darkness at the windows was softening slightly.

She sat back down beside me and sighed. 'Listen,' she said quietly, 'you said something in the car, when we were driving away from that warehouse- you said you 'had some idea' who it was that beat you up.'

'Yeah.'

'Well?'

I muted the television and looked at her. I took a deep breath. 'When we were fighting... before he got me down on the ground... he was *focused*.'

'What do you mean?'

'He was spending most of his time aiming for my left.'

'What?'

'Yup. Whoever he was, I think he knew me or of me. He knew about my injuries, he was aiming- hard. It hurts like a motherfucker- I can barely move that side of my body at all. He knew all the spots to hit.'

'So you think... he knew how to target you... specifically?'

'I'm not sure. But I believe my presence there was a surprise-which is almost worse.'

'How so?'

'If they were following me, or trying to take me out, they had plenty of other opportunities- better opportunities- all day. I was alone until you picked me up, I ran errands, I was in and out of my building. They could have gotten in and waited for me here. They might have planted that guard in anticipation of me possibly breaking in. They left him with no vehicle outside to indicate there was someone present. It means that even though they weren't expecting me there at that exact moment, the guy who beat me up knew me... maybe even *personally*.'

'Oh, man, that is bad.'

'Yep.'

'Like, really bad.'

'I know.'

'Fucking hell, what the fuck?'

'Yep.'

Becky leaned forward with her elbows on her knees. She was wringing her hands.

Her eyes were wide when she looked at me again. 'Well, what do we do now? What do you think?'

'I'm working on it, I promise.'

No One Likes to Talk About It

'How come none of your old work buddies ever come around anymore?' Becky asked quietly, holding her coffee in both hands as she watched the cars drive by out front.

With the arrival of the dawn, we'd shaken off some of the fear that had come over us; funny how the sun high in the sky, no matter how cold it still was outside, could make things seem a little better than they really were.

'I guess it's hard, you know?' I ripped kale leaves off of the stem and rinsed them. Then threw a handful of berries and some oat milk into the blender. I squeezed in some honey last.

'What's hard?'

'To be reminded. People just don't know what to say.'

'You'd think they'd make some effort to figure it out.'

'It's easier to move on, I guess. Coming to visit would mean being reminded- of what happened to me, of what happened to Perkins. It's easier to forget it you're not staring at a reminder day after day.'

'You're probably right. Still sucks though. You spent a lot of time with those people, and then, poof, they're nowhere to be found.'

'Yeah, it stings a bit now and then. But I try not to take it personally.'

'Hm.'

I switched on the blender and let it finish before I tried to talk again. I offered Becky some of the smoothie but she shook her head.

As soon as the hour was decent, I'd called Lennette to tell her what was going on. She hung up quickly, but before we disconnected I heard her husband's voice asking 'Whats wrong?' just as the call clicked off.

We decided to wait to tell Chuck. I knew he'd be sleeping, and I didn't want to wake him when there was nothing he could do about what was going on. Better to let him be well rested, and fill him in when he got up which was usually sometime in the afternoon.

'I'd better head home,' Becky said. 'Robbie will be back around dinnertime, and our fridge is empty. I suddenly feel like cooking a giant meal and having at least two bottles of wine.'

'That's a great idea,' I said. 'I'm going to take it easy. I've got enough stuff to go over, and I promised Beth I'd rest for a few days at least.'

'I'll be tracking you, so I'll know if you lie to me about going out and investigating.'

I flexed my aching shoulder. 'Don't worry,' I said. 'I *promise*.'

THE GIRL WHO DIDN'T GO

I Promised!

I did as I was told. For a few agonizing days I stayed in my building, all the doors and windows locked except when Chuck opened up to accept some food delivery, or walked next door to buy a few groceries.

We huddled together, both of us healing (his cut was basically non-existant but he was milking it; he was enjoying having a few medically necessary days off of work).

We fine tuned the data on the whiteboard, edited wherever necessary and confirmed dates, times, points of contact.

I filled out as much as I could so far on the paperwork I usually do at the end of a case when I wrap things up. No reason to not get a head start on it.

Toward the end of the day, I was going completely stir crazy. There was only so much I could do from the comfort of one of my couches. I needed to get out, and make some progress. I'd taken another look at Valmer Boulevard, and tried to ascertain where Shanks might have been heading the night he'd been caught on the traffic cam. If the spots I'd found under luminol at IEI were from an incident involving Janelle, maybe Shanks had something to do with the cleanup. Hell, maybe he was the one who hurt her, got rid of her.

As soon as I thought of that, I dismissed it. I doubted an alcoholic, who barely could make the rent as a forklift operator had the wherewithal and the power to plan Janelle's fake trip to Mexico, much less pull it off.

On my screen, I traced a route that would take me to where his car was photographed, perhaps I'd continue along that road heading East, and see if anything popped.

Maybe there were some properties I'd missed, or some areas that might be good spot to ditch a body. If not, I figured I could take a look at some of the properties I did know about, and try to catch some faces on camera, and get an idea of who might be working security, smoking cigarettes, and handing out pummelings.

Inspiration

There's a traffic light the leads to the interstate on-ramp, and if you're coming from one particular direction, the light change takes forever. Guess which direction I was coming from?

As I sat there, becoming increasingly angry at the amount of time I had to wait for the light to change, I absentmindedly started counting the rigs sitting in the lot of the truckstop, slightly downslope from where I was waiting. The intensely bright signs for the gas station and fast food restaurants glowed, a humid haze of many colors. The sky was rapidly darkening to an inky black, and the lights stood out against the unbroken sky, standing absurdly higher than everything else around them, so they could be seen from the interstate.

My windshield was foggy in the corners. It was becoming bitterly cold out. Dangerously low temps, the weather reporters had been warning. The heat pumped out of the air vents, making my eyes feel dry. At the risk of increasing the condensation in the corners of the windows, I turned the heat down. Just then, I caught a glimpse of a thin woman, darting between two rigs. My first thought was concern for her, she was not dressed warm enough for the weather. Then, I laughed at myself, and shook my head. Idiot.

The light changed and I moved to turn left, then was struck with an idea that I was actually angry I hadn't thought of before now. I jerked the wheel back to the right (I was all alone at the intersection) and drove straight to follow the slow, wide turn into the truck stop. It was the only one for miles.

I pulled into one of the car parking spots and killed the engine. There were only a few cars parked toward the rear of the main building, most likely employees.

Inside the rest stop were a handful of the customary shops

that can be found along the sides of every highway across the country; they sold fast food, donuts, coffee, convenience items such as phone chargers and bags of trail mix. In the open seating area spread out in front of the counters, with restrooms at either end, were shitty blue laminate tables surrounded by those crappy chairs- you know the ones. Always covered in fingerprints, always sticky.

A small group of women, underdressed for the weather, sat at one or two tables, drinking coffees or tall sodas, talking amongst themselves or scrolling on their phones.

I went inside, and gave a half-smile at the few of them who looked up at me, then, figuring I was not a customer, back down at whatever had held their attention the moment before.

One or two of the attendants behind various sleepy counters glanced at me expectantly, but when I didn't move toward them to buy their coffee or greasy hotdogs, they quietly went back about their business, expecting very little and getting exactly that.

I approached the tables, and some of the women eyed me warily.

'Hi, honey,' one said, giving me a winning smile.

'I'm not here for a date,' I said, smiling back apologetically.

'Too bad,' she replied, 'I wouldn't mind getting inside that coat with you.'

'Oh, here we go,' said another one. 'Don't start preaching at us either, or I'll puke right on your fucking face.'

'I'm not here to do that either.'

'Be quiet Dezzy, she's not one of those churchies. They don't wear boots like those,' said the one who'd wanted to get in my coat with me.

I chuckled a little. 'I'm actually a P.I.,' I said, pulling a few cards out of my pocket and placing them on the tabletop. 'I'm-'

'Oh no, fuck this,' Dezzy said, and tugged on the sleeve of another's coat. 'Let's go Crys. We don't want *none* of this.' Crys rose and pulled her faux fur coat tighter around her shoulders. Dezzy leaned close to my face and flipped me off; her bright press-on nails sparkled with rhinestones. 'Get fucked,' she said, and spun around. She and Crys left through a far door, and now the group was decreased by half.

'Sorry about them, they just got pinched last week,' said Coat Girl.

'It's alright, I understand,' I said. 'I'm looking for a missing girl, and I was wondering if any of you might have taken some weird jobs lately.'

'You're really gonna need to be more specific,' the one said, who'd so far remained quiet.

I nodded. 'Fair enough. What's your name?' I asked Coat Girl.

'Tigerlilly.'

'Her name's Gina. Don't mess around, she's looking for a missing girl, I'm Annie,' said the quiet one.

'It's okay, I'll call you Tigerlilly if that's what you prefer,' I offered.

'You can call me Gina.'

'I need to know if any of you have been to Mexico lately, or if you know anyone who might have flown down there and then come back home straightaway.'

The women glanced at each other, and I could see a few flashes of concern pass across their faces.

Annie began, 'I know someone-'

'Don't say anything! She said no one was allowed to know,' Gina interrupted.

'It's okay,' I said, 'she's not going to be in any trouble, I just need-'

Gina stood up. She was already tall, and had on really high heels. She fluffed her tiny, tidy afro and leaned forward, to tower over me. 'No offense Squirt, but you can't guarantee shit. I think you should go.'

'Sit down, Gina, sit down,' Annie said, gently taking hold of her friend's wrist. She looked at me. 'You too. Have a seat. Listen, there's a new girl, she's only been working here for like, a few months. Her name is Sue but for work it's Sugar. She told us about a job where she just had to fly to Mexico using one passport, then fly home using another. And that was it. She got home like, two days after she left- I know because she rooms with another girl- a girl I'm friends with. And we were both worried, you know? We tried to talk her out of it, I was sure it was something to do with trafficking. That it was too good to be true, and that we'd never see her again. Girls like us go missing all the time doing shit like that. She said she was getting good money, and, well, probably some rock too, to be honest. She insisted it was all good, and then, you know, she *did* come back. So we were relieved. She's out with a john right now, if I see her again tonight, I'll tell her you were looking for her.'

'Do you know who hired her?'

Their heads shook in a 'no.'

'Can you tell me where she lives? Or her roommate's name?'

Annie looked at me for a quiet moment before responding. 'Look, we don't want any trouble. I can't just have you going after her, okay? I need to talk to her roommate first. I *knew* it was something fucked up.'

'What makes you say that?'

'Well you're here now, ain't you?'

'Good point.' I held up my hands in a mock surrender. 'How about this, take my card, and please call your friend- the roommate. Tell her I'm not going after any of you, not trying to report you or mess with your lives. I just need to find out about this Mexico job, and then I'll be on my way. How's that sound?'

'Alright. We'll see.'

'Thanks. You've already helped a lot. Stay safe out there,' I said as I rose to leave. 'Actually, here- coffees and bagels on me. Make sure Dezzy and Crys get some too, okay?'

I went over to the nearest counter, ordered and paid for a box of coffee and a dozen bagels with assorted toppings, and told the attendants to take it over to the girls when it was ready, and to make sure they had all the cream and sugar they wanted.

I waved on my way to the door, and called out 'Thanks again!' As the worker at the bagel counter brought the food and drinks to the women, with a pile of plates, cups and napkins.

The Feds are Back, well, One Fed

I wasn't as startled this time when I saw the unmarked SUV come into my lot. I was surprised, however, when only Agent Grant emerged from the driver side door. Her hair was down this time, it was a long bob and had a bit of a wave to it. It was shiny.

I unlocked the deadbolt and let her in. 'All alone today?' I asked, as she walked past me. She smelled like sandalwood and flowers. But not a perfume- it was gentle, like it was her soap or shampoo. I stopped myself from taking a deeper breath, because that was kind of creepy. I walked around her to sit in my desk chair. 'Where's your friend?'

She sat down in the guest chair. 'Not everyone at the Bureau is my friend.'

I took that to mean exactly what she wanted me to understand, and I nodded. 'What can I do for you Agent Grant?'

'I'm not here. You never spoke to me and I'm not helping you.'

Oh, good, we are getting right to it. My favorite.

'The scope of our investigation has broadened considerably. I know you broke into IEI recently- don't bother to deny it- and I know you found something. Bowman wanted to have you incarcerated until we are done building our case, but I talked the Chief out of it.' She paused and made eye contact which made me feel like my teeth were going to rattle out of my skull. 'You need to understand- the Chief *considered* it.'

'Oh, is this where I should thank you?' I asked.

She snorted a small laugh. 'No thanks necessary, but yeah, you're welcome. Listen. I'm sure you've uncovered some serious stuff in your investigation. I read your police file. I know you're a great detective. But you need to be aware that the Bureau has a lot more resources, hours and power devoted to this than you could ever have, and we're getting farther every day than you can possibly go.'

'Wow, one minute I'm a great detective, the next I'm sounding pretty pathetic.'

'Cut the attitude. I'm here to help you.'

'This is the weirdest help I've ever gotten, and I've had cranked-up drug dealers as CI's.'

Grant's mouth moved ever so slightly in the smallest smile ever smiled. '*Our* concern is taking down the whole operation. I'm going to assume you know what I'm talking about when I say that, considering the properties we've seen you break into. I know I sound like an incredibly huge asshole when I say this- and you need to know these are not my words but our *directive*- but we are not currently concerning ourselves with the absence of one administrative assistant, who went missing during a trip to Mexico. The Mexican authorities shared their findings with us, and frankly, that trail is as cold as it gets. It's an unfortunate truth. We sent an Agent down, but whatever happened there was not...'

'It was all done rather purposefully, I know you're dancing around saying that. There was no way to pick up a lead, no way to track the so-called kidnapper, no CCTV, no witnesses. I was there, and I know you know that. So now you're telling me to stop looking into the what- smuggling? Human trafficking? Massive drugs trade? And just focus on Janelle?'

'Your words, not mine. Again, I'm not here right now.'

'She's not the only one who's missing.'

Grant frowned at me.

'There's a second employee of IEI who is unaccounted for- a forklift operator.'

Grant said, 'How did you know...' and her voice trailed off. Then, 'Nevermind.'

'What if she was murdered, right in the property you're investigating? The forklift operator might have been paid to get rid of her, that's why *he's* taken off. I got a last known on him, he was pinged on some traffic cams on Valmer, but I can't tell where he was heading. Would that be an opening for you to start arresting people?'

Grant's eyebrows twitched ever so slightly, so so so tiny of a twitch. So, there was something, *something* about Valmer Boulevard. 'It wouldn't hurt. But, it would be simple for some of these individuals to pay a guy to take the rap, make up some story about covering up an accident, and leave them all to continue engaging in what is a rather large operation. Do you think that's a good idea? Because I can see that working out not so hot for you.'

I stifled a shudder. I get it, I get it. I'd most likely have an 'accident'. I got up and retrieved two plastic bags out of a locked file cabinet located along the back wall of the room. I spread out a clean sheet of paper atop my desk, and grabbed two empty bags from my desk drawer.

Grant didn't ask me what I was doing; I guessed it was obvious to her, as I pulled on gloves and took out some sterile tweezers from their sani-wrap package.

I transferred half of the contents from each bag into the empty ones, and sealed all four, then I handed the two new bags to Grant.

'DNA sample from Lennette Golding, my client and Janelle Stevenson's paternal aunt. And paint scrapings from the floor at IEI warehouse, where luminol showed fluids had been spilled. A good amount. If you can swing it, and then share the details, I'm hoping - you know what I mean-guessing- there might be a familial match.'

Grant tucked the bags into her coat pocket and nodded. 'I can't guarantee I'll be able to get these processed, but I'll try. I'll need to add them to a file and it might not go unnoticed. We're looking at conspiracy, racketeering, tax evasion, and so forth. Those charges don't usually involve DNA matches.'

'I know. I'm sure you can come up with something. Sometimes you need to prove who handled documents or property so... maybe that's a spin.'

Grant sighed. 'Don't think of me as harsh, I care that Miss Stevenson is a victim in all this but my hands are tied here.'

'I understand.'

'Do you have a suspect, besides Stanhope?'

'Possibly. What are you looking at regarding Kevin Werth?'

Agent Grant raised her eyebrows just a smidge. She was difficult to get a read on, but I didn't mind studying her face. 'We know the firm that employs him as Director has been the one doing security for all the companies and properties we've been investigating. And moreso, he has, let's call them... *problematic* habits.'

It was my turn to take a beat. 'Regarding substances... or humans?'

'The latter.'

'And why aren't you doing anything about him?'

Grant waited again before she spoke. This lady likes to measure her responses. 'Once again, we can't risk the whole case by going after one guy who treats the women he hires *poorly*.'

I felt my cheeks turn red, but I controlled my voice. 'What could you possibly hope to gain, going after these white collar dudes? A slap on the wrist? They'll call their dad who will pay a hefty fine? If you even catch them that is, cuz they've probably got accounts in the Caymans and access to jets and fake passports? That's worth letting people be killed, or abused? How high could this possibly go?'

Agent Grant looked at me for a quiet moment, and I saw a flicker of something pass through her eyes; sympathy? Or perhaps, deciding to take a calculated risk? 'Do you ever read a lifestyle magazine called Abundant Life?'

What a Lovely Bouquet

It didn't take long for Annie to reach out to me, on speakerphone with her friend whose name was Helen, who had rented rooms to Sugar. Helen was retired from being a working girl, and had scraped together enough money during her tenure as such, to go to school and become a medical technician. She stayed local, working a late shift at a clinic, and helped support the girls who needed medicine and treatment, and sometimes offered the modest spare room above her garage to women in need, which is how she met Sugar.

She told me the same as Annie had, that Sugar had rolled in on a rig a few months ago and gotten stuck in town, but was doing alright all things considered. She had issues with substance abuse, which Helen was hoping to help her with, but hadn't been successful so far.

'What does she look like?' I asked, but I suspected I already knew.

'Short, kind of skinny, long brown hair, olive skin.'

Just like Janelle. She probably looked similar enough to Janelle's passport photo that an impatient flight attendant or tired security guards wouldn't notice any differences.

'Is she home now?' I asked.

'As far as I know- you can come by if you want. I'm off to work so I won't be here but just keep in mind, she's a little jumpy.'

'I understand.'

Helen's property was small and affordable, but well-maintainted and orderly. She had tiny, dry flowerbeds that showed the spare, hibernating branches of young hydrangea bushes, and an empty flower pot on the step. There was a front porch which was enclosed sometime in the seventies, with heavy glass louver windows, one of which was open, I guessed because the mechanisms were probably broken. There was heavy plastic taped on the inside, to minimize the heat leaking out of the open window panes.

I followed the driveway around to the rear of the house, where a detached garage with a manual door was situated. Based on the state of the large door I guessed Helen didn't park her car inside, and a quick glance in one of the dusty windows confirmed this; the garage was used as a storage shed, and contained boxes and crates, some landscaping tools and a ladder, and other sundries one needs to take care of a house and yard. A locked side door was clean and had a newer doorknob, and it was clear that was how Helen went in and out to access her things.

There was a narrow staircase against the other side, at the top of which was another dull white steel door, the twin of the one on the ground level. I ascended the staircase and pushed the doorbell, which had a soft orange light glowing in a circle around it.

I could hear its chime inside the apartment, and then silence. I pushed it again in a minute, and stood on my tiptoes to try to see through the small windows in the upper portion of the door. There was movement inside, but the person didn't answer. I rang again.

'I don't want it!' a woman's voice screeched.

I rang again.

'I said fuck off!'

'I'm not selling anything, I'm friends with Annie and Helen!' I called back.

A moment passed, then I heard the chain scrape across the inside track, and the door opened a bit. A woman, about my height, squinted at the morning light. I caught a whiff of the interior; the stale blend of old carpet, smoke of all kinds, fresh cigarettes, cheap floral candles, a full garbage can.

'What do you want?'

'I just have a couple questions about your trip to Mexico.'

'I ain't ever been to Mexico.' She moved to shut the door but I stuck the toe of my boot into the gap.

'I know you have, I just want to know who hired you. I'm not here to bust you, I'm looking for a missing girl.'

'Get fucked.'

'Look, I won't ever bother you again. I just need to know who hired you.'

'I said, 'get fucked!'' she yelled, as she repeatedly slammed the door against my boot with each word.

I was now tired of her shit, and when she pulled the door back to slam it again, I gave it a hard shove toward her instead, which doubled its inward momentum. She stumbled into the darkness of the apartment and I charged in after her.

'Get the fuck out!' she yelled, her voice cracking.

'No! I need answers, and you're gonna give them to me, so *you* sit down and *you* shut the *fuck up*!' When I yelled, I lowered the pitch of my voice, making it sound much louder and more commanding than hers. It was a trick I learned on the force. I was painfully aware of what a huge asshole I was being.

She took a few steps back and sat down hard on the edge of an old recliner that had seen better days.

'Now, listen,' I continued, incrementally lowering the volume of my voice to deescalate the tension. 'I'm not here to bust you and I don't give a shit how you make money or what you're on. I am looking for a missing woman. I know you used her passport to go to Mexico, then came home on a different passport.'

'I don't know nothing about no missing girls.'

Her last word was like a spear of ice straight into my heart. 'Girls'- plural. I carefully held my composure and stayed focused. One thing at a time. 'I believe you. I just need you to tell me how you got the job, and anything you know about who it was that hired you.'

'No one hired me, I never been to Mexico. I want you to leave.'

I took a breath and looked around. A photo was taped to the wall next to the tv. Sugar- Sue- in happier times, her arm around another young woman. 'Who's that? In the picture? A friend?'

'My sister.'

'When was the last time you saw her?'

'Before I left Michigan. We talk sometimes on the phone. But uh, she says I need to get straight. I'm trying but, you know.'

'I understand. Do you like it here? Or do you want to go back to Michigan?'

'I don't know.'

'Sue, if *you* were missing, your sister would want me to find you. I *need* your *help*.'

Sue glanced over her shoulder at the smiling faces in the photograph. 'Fine,' she whispered, her voice hoarse. 'Please, just, just keep me out of it. If he finds out I helped you, I won't go missing, I'll just be dead.'

'I promise.'

She fumbled on the table top beside the chair, and grabbed a cigarette and lighter. She took several long draws before she spoke again. 'The john. I met him working the I88 stop on Culmer Ave.'

'Do you always work from there?'

'Yeah. It's easy to get to, the number seven bus stops there right around dinnertime. It's usually the truckers but sometimes guys will come in with a line on a party or something, they'll hire a couple girls.'

'Has this john come to see you multiple times?'

'Yeah. He had other girls, then he started asking after me. After the first few times we made a standing date. I wait there every Wednesday 'til seven. If he shows, he wants me. If he don't, I got time to pick up another customer.'

'How does he treat you?'

Her eyes flicked up to my face, then back down to the floor. 'It's not a big deal.'

So, badly. 'How does he pay you?'

Her eyes stayed glued to the floor, but now her ears went a little red.

'He pays you in product doesn't he?'

'He says he's helping me manage...'

'Manage your habit? Does he give you money as well?'

'Yeah, but also other things, like groceries. Or clothes.'

'Do you know anything about the other girls he hired before you?'

'A girl named Candace. She went back home. To Indiana.'

'How do you know?'

'She was friends with Annie and Helen. They got a text from her after she cleared out.'

'How many other girls have gone missing from the I88 group?'

'I don't know. Sometimes they come and go a lot, you know? Especially in the summer. It's easier to travel in the summer. It's harder when it's cold.'

'In your core group, the girls who are there all the time. Who has 'gone home' or otherwise relocated lately?'

'Besides Candace, there was another girl, called Leelee. I heard she texted some friends too, but I don't know where she went.'

'Who is this john, Sue?'

'Everyone calls him Sarge. But I know his real name.'

Sinking Feeling in My Guts is More like an Anchor

Back at the I88 stop the next day, just as the sun was going down, I knew I'd catch the early girls, and planned to spend a few hours, so I could speak to as many of them as possible. I brought multiple blank pages of the preliminary reports I fill out when I get a new client. For each girl who was missing or whose location was unknown, I filled out a separate sheet with whatever info the girls could give me. I was even able to get some pictures from their phones, of selfies or so forth for a few of the names.

Regarding the one girl that Sugar had mentioned, Leelee, those who knew her told me the same story. Leelee had worked there for a few months but had texted some friends that she was heading out west.

A few of them had her last number saved, and shared it with me, but only Gina had a text conversation still in her mobile.

She let me read it, and it was nothing out of the ordinary; check ins and plans to meet up, jokes and funny pictures, normal things sent back and forth between friends.

The last message was forthright, simple plans to head to California, see a cousin, stay a while. The message was informative and at first glance seemed fine, but with Gina's permission I snapped screenshots and sent them to myself. There was something a little colder, less familiar about the last message, and what bothered me was exactly that- it was the last. Leelee didn't respond when Gina asked more than once, if she'd gotten there okay.

The girls who had come to work tonight, who knew him, told me similar tales about Kevin, a.k.a. Sarge, and his predilections. As long as you did what you were told, you got back to the truck stop okay, and usually, but not always, were fit enough to see other customers.

The girls were unimpressed with my interest in tracking down their missing members- not that I needed their admiration. There were no expectations or enthusiasm that a positive result was forthcoming. If nothing else, these women lived firmly within the confines of reality, with no delusions of anything grand.

I didn't try to ply them with platitudes or meaningless positive drivel. It was true, and would continue to be so, that they were the cast offs of society, largely ignored and overlooked, and I wasn't about to try to pretend it was any different.

However, my investigation had led me here, and I was going to follow it until my legs fell off, and I think, at least one or two of them recognized that in me.

By the very nature of this situation, it's difficult to track people down who don't want to be found, don't live on the books, and don't move in the social circles that get photographed and put in magazines or plastered all over social media.

I mean sure, it's not impossible, but the barriers these women face include difficulties getting rentals, car leases or loans, any credit at all in fact, and it's due in part to working for cash, as much as it is the persistent degrading and demeaning treatment from judgemental people.

They often use burner phones, stay with friends, buy cars used straight off the lot or stick with public transportation. They shop with all cash, and often manage to stay under the radar until some overly enthusiastic cop decides to make an easy collar.

Sure, there are investigations into large scale trafficking and other seedy businesses that involve the sex trade. Vice divisions in police departments all over the place try or succeed in busting up far-reaching or organized operations all the time. And there are often handlers, lurking in the dark, threatening and abusing their workers and taking all their earnings. But also, a good number of working girls manage on their own, in places like this, and come and go frequently.

When their bodies are found, they're not treated as high priority, when their bodies are violated, they're asked, 'Oh so a normal Tuesday?'

No one picks this as a profession without circumstances in their life leading them down a path where there was only one solution to stay alive. This isn't the movies, and these girls rarely make it out alive.

When I left, doing my best to hide my feelings of abject misery, I had four names- real ones- and two false names from girls who didn't stick around long enough to make friends, and share their given names, or anything much about themselves.

Not Used to This

The investigation had taken a drastic turn. One that I could never have seen coming, not in a million years. My conversation with Agent Grant had sent shockwaves to my core. The FBI didn't make a habit of wasting time and resources but the potential involvement of a congressman? That was heavy. I took Grant's suggestion to back off a bit, but focusing on the working girls who might know something about the people who orchestrated Janelle's disappearance kept me well in my lane.

I found myself, late into the morning (four cups of coffee and two cherry pie slices for breakfast) eyeballs deep into missing person reports, burner phone traces, and sparse background information on the handful of women I'd learned about from the truck stop.

How did this connect to Janelle? Well, I figured if there were some guys mixed up in the stuff the FBI was investigating, using prostitutes for doppelgangers, and possibly being people who weren't afraid to get rid of a couple of bodies, one more wouldn't be that hard.

I had circumstantial evidence connecting Kevin to these people but nothing that would stand up in court. I had rumors, ideas, theories and fears. But no evidence.

On paper, The Solution Security Services was a top notch firm, offering in-person guards, risk assessment, travelling security teams and safety consultations.

Kevin was not listed on the public records, but he appeared to be the one running its operations. Carter Linhurst, of cleverly named CL Consultants, didn't appear to be involved in the day to day. I had no idea how these two knew each other, but that didn't matter as much as figuring out what Kevin was up to in his spare time.

My last meeting with Agent Grant left me, in no uncertain terms, fully informed that if I was considered to be 'getting in the way', I would be quickly removed from the picture. And I wasn't interested in sitting in a jail cell, courtesy of Agent Bowman, on some trumped up charge for the next few weeks or months, depending on how long their case took to build.

I needed to focus on one small thing, that perhaps might lead me to something bigger. And that one small thing was Kevin's treatment of working girls.

There was no chance I could speak to Linda, Kevin's wife of the last couple decades. Or his kids. Or friends. Or former partners. I had to stay as far away from him as I could while trying to learn as much as possible. Sounds super fucking duper easy.

Where to start? He'd pick up on a tail really quick. His company was a literal security firm- no way I had the skills to break in. Even Grassy was unsuccessful breaking in remotely.

Then, I had it. Back to basics. Treat him like any other unfaithful spouse- just with a little more distance.

I dug through my equipment lock box and pulled out a couple of older model GPS trackers. Ones whose tech wasn't top of the line and current- which might not ping if a person, say, ran regular sweeps of their vehicle for devices. I tested their batteries and capabilities, and packed them to go. I was going to have to choose my opportunity extremely carefully, or, I thought (maybe a little maliciously) I could create one.

The Opportunity

I reached out to Becky to bring her up to speed on everything; she was just finishing a DIY renovation of their upstairs guest suite.

I told her she was officially benched, which didn't make her happy but I knew Robbie would be at least. One out of two ain't bad.

Chuck, on the other hand, I needed, but only for one small favor. Jasmine, the dancer at his club, had told me that Kevin, or Sarge as she knew him, was a regular. I needed Chuck to let me know when he came in, and make sure he had a few drinks that were extra strong.

It only took a few days for the situation to transpire. Kevin, apparently, had needs that were compelling to say the least. The bartender didn't ask questions when Chuck told him to make Kevin's usual drink a triple, and Jasmine texted me that she kept his eyes busy while he'd downed it in a gulp or two, and she made sure he was immediately provided with a second.

Chuck gave me the heads up once Kevin was wasted, and set up in a private booth to chill for a while. Jasmine enlisted one or two more dancers to keep Kevin distracted while she lifted his keys, which she told me later proved to be rather easy. She handed them to me where I was standing out at the back door, freezing my absolute ass off.

I started by installing a GPS tracker as high up inside the undercarriage as I could reach, in a spot I knew they wouldn't be seen by a cursory glance at the underside of the car, but also would not interfere with any mechanics.

It helps that I'm petite; I was able to slide my entire body completely beneath the vehicle, and still have some room to manevuer my arms. But goddang the asphalt was cold.

I went through his car as quickly as I could. I photographed any and all receipts for toll booths, lunches, convenience stores. I shuddered a bit when I found an (unsecured) weapon tucked into the glove compartment and another under the driver's seat.

I leaned down and sniffed the carpet in the backseat and the trunk; I practically had my nose buried in the fibers. No smell of industrial cleaners, or of recent shampooing. By all accounts the vehicle was 'lived in'; not recently cleaned, dirt in the corners and crevices, old and newer splashes of coffee near the cupholders, a few fast food wrappers and other trash here and there.

So it didn't appear he'd used it to transport any bodies recently, then followed with a thorough cleanup. (Which was annoying; I'm aware of how odd it is that this would annoy me.) I couldn't risk using any products to conduct further tests. A lot of forensic testing chemicals leave their own smell or residue, and even though Kevin was toast right now, he would be sober again soon, and if he suspected anyone was in his car, or sprayed something he would definitely know the smell of, the jig would be up.

Once I was done, I locked the car and hurried back to the

front door, where Chuck was waiting for the keys. 'How's he doing?' I asked as I handed them over.

'Sleeping like a baby right now,' he replied, laughing. 'Gonna wake him up in a minute and get him the fuck out of here. Might even confiscate his keys and force him to call a cab,' he added, jiggling the keys around in his massive hand.

I shook my head and laughed a little, but with a wave I hurried away. While Chuck could, and should, confiscate the heavily inebriated Kevin's keys, I knew Kevin would call the finest taxi service around, and his car would be thoughtfully driven home also. So the GPS tracking was set to begin, and I needed to be well out of the way, out of sight and ready to watch from a safe distance once Kevin's buddies in blue arrived.

Motel, Hotel, Holiday, How's it Go?

Kevin's movements were nothing out of the ordinary for a couple days. From what I could tell, he was unaware of the tracker. He went between warehouses, offices and other business locations whose addresses I was acquainted with, his home and some restaurants, gas stations, random stores, et cetera. Nothing interesting or noteworthy.

Until one particularly bitter night when I watched from the safety of a screen in my office, the little arrow that indicated his vehicle headed to the I88 truck stop then off to somewhere I wasn't familiar with, but the address rang a distant bell.

A quick internet search showed me it was a motel, which made me remember where'd I'd seen that address before- it was a CL Consultants holding. A satellite view gave me a few options for surveillance.

I hurried to the location, not ashamed to admit I was a little anxious and sweaty despite the weather.

I was able to park in a busy lot for a strip mall across the road; the businesses located therein included a bustling sports bar, some boutiques and a salon, all thankfully open a little late, making the lot busy and full.

I had an okay view of Kevin's car. The motel was a two level, exterior walkway type of place along the side of the highway. It had seen better days and was probably easy to get a room in, if your standards weren't high. My guess was that Kevin had a standing reservation.

I could see a few people coming and going; they too looked like they'd seen better days, and I gathered that the motel offered long term stay options in addition to hourly rates.

I didn't arrive in time to see which room Kevin went into, but his car was parked close to the low numbers, and knowing he frequented women and most likely places like these, I guessed he stuck with some routines, which would translate to parking spots also.

When you spend time watching people as long as I have, you get to know their idiosyncrasies pretty fast, and most of us are creatures of habit to a much larger extent than we ourselves even realize.

It's the same when two spouses share a driveway, bed, living space; they pick a spot for their cars, they sit in the same place on the living room furniture or at the dining room table, sleep on their preferred side of the bed. Habits form and stay with us, sometimes for life.

I remembered from my conversation with Sugar that Kevin picked her up regularly, and I wondered if tonight was one of their recurring dates.

I kept watch there, in my increasingly cold car, for hours. My ass was sore, and I had to periodically kick the heater up to relieve the tension and chill from my achy joints.

The sports bar was thankfully, consistently busy- go sports- so my car was well hidden, tucked in amongst a swath of other boring looking vehicles. I'd purposely parked in between two larger model SUVs, the heights of which blocked the street lamps and kept the cabin of my car in darkness.

After an eternity (my guess was that Kevin had a prescription to keep him going this long) a door on the second story of the motel opened, and Kevin stepped out. I snapped dozens of pictures of his every movement while he was in my line of sight. He turned back to say something to the person still in the room, then he shut the door and headed along the walkway in the direction of his car. I was grateful for the fact that I would be home soon. No one else exited the room immediately, so instead of starting up my car with a mind to leave, I decided to stay to get a glimpse of who he'd spent so many hours with.

Then, Kevin shocked me by going past his car, walking to the curb, looking left and right and running across the highway - straight toward me.

Oh Shit

Kevin did a half-jog across the empty lanes of traffic, and was moving directly toward my car. I scrambled to figure out what to do- I started with making sure my doors were locked. I fumbled in my pockets for one of several self-defense tools I always carried. Just as he arrived at the row of cars in which I was sitting, he moved further to my left- four cars away from where I was- and cut through the rest of the vehicles on the lot, then went into the bar behind me. 'Fucking hell fuck fuck fuck shit fuck fuck,' I said out loud, probably too loud, letting myself breathe again normally. I really thought I was fucked this time.

In my mirror, I watched Kevin smile and act friendly to the young hostess, and again to the similarly-aged server. It gave me some serious creeps.

Being middle-aged is weird sometimes; you miss the vitality, the flexibility and perky boobs of your youth, but I have found an enormous amount of comfort in being less visible; and what I absolutely *don't* miss is having to put up with creepy old dudes who don't hide the fact that they like to look at the perky boobs of young women.

Kevin sat alone at a table off to the side of the dining room, and ordered a drink and dinner. I kept an eye on him through the wide, plate glass windows of the bar while also watching the door he'd come out of at the motel. Eventually, a cab pulled up to the motel, and waited near the bottom of the staircase. Kevin was nearly finished his steak and potatoes and third beer as Sugar emerged from the motel room. She wore large sunglasses even though it was late at night, and a fluffy, brightly colored faux fur coat. She held her shoulders high, using the fluff to surround her face. Either for warmth and comfort or to obscure injuries, or both.

I watched her go slowly- painstakingly- down the stairs and into her waiting taxi. It looked like it hurt to walk, and my heart broke for her. Whatever Kevin was doing to this woman, in exchange for money and drugs, she didn't appear to be what I'd call an enthusiastic participant.

I covered the viewfinder of my digital SLR with my hand, so the screen didn't light up my car, as I snapped as many pictures as I could, feeling horrible for doing so; I was capturing someone else's pain, without their knowledge. But I needed the proof, and I consoled myself with the thought that my goal was to get Kevin out of this woman's life, so he wouldn't have this power over her anymore. It was a shit way to make only myself feel better, and I was well aware of that.

One last glance in my mirror showed Kevin cleaning his plate enthusiastically with a bite of medium rare steak, scooping up every last bit of potatoes, mushrooms and gravy, and I was pretty sure I'd never eat a steak again, as long as I lived.

Now What?

So I had photographic proof, as well as a statement from Sugar of Kevin's infidelity.

But who cares? Morning light is an incredible clarifier. Last night I was sure I was onto something, had an avenue of inquiry. Kevin was an abuser of women; but with a clearer head this morning, I knew that didn't make him a murderer. And Sugar wasn't going to press charges. I needed to catch

Kevin doing something that could build a case that the feds would be interested in.

I needed to see what he was doing with people who displeased him.

I wondered if maybe Sugar would be willing to talk at least. I pulled on my coat, grateful for the repaired button, and jammed my watch cap low over my ears. I headed across town to a good bakery, where I had the workers put together a small offering; a box of coffee, all the fixings, some breakfast foods both savory and sweet, and then I drove over to Sugar's apartment.

Unsurprisingly, she wasn't super motivated to let me in. But when I held up all the hot food I'd brought, her frown dissolved a bit, and she somewhat reluctantly opened the door.

The morning sun did little to cheer up the conditions she lived in.

Sugar lit a cigarette and motioned for me to follow her to the little table and chairs set up in the kitchen. She was in lounge clothes; a small black tank top and loose cotton pajama pants, tie dyed in pink and green swirls. Her wet hair hung in limp waves around her face, and I could smell a brand of coconut scented moisturizer I was familiar with.

She hadn't spoken much, and neither of us mentioned the elephant in the room. Her battered face and the clear signs on her neck, chest, upper back and arms, of the almost-too-far treatment that she'd received from Kevin the night before, spoke for themselves.

I washed some dirty mugs and plates that were sitting in the sink, and dried them with napkins I'd brought with me, then, still without speaking, I served her a heaping pile of bacon, sweet and savory baked goods and steaming hot coffee, made the same as mine- plenty of cream, lots of sugar.

She started slowly, picking a bit here and there, but it must have awoken a ferocious appetite because about thirty minutes later her plate was clean and her mug had been emptied twice.

'He's not always like this,' she said, finally. A statement uttered too many times, by far too many women.

I nodded.

'There was something... on his mind. Usually,' (That means not always, I said to myself) 'he's alright. Like any other john. Gets what he needs, pays and moves on.'

'It doesn't make any of this okay,' I said, touching my own face to indicate the worst of her injuries.

'It's par for the course.'

'I understand.'

She eyed me for several moments then looked back down at her plate. 'No, you don't. You *don't* get it,' she said.

'I was a cop for years, I-'

'No,' she said, firmly. 'It's not about sex. He never wants *sex*.'
Confusion must have played across my face, which I
tried to hide, but I knew I'd failed. When you spend all
your time gauging the reactions of the people in your
immediate vicinity, you learn how to read the most minute
expressions, and Sugar saw mine. She stood up slowly,
carefully, and retrieved her cigarettes and lighter from the
living room then rejoined me at the table. I made her
another cup of coffee but she just stared at it for a while,
smoking in silence.

I took the opportunity to say, 'Even still, with that kind of
lifestyle, there's consent, boundaries, there are safe words,
it's not about-'

'I *know*, I know.'

I let her words settle on the air for a few moments and
finished my coffee before I spoke again. 'I know you don't
want to press charges, or get involved in anything. But
would you mind at least, answering some questions?'

She looked at me, world weary and sad, but didn't answer.

'Okay, how about we do it this way,' I offered. 'I'll ask some
questions, and you answer the ones you want to answer, but
I promise, I won't tell anyone who you are, or where you
are, or how I got the info. Look, I brought NDA's with me.
They're standard forms I offer as part of my employment

agreement. You got a dollar?'

She frowned in confusion but reached down behind her to the pocket of a coat which was hanging on her chair; the faux fur one she'd been wearing the night before. I pretended not to notice the droplets of dried blood that were caught in the longest strands of the fur around the collar.

She pulled some crumpled bills out of one pocket and slid a single across the table to me.

'Good. Now, you've hired me. My salary for this case is one crisp dollar. I'm bound by confidentiality regarding anything you say to me.' I handed her the agreement with my signature, and showed her where to put hers. She did so, a bit hesitant at first, then handed it back to me.

'I don't know what I can tell you,' she said, sighing.

'It's possible you know things without realizing you know them,' I began. 'I'm hoping some of my questions trigger some memory or help me make some connections.'

She nodded, and we began.

A little less than two hours later, it was clear that Sugar had reached the end of her tolerance for me. Fatigue had replaced what little energy she'd gotten from the food and coffee, and she was slowly becoming irritable and impatient. I knew a cue when I saw one.

I thanked her for her time, and left a business card on the

table in case she needed anything, and I went outside to my car.

Helen was leaving for work, so we exchanged a few pleasantries outside in the driveway, and I carefully and quietly relayed my concerns for Sugar's physical wellbeing. Helen promised to stop in and see her right away, and we parted.

Sugar, like any good escort, knew how to fawn and cater to her clients. She gave them what they were looking for; in Kevin's case he sometimes took more than what she'd been willing to give him, but he paid well, and regularly. I knew this was a more common scenario than anyone wants to admit, and me being mad about it was going to do exactly jack shit to fix it.

Another thing that most johns don't give escorts credit for is that they have brains in their heads. They listen, they understand; if anything, they have that skill honed in a short time, sometimes out of pure survival.

Like a good investigator, they can tell from your shoes, hands, fingernails, teeth, clothing, odor and attitude a lot about your life. They can tell how you want the exchange to go, how long and how intense. They work to keep your attention, satisfy your interests and then get the fuck out; it's all in a day's work.

Sometimes, the more perceptive ones, like Sugar, can figure

out your triggers and your pride, your fears and hopes. Kevin, I now knew, was concerned with his partners' perception of himself; of how well he was conducting his business, of his ability to fit in with them. And he also had a boat. Which would provide a nice, solid way to get rid of a body.

Now I just had to find it.

Cigarette Man was Back, Yeah I know it's a Dumb Name

I'd moved the angle of my security cameras to show more of the parking lot of my building, and I'd also tucked one or two more in various spots showing different sections of the property.

They were picking up a lot of traffic from the deli next door, but thankfully, since Nasir wasn't open too late, I had a pretty good window of time for when to check and see if someone was watching me still.

I was spending what I'd refer to as 'a collosal waste of time' scrolling through video footage, and was ready to quit - I'd gone through several days worth of recordings with no sign that anyone had come back to watch my building, when I got lucky because Tough Guys (™) are sometimes very dumb.

The night when I had been out watching Kevin, Cigarette Man had returned. He parked or was dropped off somewhere way off camera, and walked along the back fence around the deli. He slinked around like a shadow, following the fence until he got to the front of the property, where you can see inside my office when the lights are on.

He stood where he had before; under the trees in Nasir's flower bed. I fast-forwarded the video; he was there for several hours, shuffling from one foot to the other in the cold, and smoking many cigarettes. During the course of the video, I watched him pace a bit along the edge of the fence; sometimes I'd lose sight of him, he was careful, he stuck to the shadows. Only when he came back to the flowerbed did I get a better look, and even then, he was still slightly obscured.

But my eyes dragged around the edges of his silhouette, burning it into my memory. The way he moved his arm as he drew on, then put the smoke down, the way he cupped the cherry, then eventually flicked his butt. I noticed he would tap the toe of his boot, first one, then the other, to shift his feet inside them. He never rubbed his hands together or ran in place, or any of the other things people do when they feel the cold creeping into their limbs; he was tough, the cold didn't seem to bother him too much; rather, (my stomach turning a bit) it was the boredom.

He wasn't here for fun, he had a job to do, and while he stood there, unable to do it, he was getting antsy.

Eventually, when I hadn't returned, he gave up, and I saw the light from a phone screen in front of his face. I knew that face; I'd photographed that face - behind Cornwall Imports.

A few moments later, a car drove across the deli lot, illuminated brilliantly under the security lights, wherein I got a perfect high-res image of the license plate number, and he climbed into the passenger's side, looking annoyed.

They missed me by twenty minutes or so, and were long gone by the time I watched my own car pull in and park, and myself go into my front door.

This told me two things: I was still of interest to the security firm and they weren't tracking my movements via my phone or a tracker in my car that I'd failed to detect; so at least that was something.

Becky is Back in the Game

Way too early the next morning, before the sun had broken the horizon line, I sat at my desk forcing myself to drink some of my breakfast smoothie. I was wrapped in a blanket from upstairs, as for some reason when I was coming down I thought keeping my bathrobe on against the harsh chill in the air was unprofessional. To my addled brain, being in a blanket burrito was apparently not the same thing.

My guess was that Kevin took a lot of precautions with his personal finances, not unlike how the Security firm was run. But that didn't necessarily translate to how careful his spouse and children were, and I got started hunting them down on the internet.

Becky was done sitting on the sidelines (I was glad she'd taken a few days to herself). She had finished installing the crown molding in her guest room, and was bored. She began texting me for updates around eight, and I filled her in on what I'd been dealing with. She was mad that I hadn't let her know what was going on sooner.

'I was glad you were taking some time off!' I lied. I was glad she'd been out of harm's way. She knew this. I could feel her tone through the text messages: 'Oh shut up Dea i know what you really mean i'll be by in an hour'

'Sounds good' I replied. Truth be told I was looking forward to having some company again.

It was definitely icky to look into the activities of the two college-aged kids and wife of a suspect but it was the fastest way to find out if Kevin's boat was enjoyed by the whole family. Tracking them down and sorting through their social medias was Becky's forte, and she was glad to be back and able to help.

In a short time, she had found them online, and we began the very creepy task of scrolling through their lives to find out anything about their routines and movements that might relate to Kevin's.

Linda was cautious, and didn't have much of her life online. Some images of fancy foods at nice restaurants, a sweet deal at a store, some nice posed pictures of her and the family at an event like a wedding or a shot of a beach with her feet in the sand. Pleasant (if boring) stuff. Their daughter, Eva, had substantially more of an online presence, going back years. A lot of fun: partying, clubs, travel and drinking. Shoes, 'fits, manicures, days spent doing volunteer work, bags of trash collected along the highways, peace signs up while protesting for women's rights. Lots of group shots with her friends, heads close together.

I was thrilled when Becky found several images of her on a boat- and some of the pictures might have had Kevin, or Linda, in the background but it wasn't possible to be sure. The angles were funny, or the person was cut off, and there was no sign of the name of the boat, or a registration number. To me, it looked like every white and chrome boat with blue cushions I'd seen in my life.

The son, Harry, was harder to track down than Eva had been, but he couldn't hide from Becky for long. He posted under usernames that didn't include anything about his real identity and he had his profiles set to private. Becky circumnavigated that the good old fashioned way: by stroking his ego.

She had a couple of profiles she had invented- of beautiful, leggy women (models she'd hired- she's not a monster who steals other women's pictures without their consent). She used the images to craft fake identities and would post often enough to make the page look legit but not so much that it took up a lot of her time. She'd delete and repost to reuse images, had a backup of fresh pics, kept them private so she wasn't inundated with random followers, and was careful about who followed the account. She used them for this express purpose- to request permission to follow guys whose profiles were set to private. Within the hour, Harry had approved her follow request. (Sorry, Harry.)

His social media was a bit more enigmatic; odd things he'd seen or found, stuff about his work, short captions or none at all, nothing about a girlfriend, very few pictures of other people. But plenty out on the boat. Apparently, he and Kevin spent a great deal of their time on fishing excursions, and Harry was the kind of guy who liked to photograph his catches. So many pictures of him holding up glistening, wet fish.

It didn't take long for Becky to locate enough pictures that when we saved them, sized them to match, printed them out and pasted them together, we'd basically puzzle-pieced what almost the entire boat looked like.

Now I could see the flag Kevin had flying from the pilot's seat, the color of the fabric on the top, the orange and yellow paint stripes that ran down the side, the devices they had set up around the controls, and the sticker they had on the door that led below. But most importantly, the name of the boat- was it funny? Stupid? An inside joke? It was called 'My Solution'. Whatever the reason, I hated it.

While Becky was combing through the socials, I dug up info on all of the marinas that were close enough to Kevin's house to make the trip manageable. Being that we were not far from the coast, there were plenty to choose from, but I couldn't spend the rest of my life going through each one. So I picked the ones that appeared to have access to a bay or inlet that, according to satellite images, was shaped similarly to some of the pictures from Harry's account.

'Now I have a lot of driving to do,' I sighed, writing down the location for the furthest marina, which combined with all the rest, I wasn't even sure I'd have time to get to in one day. '*We*,' Becky corrected. '*We* have a lot of driving to do. I'll pack snacks.'

We had to wait until the following day to head out on our mission. I wanted one more thing to bring with us, and it took a little time to get it. In the meantime I showed Becky the footage of Cigarette Man and, now that I had a license plate number, I gave my friend Gary at the impound lot a call. I didn't want to call Doris again- it was unfair of me to lean too much on individuals from my old life, and also, I worried they might face repercussions if it was found out they were helping me- cuz they definitely weren't supposed to do so.

'Hey there,' he said good naturedly when I identified myself. 'Two convos in such a short time? Why am I so lucky?'

I smiled at his pleasant demeanor, and told him I was sorry, but it was still a business call.

'I see,' he said, his tone softening. 'You still looking for that missing girl?'

'Yeah. That's why I'm calling, I was hoping you could run a plate for me. I know it's a big ask, so if you can't-'

'No, no, lay it on me D. That Lennette lady was nice, and I'd like to help.'

I gave him the details, and I could hear him shuffling some stuff around in his tiny office. 'Hold on, hold on, I'm looking for my readers, ugh, ok, I got 'em, give me a sec here.' He typed slowly, I could imagine him jabbing the keyboard with one single finger. 'Alright. You got a pen?'

'Ready when you are.'

Gary gave me the name that the registration was filed under- he said there was no associated business name, however. I was surprised, as I fully expected the car to be registered to Kevin's security firm. 'Be careful with this one, D,' Gary said quietly. 'He's got a record. A nasty one at that.'

'I appreciate you, Gary. Give Hettie a kiss for me.' Hettie was his wife.

'Will do.'

I didn't recognize the name of the person to whom the car was registered. I did some internet searching, however, and found multiple arrest records. Gary was right, this guy was serious. And if he was playing chauffeur to Cigarette Man, that made *him* a pretty serious player as well. My dark thoughts were interrupted by a message from Grassy.

Welp the Feds are Gonna be Pissed I Know This

'In nasirs. this was a weird one, im almost curious'

I left Becky in the office and walked next door. I placed an order for two sandwiches at the deli counter, then casually approached Grassy, who was browsing the bagged snacks. How funny is that, I happened to want the exact same chips that he picked up so I grabbed a bag as well (along with the thumb drive and adaptor that Grassy placed behind the bags on the shelf). He paused for a moment and I leaned a little closer as he spoke, his voice so low I barely could make out his words over the din of the store's activity.

'I've got the name for Seaside Optics,' he said quietly. 'I finally got it right before I left to come here. I'm just telling you now, I'm officially out, okay?'

I nodded once in reply.

'Hackerman.' Then he was gone before my sandwiches were even done being assembled. Welp, I'd love to say I was surprised but too much had happened recently, and my threshold for bullshit was in the stratosphere.

It was an hour drive to the first marina, and then there were at least thirty or forty minutes of drive time between them, if not more. We knew we were about to spend the entire day in the car, so we also mapped out where we could stop for bathroom breaks.

I brought everything I had that could help me examine a crime scene. All the luminol, wipes, testing kits I could come up with, most of which I put together myself using techniques and materials I learned about all the way back during my investigating and forensics courses before I even got a spot on a beat. I knew Kevin's boat would be ripe with biologic materials and it was going to be a challenge to check it over. If we could even get onto it, that is.

Two marinas down with no luck, and we pulled over to eat the sandwiches I'd picked up from Nasir's in the morning, at a lookout point along the coast line which had a nice view of the land dropping off into the water below.

We took our time; I was tired of driving so Becky was going to take the wheel from this point on. My left arm and shoulder were aching a lot more than usual; and we all know why.

At each marina, we told employees who noticed us and asked if we needed help that we were interested in buying a boat, and that a friend had recommended that particular marina for storage and accessibility; and could they tell us more about it? I was already tired of hearing about tides and wakes and docking fees and wintering services, but we still had three stops to go.

It was late afternoon and the sun had dropped behind the trees that lined the long, desolate road we were traversing, instead of using the main thoroughfare. We were close to the fifth marina, with no luck so far. This one was the furthest from Kevin's house, and not the most affordable either- large yachts and fancier boats than were docked at the other locations were moored here; and if their website was any indication, their services were of a higher-end variety.

Being the harshest part of the winter, all of the marinas had less vessels active in the water than they did during the nicer weather months, when more people spent time out on the water. This had been helpful, as we'd thus far been able to look through the boats that were in the water for the one named My Solution; and we hadn't had to ask after it. There was always a chance, not knowing where the boat was, that if we asked the *one* harbormaster who was friends with Kevin, where *his* boat was, he'd be alerted right away that someone- and he could probably guess who- was out looking for it. Not giving out its name, or mentioning Kevin at all, was our only chance of him not being made aware that we even knew he had a boat, or had an interest in this line of inquiry.

Becky and I could see through Harry's social media, that he and Kevin went out in all weather; so we were confident their boat was not in storage- although with every marina we left with no joy, we were losing that confidence.

I began to fear that with my luck, he had in fact had it put up somewhere, wrapped in thick blue shrinkwrap in some lot or facility someplace, completely inaccessible to me and my forensic kit.

I was just about to vocalize this complaint when Becky made the last turn, the trees gave way to sand and marsh, and seconds later, the tall masts of sailing ships came into view.

The marina was lovely- it had a small, elegant club and dining room, a parking area made with paving stones that were laid in a looped design in alternating shades of gray, and a walking path that went along the water's edge.

As soon as we pulled in I could have laughed; *of course* this is where Kevin would park his boat. Rubbing elbows with the upper crusts. The people who learned to sail when they were toddlers, who went to schools where you wore a crest on your blazer, who were on rowing teams in their ivy league colleges.

Becky is Not a Fan of This Idea

We could see Kevin's boat from the parking lot; we didn't even need to get out of the car to know we'd come to the right spot, it's dumb name shined like a beacon.

Becky grasped the door handle and moved to exit the vehicle but I stopped her, and shook my head when she frowned at me.

'The sheer number of security cameras and employees here is absurd,' I said. She situated herself more comfortably in the drivers seat again. 'I think I'll wait until nightfall. There's little chance I can completely escape scrutiny but I'll have better odds. I need to spend a good deal of time on the boat, and the less people see me, the better.' Then I started to get annoyed. There were marinas we'd visited earlier that we'd wandered the entire property and didn't see a single employee. Other ones where the lowly, bored guy on shift was happy to speak to us at length, who had no clue about us. But this one? Security was tight, and while that bothered me because it slowed down my plans to examine Kevin's boat, what bothered me *more* was that I'd spent this whole day thinking this was how Kevin got rid of Janelle- but there was no way he was getting a body past all these cameras and people.

I sighed. 'Let's go get some coffee - GPS says there's a diner a few miles down the road. We'll come back later, once the sun is down.'

The diner was old, a classic chrome and vinyl joint straight out of the fifties. It had been renovated, but done in a retro style so it was kitsch. It was everything you want a diner to be- twenty four hour breakfast, lunch and dinner, coffee always ready.

I actually meant to only get coffee but the smells coming from that kitchen changed my mind, and Becky and I ended up ordering dinner as well.

We didn't converse much; we'd spent all day in the car with the possibility looming over us that we might not even find Kevin's boat. Now that we'd located it, a new cloud hung above our heads: discovering evidence that my theory was correct.

But the problem was, how to get onto the boat without

being spotted by the alert employees, who were no doubt paid very well to keep an eye on these expensive seafaring vessels? The dining room at the yacht club had people milling about inside; clearly those for whom sailing was life weren't put off by a little winter chill. The cars in the lot were high end; the cameras pointed in all directions. Every precaution was taken.

Once the sun was down, and the shadows between the trees and behind the buildings had grown deep, we got into the car and began the drive back. We were a few hundred feet from the entrance to the marina when Becky asked me, 'So what's the plan?'

And I was about to reply, 'I'm still working on it'- but something through the trees caught my eye, and I cried out instead 'Pull over!'

There were no other cars about so Becky was able to do so immediately, and she was slightly panicked when she said 'What is it?'

'It's okay- I've got it! Reverse! There's a driveway back there- go down it.'

Becky didn't ask questions, she just threw the gear shift and hit the gas, then turned right down the driveway I indicated- the only one around.

When she saw why, she smiled and shook her head.

At the end of the drive was a small cabin, the windows were

dark and there were no security lights on either. The leaves piled up at the door and along the front walk told us this was a summer place; a quick peek in the windows showed four no-nonsense built-in bunk beds against one wall, with bare mattresses piled high on a top bunk- a small effort to keep mice or other little creatures from making them a home in the winter. A modest living room area with a wood burning fireplace opened into a small kitchen, which was all that made up the rest of the space.

The shed to the side, with two canoes and a rowboat chained to a rack and the boat launch behind the house, told Becky everything I was thinking.

I showed her an image from the satellite pictures I'd used earlier in the day to locate the marinas- in the trees to one side of the marina I could see the roof of the cabin where we were standing. It might be a little hairy, but the estuary behind the house led directly in the water where the marina began, and if we hugged the shore we wouldn't have to fight too hard against currents.

Becky was not a fan of the idea. 'First of all, this is stealing-'

'Borrowing.'

'-and secondly the water is freezing. If we fall in we will die! In like, a few minutes.'

'We won't fall in. Plus, we'll only be in deep water for a short distance- just to get around the dock.'

'Also, you can't row *anything* with your bad arm, so obviously I'll be doing all the work.'

'Yes, although I think that boat is wide enough that if we had to, we could sit side-by-side and row together.'

'Robbie is going to kill me. Then he's going to kill you, then me again.'

'Correct.'

I fished the bolt cutters out of my trunk (a vital part of any decent PI kit) and cut the chain off the rowboat. Not the lock- the chain.

Then, I looked inside the shed- and spotted something that was going to make all of this way easier. I turned and grinned at Becky, then pulled my lock pick set out of my pocket. 'In for a penny,' I said, chuckling.

She sighed and shook her head, keeping an eye on the driveway and the road beyond. The darkness was settled heavily, though through the bare trees, we had a good sight line pretty far down both directions of road. No headlights would be able to come near us without us having advanced notice.

She moved the car behind the cabin to hide it from the street, and then helped me carry the rowboat down to the water's edge, where we attached the small motor I'd found hanging on a rack inside the boatshed.

The cabin owners were well-prepared people; there was

even a little gas can in the shed with enough fuel in it to fill the reservoir in the motor.

I felt a bit bad about what I was helping myself to, however, I made a decision that at some point in the near future, I'd come back with a full can of gas to replace what I used, and that I could repair the chain by putting the two lengths back together with a fresh padlock. The keys of which I could leave inside the shed, just to be you know, neighborly.

I could have laughed - it would have helped to relieve some tension- as Becky accepted the dark watch cap, a duplicate of the one I was also wearing, that I handed to her to hide her long blonde hair. In our dark coats, scarves and matching hats, we looked like cat burglars out of a sixties movie.

It didn't take much to get the well-cared-for motor going despite the cold and in a few minutes, we were away. I was much less afraid of the journey now that we didn't have to manually row there; but caution was still the best friend we could have. Becky steered well and stayed close to shore- she had more experience with boats than I.

Then once we were out of the estuary and heading for open water, she braved the crossing and moved away from the land to take the most direct route. When we were close to the dock, she cut the engine and began to row. She closed the gap fast, and then slowed carefully, maneuvering us near to the side of My Solution. I put both hands out to stop us so the boats didn't collide, and then Becky held us as steady as she could. I reached up and tied a line to the rail along the gunwale of My Solution so Becky and the rowboat wouldn't drift.

There was a light and a security camera on the nearest pole, so I pulled my hat down to my eyebrows and kept my chin down as I stepped out of our borrowed rowboat and slipped over the far side of My Solution.

Mae West Was Wrong

All was incredibly quiet, but for the the gentle lapping of the waves against the fiberglass hulls. I was grateful for the relative stillness of the water and for the quiet of the season. I could hear the laughter and conversation from the yacht club dining hall when people opened the door to go in or out.

I first checked to make sure I was, in fact, alone on the boat. That was easy; it was modestly sized, and picking the lock to go below was a cinch. The cabin had a stale odor of cigars and saltwater damp, but it was clean.

I took a look around on the deck and seating areas, and the pilot's chair. The only thing that seemed out of the ordinary was a series of deep gouges in the fiberglass of the gunwale on one side; they caught a bit on my jeans as I'd climbed over. I made sure I hadn't left any fibers in the scratches, and moved on to the cabin.

I opened and closed a few cupboards until I found what I was looking for- Kevin had a fancy depth checker fish finder thingamajig- equipped with GPS tracking. And if I knew anything about modern devices, it's that they keep tracking you even when you think they aren't doing so.

I powered up the machine, pulled the thumb drive and adaptor out of my bag that Grassy had put together for me, and plugged it in. The thumb drive contained a program that Grassy wrote, which mined the data from machine and downloaded it. When that was done, I tucked my device back into my bag, and put the tracker back in the cupboard where it had been stowed.

The ports had small curtains on them. I made sure they were tucked closed, so the beam from my flashlight wouldn't show outside, and I started easy, with luminol. Well, joke was on me because Kevin liked to party, a little tidbit I'd nearly forgotten. The place was a mess under the blacklight, and I wanted to throw up.

I could tell by the colors of the spots as they fluoresced what they were; and I didn't care much to find out about the origin or owner of most of the fluids; but the quantities of blood were disconcerting at best, horrifying at worst, and were my priority.

I had to re-spray the luminol multiple times to photograph the blood spatters against the walls surrounding the cushioned bed area, and the places on the floor where some of it had pooled. Nothing was large enough to be considered drastic blood loss; but blood doesnt have to pour out of a body for the person to not be alive anymore. I didn't allow myself to picture in my mind what the fuck Kevin was up to in this place. Letting my imagination go would mean less room for reason and cold judgement, two things I currently needed more than speculation.

I set up my phone to take video, speaking quietly to narrate my actions, and stating the date and time. I used miniature markers and photographed myself taking the samples on swabs, placing them in tubes, then writing on the tubes' labels the numbers on the markers. I worked as quickly as I could, but it felt like I was in there for an eternity.

My hands were shaking at everything I was seeing; I had been out of this kind of game for years; my tolerance to it had worn off. I was pretty sure, though, that that was a good thing.

Thanks for All the, Well, You Know the Rest

Becky pushed the motor hard returning to the little cabin.

I wondered if I was going to have to replace it too; but it didn't sputter or even register discontent. Under other circumstances, I imagined this would be a pleasant experience; the sky was a vast dome of stars, black as ink between the twinkling lights, the trees, bare of leaves reached their winding, twisting limbs up, the water was calm and the energy of the yacht club was festive.

It was probably lovely (especially if you were fortunate enough to own a small cabin with its own water access) to spend the days and evenings here, out on the water, listening to the way it rolled around, and how the tiny waves moved along the shore. The air was fresh and tonight the breeze was mild; even in the winter this place was darling.

However much I'd have liked to keep musing, our current errand was too overwhelming to let me enjoy this seafaring adventure; the quiet thunks of the plastic vials and bottles rocking against one another in my kit as we rode the low waves back to the cabin were more than enough to keep my mind from wandering too far from what was at hand. We made it back quickly, and relatively unscathed.

Relatively because Becky was definitely freaking out a little. 'Ohmygodohmygod,' she said. 'I'm gonna pass out, I was so scared!'

'It's okay, we're okay, we're okay,' I tried to reassure her, 'let's just get out of here.'

'You don't have to tell me twice,' she said, replacing the oars in their bin, and running back to the water's edge to grab the bow of the rowboat. She heaved it up onto the shore, and I removed the motor from the back end. She helped me carry it back inside the little shed. We ran back again, (I was not a fan of all the running) she grasped the bow and I took hold of the stern, and together we put the boat back where we'd found it. I did my best to wipe down every surface either of us had touched with a spare t-shirt I had in the car, and then I locked the doorknob of the boatshed and pulled the door shut.

I set the chain up around the boats to make them look like they were still locked up, and we both took a quick look around to make sure everything sort of looked how we'd found it.

I stowed my forensic kit in the trunk while Becky started the car, and I'm pretty sure she peeled wheels getting us out of there and back on the road.

There was no way I was getting any sleep tonight. Becky went home, and once I had confirmed via the tracking software that she was there, I sent her a coded message. 'Im home' was too easy for someone to imitate- instead we said something weird like 'cats shouldn't wear shoes.' Her response was in the affirmative: 'yes they should when necessary'.

Robbie was spending a lot of time in his home office lately, putting the finishing touches on some expensive lawsuit his firm was handling, and she told me later, she was grateful for how intensely he was concentrating on his work, for it gave her time to let the tension leave her voice.

I was asking too much of her, I thought, and of myself. This whole case was too much.

In the wee hours I was trying to teach myself how to read tidal current charts when suddenly I could no longer comprehend what I was reading because my brain was close to hitting its shutoff switch, so I forced myself to lock everything up, and go to bed. I stared at the ceiling of my bedroom for a while, and just when I was wondering if I should give up on sleep and go back downstairs to keep working, I finally nodded off.

I'm Good But Not That Good

Way too early the next morning, after a pre-dawn shower that did nothing to revive me and coffee that was barely making a dent, I sat angrily staring at a pile of evidence with no way of finishing what I'd started. I'd have liked to sleep longer, but my 'twelve angry squirrels fighting on a merry-go-round' brain decided I'd had enough rest.

I was flush with forensic evidence with no way of processing it. The irony was painful. Of course I knew of several labs that I could pay to analyze all the samples, but without something to compare it to, the results would not be useful at this stage.

I decided to get focused on tracking my suspects again, and try to figure out wether it was Stanhope or Kevin or Carter Linhurst, maybe? Should I start a case on him? He hadn't even popped up in my investigation yet with the exception of his name and face on a website. Did this guy even exist? I made a mental note to sic Becky on him ASAP.

I needed to figure out who was paying goons to keep an eye on me and perhaps hand out beat-downs, or worse.

It was a relief that Kevin didn't appear to know that I'd placed a GPS tracker. For someone whose job was security he didn't do enough checks of his own vehicle. Call me paranoid but I'd been sweeping my own car twice a day since Cigarette Man first showed up at my building.

After a while of watching Kevin's car sit in a parking lot of one of the warehouses who were paying his company for security, and scrolling through surveillance footage of Stanhope's car sitting in the IEI parking lot, I lost the fight against boredom and switched gears and pulled up a map of Valmer Boulevard, and dropped a pin where the traffic cams were that caught Shanks' vehicle.

I zoomed out and followed the road East, but most of the land it went through was undeveloped county property, trees, marshlands, low lying wetlands that bordered the coast. I was becoming despondent at the prospect that he could have dumped a body literally anywhere in those hundred of acres, when I noticed there were a few structures on the map where the boulevard terminated. I switched from a street to a satellite view and my heart heavily thumped once, twice in my chest.

It was an industrial wharf- not a private or recreational one- a small, lesser used shipping port- out of date and not well-equipped for modern shipping needs.

According to some articles I speed-read online, I discovered it most recently was used to service local fishing charters; smaller vessels that didn't carry large containers.

Now, what to do about this?

Well, there was only one thing I could do right now- look at this spot with my eyeballs- so I geared up and out the door I went. When you're investigating a case where there are boats, and shipping and mysterious car rides in the night, and you find a weird old location that involves boats, shipping and a late night mysterious car ride, well, it's a good idea to check that spot out. If the road terminated in a petting zoo, or a nail salon, it would probably not be related (well, you never really know).

The sky was clear and the early morning sun shined brightly but did little to dispel the bitter cold that whipped along the roadway. Swirls of snowflakes that had fallen in the night danced across the empty highway ahead of me.

It was a weekday; people were at school, or work, no one was traveling along Valmer Boulevard to the waterfront at the end.

When I arrived in the approximate area, it took me a while to figure out what I was looking at. Access to the vicinity was blocked off, closed due to dangers of falling debris; the whole area was out of commission.

It took me several minutes to even find the entrance; I parked at the end of what appeared to be a driving lane; it was blocked off by a large metal gate. A simple push was enough to open it- someone else had come by before me and busted the lock. The buildup of rust in the dangling padlock told me it had been a while ago- possibly even years.

I drove along the small road, noticing the lack of signs of recent activity, looking in patches of dirt for tire treads or fresh trash, and seeing nothing but neglect and decay.

Old, broken down brick buildings, which must have stored the shipped goods or perhaps were cold storage for fish, sat in overgrown lots, their windows long gone, their floors overtaken by vines and underbrush. I stopped my car a good distance from the water, where the ground was firm. Definitely couldn't risk driving over a rotting structure by accident.

I felt confident I was alone, well alone. Not even birds flew around in the rafters of the empty buildings, for they had all migrated for the season.

Small animals flitted about when I came too close to a pile of trash or debris; which I took as a good sign that there were no other humans besides myself disturbing them.

I photographed the area as I went, following the sounds of the water lapping.

I rounded the corner of a building, and found I'd arrived at the wharf. To my left was the rusting structure of what might have been a crane, to my right, the wood and metal ran along for a few dozen yards and then ended in rotting, empty pilings jutting out of the calm water.

When you hear 'waterfront property' it's easy to think it's valuable and that someone would have bought this place up and made a bucket off it, however, I could see where the land was denuded, it was soft muck, impossible to traverse or build on, the structures were all destroyed, out of date and unusable. The amount of money it would take to tear this place down, fill in the land and make it usable again was, I imagined, far more than it was worth, when there were much larger modern shipping areas not that far away.

I photographed the area, and, stepping as gingerly as possible, I walked over to the edge of the still-standing wharf.

The bottom was not visible, at all. The murky water, many feet below me, rolled around the pilings holding up the surface I stood upon, appearing deceptively lazy. I could tell it was incredibly deep. This made my stomach flutter, and I backed up quickly.

There were no tire markings or skids along the edge; not that I'd have been able to see them. Much of the ground was covered in rust and filth, the surface of the tarred boards was impossible to see minute traces of things that shouldn't have been there.

I hurried back to my car, feeling spooked and jittery. If Shanks had driven here, I didn't have any proof that he did so; the crawling feeling all over my body didn't count as evidence.

Surprise Lunch

I was far past being irritated at following leads that led me nowhere, or to more questions, or to empty rotting docks, or to empty smelly apartments. I was annoyed at not hearing back from Agent Grant about whether the DNA from the warehouse floor was viable, and matched or didn't match Janelle's.

I tried not to think on it too much, lest I convince myself it was going to be a definite match, and then if I was wrong to have to deconstruct that in my mind, but it was impossible to cease the hope entirely.

I was frustrated and exhausted from the disconcerting sensation of standing above the ominous darkness and depth of the water beneath the wharf; it had made my legs feel wobbly and my stomach lurch a bit, and on the way home I was plagued by intrusive thoughts such as 'what if the boards had given out' 'what if I'd fallen in' and I had to sing out loud to shut my own brain the hell up.

I sat down and resumed scanning through my security camera footage from Stanhope's home and office. I finally caught up to the last few days or so of video, when I noticed something was amiss.

He'd eschewed his normal routines. I grabbed a pen and legal pad, and made notes as I watched the images move across the screen in fast-forward. His schedule was off, and though the view of his house was slightly obscured by some trees, I could see that his lights had been on well into the night for almost a week; as late as three or four am. I could sometimes make out his silhouette moving past windows.

He was showing up late to work, and leaving early. I frowned as I watched his face on the screen while he sat waiting for an opening in traffic to leave the IEI parking lot. His eyes were sunken, he looked pasty and jittery. I'd have said he was struggling with a coke habit, but without seeing him in person and having a conversation, it was impossible to say for sure.

When I arrived at the video files which were about a day old, I paused the recording, and tried to think up with a way of interviewing him again; knowing the FBI was watching made it incredibly difficult. I leaned back in my chair and wondered if I could come up with a way to plant a tracker in his car, to maybe catch him at lunch or someplace the FBI wasn't watching...?

I was stewing over this particular thought, while on a separate screen I watched Kevin leave the warehouse and drive around town, when a blocked number called my mobile.

'Hey Ms. Oshtrovsky. It's Agent Grant.'

I heard myself say 'Please call me Dea.'

'Dea. I don't have time to talk right now, can you meet me in a little while?'

'Sure, uh, when and where?'

'Do you know Lorenzo's?'

'Yep.'

'Three o'clock? I'll have a table in the back.'

'I'll be there.'

She clicked off without saying goodbye, and I looked at my clock. Oh man, it was going to be absolute hell waiting to leave. I was going to be climbing the bloody walls. I tried to stay busy, but it was impossible to focus on anything. I was sure Grant was going to share results of a DNA test, and I practically ran to my car, more than twenty minutes earlier than I needed to leave.

Obviously, I was way too early for our, what was this, lunch? I don't know, who eats lunch at three? So I spent a few minutes in the car to tidy up, which I had been too anxious to do at home. I'd gone upstairs to my apartment and changed my shirt into something a little less lived-in, but I didn't want to look like I'd tried too hard. Then, catching sight of myself in my vanity mirror in the car, I decided I hadn't done *enough*, so I primped a bit. Like, fluffed my hair and put on lipgloss. Why, you ask? If it's not obvious, I'm not explaining it to you. I sniffed my armpits and touched up my deodorant. (When you spend hours in the car doing surveillance, you keep a toiletry bag in there. The more you know.)

Soon- right on time- I saw Agent Grant pull into the lot and head for the door. I gave her a minute; she was the one with the table so I wanted to give her the opportunity to go to it first, then I followed her in. She was still taking off her coat and scarf when I came in, and she smiled (!) at me, then dropped it just as suddenly as it had appeared. I took that to mean our meeting wasn't going to be a happy one, even if she was glad to see me.

We exchanged our hellos and sat down. Grant told me the chicken piccata was excellent, but added, 'Unfortunately I don't have time to get it today, I need something quicker.' I had scanned the menu before I left my office, to expedite the lunch. The server asked if we'd like to start with beverages but we both said we were ready to order, and we each requested the grilled chicken wrap. The server made a joke about how we were probably going to be her easiest table that day; and she scooted off. After she'd brought our drinks and disappeared again, Grant's face became solemn and she began.

'I'm sorry for the rushed meeting,' she said. 'I didn't have any time today to come see you at your office, and couldn't risk wasting the trip, if I missed you if you weren't there anyway. The only time I could get away would have to be my lunch break and I didn't want to swallow a burrito while driving so I thought this was better, plus it's close to my office.'

'This place seems nice.'

'It's a favorite.' She sighed. 'Is Stanhope still on your suspect list?'

My spirits sank. So no DNA results. 'Yeah. I've been

monitoring him but he's getting jumpy. He doesn't look so good, I'm not sure what's going on. I'd almost ruled him out but now... I'm thinking of putting him back in the running.' Grant nodded. 'You're not wrong, but investigating him further isn't possible anymore.' I was about to protest- I did not need the FBI putting more restrictions on me- but she continued- 'He'd dead.'

The news was shocking, so it took me a second to process it, then my brain became overwhelmed with questions. I'd just been looking at his face, caught on my hidden cameras, what felt like minutes ago! The videos I'd been reviewing were a couple days old- I hadn't made it to the data from the last twenty-four hours yet. 'When did it happen?' was the first question that managed to make its way through the bottleneck in my brain and out of my mouth.

'Initial examination puts T.o.D. sometime in the early to late evening, last night. As you know, we're surveilling IEI. When he didn't show up for work today, we sent an agent dressed as a door-to-door salesman to check on him. The body was found at the bottom of the basement stairs. It looks like an accident but...'

I didn't need clarification.

Our lunches arrived, and we took a few bites each in silence, then I asked, 'Do you know who did it?'

'No.'

I knew she wasn't just trying to keep the details under wraps. Her answer was definite and clear. They might have had a list of suspects, but no one for sure. A new line of inquiry must have already opened; I could imagine the hubbub at the FBI office all morning as they began to comb through the last few days of Stanhope's life, and try to figure out who made it into his house and out again. There had been no news blurbs (I still had all my active news alerts going) so my guess was that the Bureau was successfully keeping the situation under wraps for now. I sighed. 'I might be able to help,' I said.

Grant looked at me with an intensity that was unsettling, but I knew it wasn't personal. It was her professional glare- and it was effective. 'What do you mean?'

'I've had cameras on his house this whole time... I put them up within a day or so of being hired to find Janelle.'

Her eyes widened in surprise, she leaned close to me, her voice barely a whisper. 'Dea- you don't understand- Stanhope was the reason the Bureau was investigating at all- he was our source. He called the Bureau, about a week after your girl went missing- he's been giving us supply lines, schedules. We wouldn't even have a case without him. Are you telling me you have *seen* his killer?'

I shook my head rapidly; so many things were starting to make sense. That's why I had a (albeit miniscule) headstart on the FBI, even though they obviously were able to eclipse me. That's why they caught up to me, got me on camera at Cornwall, had a line on me, knew when I broke into IEI. But I'd placed my cameras before their investigation had begun. They were hot on my heels for a few days, but now, they had more than I'd ever have, because of their resources, yes, but they also had an inside man.

'No, I'm not up to date- I'm a few days behind on the recordings.' I told her where the cameras were located, and gave her a idea of the view they covered. Agent Grant didn't seem surprised that I had security cameras tucked away to watch Stanhope. I think she was mostly surprised that the Bureau hadn't made them. I'll take that as a compliment. 'I know you said you were super busy but can you make time to come to my office?'

'Let's go- now- or, do you want to finish your lunch?'

'I've had enough to take the edge off. I can finish it later.'

She waved down our server and paid the check, then we both took our food to go. Grant followed me back to my office, I'll admit I drove rather more quickly than I normally do.

I tossed my take-away in the office fridge while my laptop booted up. I'd left the heat up before I went to lunch, so it was comfortable in the room, as opposed to the blustery frigidity of the outside. Grant's cheeks were a bit pink from the nip in the air.

I sat down behind my desk and Grant shifted a guest chair around beside me so we could watch the screen together.

I fast-forwarded the last day or so of footage from Stanhope's driveway. We saw him come home from the office, early enough that the sky still held a little light from the setting sun.

Grant rewound it repeatedly; Stanhope had made a right into the driveway, like he did every evening. The angle of the camera only showed his right arm, upper thigh and a bit of his gloved hand as he straightened the steering wheel.

'What are you looking for?' I asked.

'Just making sure he's alone in the car,' was the reply.

We watched the driveway as the sun dropped rapidly, and darkness descended over his property. The trees my camera could see were illuminated periodically by the flash of passing headlights, and eventually, the lamps came on inside his house- a long time after the sun had set. He'd been sitting in darkness, doing who-knows-what, for at least an hour.

We watched the span of several hours pass, as little more than headlights or the occasional small animal or foraging deer came through the view. The lights in the house stayed on, and sometimes Stanhope passed by a window. I'll never understand why people live without curtains, but it does make my job easier, so keep those windows bare people.

I was starting to worry that the perp came onto the property by another route, when some lights stayed on the trees for a second or two longer than others had done- they weren't just passing.

'Slow it down,' Grant said, her voice just above a whisper.

I rewound a few seconds, then pressed a key and the video played at normal speed. It was unmistakeable- a car had pulled off the road and killed its lights, but outside of my camera's- and the house's- view. After a few seconds, a tiny light flashed across the bottom of the screen.

'What was that?' Grant said, rewinding the video and replying it two or three times.

'That,' I said, 'is someone tossing a cigarette on the ground.'

A moment later, a dark figure moved into view, hugging the edge of the driveway, keeping tight against the line of trees. If we were watching from another angle, he would have been incredibly difficult to see. His clothes and slow movements hid him well; someone glancing out of a window in the house, perhaps with a light on in the room they were in, would not have been able to see him.

He soon disappeared entirely, melting into the shadows of the trees and underbrush. Our eyes stayed glued to the windows on Stanhope's house, hoping for any movement, any image of the two figures. But we could see nothing but the rectangles of the windows, comfortably lit with soft amber light from within.

After what felt like an eternity, Cigarette Man emerged once again from the shadows, like an oil spill making its way down a street and pouring into a gutter. He was smoking again, and he walked confidently back under the camera. It was too dark to see his face clearly but I knew his frame, and the way he moved.

But this time, he wasn't alone. The darkness obscured his companion's face as well; *his* visage was little more than a small splotch of a lighter color in the night. Truly terrifying, that was. I paused the video through several frames but we could never see him clearly. *He* stayed well in the shadows. It was only the tiniest flickers of movement that told us that the smoking man wasn't alone.

A moment later, headlights shined, slid across the trees to the left, and were gone.

'Who the *hell* was *that*?' Grant said out loud, what we were both thinking.

'And where did he come from?' I added.

Welp, Who's on First

Grant rubbed her forehead with the fingertips of her left hand. 'I'll need that file,' she said.

'I'm already copying it.'

'Do you have an ID on the smoking guy?'

'No, I've got some clear pictures of his face, though. We need to identify him immediately cuz uh, he's been keeping an eye on me.'

'What?'

'Yeah, he's been here, watching me once or twice. Maybe more. I'll give you a copy of that video too. I got a plate off it, and I only just got a name on the driver- I had planned to try to get some names of the driver's known associates.'

'Fucking hell,' Grant breathed. 'Do you realize what that means?'

'I sure as shit do now,' I replied. I thought everything over for a few minutes while the videos copied onto a thumb drive. 'Stanhope wasn't looking so good,' I began. Grant nodded in agreement. 'He wasn't sleeping, was barely showing up to work. When I first took the case I followed him to a strip club where he met Kevin, who really laid into him. He was mad, but Kevin was madder. It was only a few days after Janelle went missing. I bet Stanhope *wasn't* involved in Janelle's disappearance- he seemed genuinely surprised when I told him I was looking for her- he may have started to suspect Kevin had something to do with it, and it was eating him up. That might be why he decided to blow the lid off the whole thing. Maybe he really did care for her.'

'I'm not his contact. It's possible he mentioned it to his handler, but I have not been informed if he had. Something tells me though, that he didn't say anything. Maybe he suspected it but didn't want to go there, you know? Didn't want to admit it. Also, he must not have known for sure; so he shared with the Bureau what he did know- the operations.'

'Right. But I'm not the only one one who can guess, that since Janelle is still missing, it's likely she ran afoul of someone. He must have had his suspicions, especially when Robert Shanks went missing as well. His fears must have worsened the longer they've both been gone.'

Grant was nodding. 'He was becoming a liability.'

'Yes,' I agreed, 'but to whom?'

Grant frowned. 'Right. Who's making the calls? It obviously wasn't Stanhope.'

'This blows my, admittedly, not-fully-formed theory of the whole hierarchy out the window,' I said, dejectedly. 'When Becky found that article in that style magazine, I just assumed Stanhope, with the help or maybe in cahoots with some of his big wig buddies, was the head of this; perhaps he didn't get his own hands dirty, but he had goons, and he also had legit security- former cops. So the goons handle the dirty work and the cops clean it up real good. It was a solid system. Protected from the top by all that money and connections, protected from the bottom by people who know the system, who know the routes, the dirt. But who is really in charge, if someone took out Stanhope? He was an asset while he had connections, and was running the company; once he took issue with the way things were handled with his girlfriend, he found his conscience and looks like he was crashing.'

'Kevin Werth?'

'I don't know,' I replied, shaking my head. 'From everything I can see, he actually *is* running the security business. Based on his movements, the places he visits, I just don't know how he'd have time to be the head of an international smuggling ring. I know that Hackerman has Seaside Optics to funnel or hide money. But is he the one running things?'

Grant breathed a heavy sigh and looked at me warily. I imagined from her perspective it was annoying how much I, as a P.I., was able to figure out.

'As far as we can tell, he's just an investor. We can't put him in the same place as any of these people, physically, or nail down how they're communicating. Werth, however, he's everywhere something is happening. He could be ambitious. Staging a coup.'

'Yes, true, but, he seems more like he's getting his jollys other ways; his interests are more tangible, more...

accessible than being the guy in the shiny office.'

'Mm. I think even the Bureau has been operating under the notion that Stanhope was the head, or close to it at least, and his, as you say, big wig buddies were simply benefitting somehow. But maybe he was inflating his own worth, to get us to take everything his told us more seriously.'

'I guess he didn't have a lot of faith in law enforcement, if he thought the FBI wouldn't be interested unless he acted like he was the one in charge.'

'Well look at his comrades. Congressman, police sergeant, et cetera. I wouldn't have much faith in the system either, if I knew all the ways it could be screwed by the people who are supposed to uphold it.'

'Good point.'

'It's time to take this all to the Bureau,' she said. 'I need everything you've got, on Janelle, on Stanhope, on all of it. I put in that DNA request for you, by the way. I attached it to some of the evidence we swiped from the trash at IEI. That way if it pinged as Janelle's it would make sense. I'm still waiting to hear back.'

I pulled up everything I had so far; the names and faces, the times, dates and movements I'd been able to corroborate. I'd been feeling so lost, so inundated with data, that seeing it all collected in front of me was eye-opening. I'd done more work, collected and collated more information, on this case than on any other that I'd take on probably the entire time I'd been working as a P.I.

'Woah,' Grant said, as she helped me copy and organize everything to take with her. 'You've been busy.'

'Yeah, until this moment, I was feeling like I'd gotten exactly nowhere, but I can see that wasn't quite accurate.'

'I second that, for sure. I can't believe how far you got with your limited resources.'

I knew what she meant and took it that way. 'Thanks,' I replied. 'Actually, let me stop you there,' I said, holding up my hands. 'I've got more forensic evidence than I know what to do with today.'

Grant's eyes bugged out a little when I gave her an extremely edited version of the story of me swabbing samples of Kevin's boat, and showed her the pictures of the luminol discotheque that was the interior of the cabin.

I explained that he had a fishing and depth tracker on the boat, and that I'd downloaded its history.

'I can't do anything with that information,' she said, in dismay.

'I know,' I replied, 'But... uh... would you like to sit with me while I find out where he's been?'

Grant chewed her bottom lip for just a moment or two. 'I need to call my chief,' she said. 'Let him know I'll be a while longer.'

Ten minutes later, wherein I watched as Grant argued in her vehicle with someone on the phone who did not appear happy with her, she was beside me again at my desk. 'Let's see what you've got,' she said, and I am one hundred percent positive I heard admiration in her voice.

I'd actually retained more than I realized about the movements of the water in the area around where Kevin docked his boat. I'd been so exhausted when I was reading the charts I didn't think any of it stuck, but I was wrong. Following the data points from the fish tracker, which indicated places where the boat paused for a short time, stayed for a while or travelled, I could see there was one particular area where he paused several times, before continuing out to sea, or returning to the harbor- the last time was several weeks ago, right around the time that Lennette hired me. The water wasn't terribly deep, and the currents were mild. Lots of fish activity.

'How much do you want to bet, that's where we'll find Janelle?' I whispered, my mind a veritable tempest.

'We need warrants,' Grant said. 'I need to get all of this evidence legally, right now. Shit, how do I sell this? How do I get the chief to look this way, without telling him where I'm getting my tips from? Cuz if he even so much as gets a whiff this came from you, I'll be filing paperwork in a back office for the rest of my career. Bowman will make sure of that. You really chapped *his* ass that first time we came here.' She stood up and paced the floor, in long rapid steps. 'Fuck, I've got it. We've been wondering about the origin points of some of the product they're bringing in. I could tell him I did a search for marine vessels for all involved parties- and that's how they'll find this. This could tie into what the companies are doing- the product we're tracking, as well. We've got some footage of dock workers, shipping containers. But who's to say they're not bringing it in on personal vessels, under the guise of fishing trips, as well? That's my in.'

I watched as Grant's mind raced and almost laughed. 'I guess it's your turn to say thank you?' I teased.

She stopped pacing and looked at me, sincerity shining in her eyes. 'Yes, obviously, thank you. I mean, of course. I'm not trying to just steal your work, right, You get that right? Once this leads somewhere, I'll make sure the chief knows it came from you- you'll get the credit you're due, I promise.'

'Don't be absurd. My priority has always been, and still remains, finding out what happened to Janelle. I'm barely sleeping because of the magnitude of crap I've looked into or uncovered. I've had the shit kicked out of me, I've had the FBI banging on my door-' at this Grant gave me a sympathetic half smile- 'I've got hitmen hanging out in my parking lot. They know what my friends, my family look like. I have people I care about who are in danger. Do you think I *want* to keep going? I'd happily hand all this over if it meant these douchebags could be scooped up and kept behind bars. I don't care about any of these people, including Mr. Gets Married in Abundant Life Magazine. I just want to find Janelle, and give Lennette some answers, and not be afraid I'll be murdered in my bed. Honestly, the less credit I get, the better. These people have a long reach, and I'm a much easier target than the Bureau.'

Grant nodded. 'It's going to take a few days to get the warrants, the paperwork in order, get on the boat. I need you to hang tight, and not do anything. In fact, maybe you should get a hotel room, hide out. Once these guys get a whiff that we're looking closer, that we're coming in, they might go nuclear.'

'I understand. I'll bring Chuck along too. Don't want him here all alone, in case anything happens.'

Grant took a deep breath and looked at me, I knew she wanted to ask me something but couldn't make up her mind. Of course I thought it was about the case, so I said 'Go ahead, ask me whatever.'

She smiled a bit and went, 'Okay, well, I was wondering... when this case is wrapped up, would you like to, well...'

What she was asking hit me like a slap- but a nice one. Is that a thing? 'Yes, yes I would,' I replied.

She smiled again, and I couldn't help but do so, also.

'Good. Great. Then you may as well start calling me Inez.'

Feet Up, TV On

Robbie's law firm had filed the suit and now it was a matter of doing a paperwork dance over the next few months, so he took some time off to rest. He and Becky decided (at my urging) to take a road trip out of state to a B&B, do some shopping and unwind. I was glad to watch the little dot that indicated their location travel for nearly five hours, then stop in a quaint little town near a low mountain range, where I'm sure it was picturesque and darling, despite the cold, the lack of foliage and the eternally gray winter sky.

I told them to enjoy their time off and get me the weirdest souvenir they could find. Then, content that my kids were safe, I let myself relax.

'Ey, yo, how'd you get the tv to work?' Chuck called from his adjoining room. He'd also put in for a few days off from work to hide out with me- and to compensate for the wage loss I told him he could hold off on paying the rent this month.

I got up from my bed and went through the open door that joined our suites, and pressed a few buttons on his remote.

'Perfect, thanks.'

'You hungry?' I asked, picking up the room service menu. 'I'm ordering dinner.'

'Yeah, I'll take the burger, extra pickles, extra fries, two iced teas, extra sugar.'

'Coming right up.'

We had dinner together and watched a little tv, then I called it a night although it was barely seven thirty. The weight of exhaustion I was carrying was taking its toll.

Inez had informed me that the DNA I'd collected from IEI was not a match to Janelle. I was really, really, *really* sick of getting negative results. 'It was an unknown male,' she'd continued. 'We sent two Agents to find something we could use to compare from Robert Shanks' apartment, to try to match it to him.'

Then, around five this morning she'd called again to inform me that no-knock warrants had been executed overnight. Offices were searched, rich white guys had been taken into custody, goons had been tracked down (including Cigarette Man), cars had been impounded and warehouses torn apart.

She relayed to me, anger and frustration apparent in her voice, that Kevin's boat had been torched. Someone in law enforcement must have given him a heads up. It was actively ablaze when the Agents arrived to examine it, firecrews still battling the flames, and he himself was nowhere to be found.

I checked my tracking software. 'I have his car-' I'd said, and gave her the location.

'No good,' she'd replied. 'That's the FBI's temporary storage facility for this case. His car was confiscated- he must have another vehicle- one none of us knew about. His wife's and kids' cars are accounted for. The good thing is we got both weapons he had stashed in there. I wouldn't put it past him to have more, of course, but right now he's got two less firearms.'

After only a few days, Chuck and I were definitely hitting the limits of our ability to deal with boredom. We'd watched movies, played cards and took lots of naps, and though it was nice to get some rest, we were getting too antsy for it to go on much longer. It was a huge relief when I got another call from Inez.

'Good news,' she said. 'We finally got results on passport activity, and we got a hit on Kevin Werth; he flew down to Ecuador the same night he torched his boat. He got out of the country right before we got his name out to the airlines and ports. So it looks like you can go home. We've got Agents heading down today to help the locals track his movements, and we should have him soon. The chief wants all the forensic samples you took from Werth's boat. He looked over the pictures you took, the video, how carefully you documented your movements while you were on-board, and with all the identifying information in the photos, he thinks we can use it as leverage against him when we find him. With the scope of this case, a friendly judge might let us bring it all in, even though we didn't obtain it ourselves, or at least, we can threaten him with it. He doesn't have unlimited resources anymore- he will have to pay a lawyer handsomely to fight everything. It might be enough to get him to talk.'

Chuck and I were grateful to pack our stuff and check out. He called work to let them know he'd be back, and he accompanied me while I assembled everything I'd gathered from Kevin's boat, and delivered it to Inez where she asked me to meet her.

Chuck winked at me after they'd been introduced, because of course during our few days in the hotel, I'd shared my feelings and hopes about her.

The Girls

Updates came hard and fast over the next day or so. Some preliminary tests had been run on the swabs, but so far, none of the blood evidence was a type-match for Janelle.

My heart sank at this news. How could that be possible? Had I missed a stain? Was I that rusty?

Blood from five different individuals, all female, was discovered on the swabs. Two more samples were inconclusive. I could have cried, or thrown up.

None of them matched Janelle's blood type. Nothing conclusive. Where the hell was she? If he didn't use his boat to dispose of her, what had he done? Did he even get rid of her? Cigarette Man- whose name was Frank Robinaux, wasn't talking. But they didn't need him to confess to make a case that he got rid of Stanhope. They had him on camera, and he had a rap sheet as long as he was tall. Maybe I had this all wrong. Maybe Kevin just gave the order, Robinaux took her out, and we'd never find her.

I sent Inez everything I had on the missing women from the I88 truck stop. The six names, and everything I'd been able to look up on them on my own in the last few days since I'd stopped investigating Kevin and Stanhope and paused the search for Janelle. I had some birth dates, last knowns, and arrest history when applicable. Some of them had prints and DNA in the system from being in fights, or other charges I don't need to explain.

It was a sad morning when Inez confirmed two matches. Kevin, apparently, didn't just take his dates to shitty motels, he also treated them to boat rides- ones they may not have returned from. At this, I let myself release all the emotions I'd been working so hard to keep in, and I cried for an hour.

Another day or so went by and Inez informed me they'd only been able to confirm one more identity. The others were to be left unknown for the time being as the FBI focused on the larger case.

I had three names. Three vulnerable women who had gone missing and no one had looked for them. Three women whose remains were as yet undiscovered, or were at best, alive but battered and hiding somewhere. But that was looking unlikely.

If they were merely hurt, they probably would have returned to work at some point. The ladies at the truck stop had told me that Kevin was rough, they knew about it. So if they didn't come back, chances were that they couldn't.

Melanie Gerald, Carly Hunt and Lilian Sodensky, a.k.a. LeeLee. Three humans, with thoughts, dreams and feelings, three faces that laughed, cried, worried and felt fear. Three people whose friends and families might be wondering where they are, what happened and want closure.

Well, I was gonna get it.

Inez told me there were divers scheduled to examine the area where Kevin's boat stopped during its travels, and that she'd keep me posted. The Bureau were hoping to find a drop zone for product, she told me, but we both feared they were going to find something else entirely.

Did I feel bad that the Bureau was basically doing my work for me? Absolutely not. They didn't know and why should anyone tell them? I didn't have the kind of money it costs to hire a dive team. I didn't need credit for taking out a woman-killer. I just needed him found, and locked up. The more evidence they had to build against Kevin when he was eventually located, the better.

Even if his lawyers fought to get it tossed because it originated from the work of a private investigator, I was sure the FBI would make something stick- I was, after all, licensed and operating fully within the scope of my duties.

It was a difficult phone call, the one when Inez updated me, that several sets of human remains had been located.

Kevin had a careful way of doing it too; he'd wrapped the bodies in chicken wire or some other kind of wire fence, weigh them with rocks or cinderblocks and drop them over the side of his boat. That certainly explained the deep scratches in the gunwale, and I shuddered at knowing I'd touched the very surface that had been used in such a way. The bay was deep enough that the fish that lived there would have a nice feast before whatever was left over would be washed out to sea with the currents at the bottom. The divers found multiple bodies in various state of decay and disarray; some only had the largest bones left, some still had flesh. All in all, there were seven cages, still loaded down with rocks, firmly anchored where they'd landed. If I hadn't found the boat, and collected the evidence that I had, chances are they never would have been found.

The bodies that had been down there the least amount of time would be the first and easiest to identify, and potentially, one could be Janelle Stevenson.

Even harder than getting the call from Inez, was the one I needed to make- to inform Lennette about the developments.

It would take a while to formally identify them, I told her, but for her to stay strong. We spoke for a while; grief is a funny thing. She was tired and sad, but glad to have news, however dreadful it might be. She cried, I cried, we spoke at length about happy memories she had of Janelle as a girl. I told her to hold onto that, no matter what the outcome was.

Time Is Relative

That time crawls, absolutely slows to a snail's pace, when one is waiting for news is a gross understatement.

But then to receive news that isn't what you're waiting for? Horrendous.

Inez informed me that the most recent sets of remains were none of them a match for Janelle. They were, however, for the blood stains on the boat.

'Every step forward is at least some progress,' she said, trying to be soothing.

'I know, I know,' I muttered in reply, struggling with the crushing disappointment.

'We'll find her,' she said.

I was becoming less convinced that was going to be true.

Robinaux, however, was teasing some info in exchange for a lesser sentence, but he'd managed to retain an expensive lawyer, so the DA was dealing with more of a challenge with him than had been anticipated.

My hope was fading that we'd ever get anywhere, as the info that Robinauz offered had to do with the location of crates of money that were waiting to be laundered, and nothing to do with Janelle.

Then, I was shocked when Inez informed me that his deal had been rescinded. The DA had claimed the money would have been found during inevitable discovery, as it was securely hidden in the basement of one of the properties the Bureau had been investigating. So, faced with his deal falling apart, he suggested that he hadn't been the one who had done Stanhope in- that he'd simply been instructed to help arrange the body to make it look like Stanhope had taken a header down the stairs.

'Now we're getting somewhere,' Inez had said, in an effort to lift my spirits. 'And the Agents in Ecuador have a trail on him. We'll find him, Dea.'

Something stuck in my mind, the way Robinaux said 'help'. Not, go arrange the body, not take care of the body- 'help'. *Who* did he help? Who had left the house with him that night? Something clicked in my mind. 'Did Stanhope's car get processed?' I asked.

'Yeah- it was weird-'

'No fingerprints, nothing?' I guessed.

'Yeah- how-'

'That's how I found Janelle's car- in the impound lot. It was wiped clean.'

Inez was quiet for a few moments. Then, 'So you think, someone *else* was driving Stanhope's car home that last night.' Her voice lowered until it was barely a whisper. 'Shit.'

I suggested, 'Stanhope's body was probably in the trunk. And the driver who we thought was Stanhope waited for Robinaux to come, to help stage the scene. Then they wiped the car down, and hoped we were all really stupid. That's why two people left, not just one.'

She sighed. 'There's a lot of repeating patterns here,' she

said. 'I'll call you later.'

Oh Fuck

I had fallen asleep on my couch, and awoke uncomfortably from a bad dream. I had had Inez's voice in my head, on repeat: *patterns, patterns. The same behaviors, the same tactics? Someone using repeated methods.* My mind rambled sleepily: *methods, patterns, behaviors, people, even criminals, tend to follow patterns, routines, rhythms, do things the same ways that they think have worked before.*

Headlights streaked across my ceiling, which I assumed, sleepily, were from Chuck returning home after work. But the engine noise was different; his van was loud. Then my brain rolled through multiple half-formed notions, a vague recollection of him getting a ride, when was that, yesterday? Earlier tonight? Oh yeah, his van was in the shop, right? What time was it, was he home or still at work? What fucking day was it?

My eyelids drooped and I took a deep breath and tried to stretch, but the throw pillows were bunched in a hard pile, and I didn't have enough room to maneuver. I shoved a few of them, accidentally causing them to fall. One hit a chopstick sticking out of fried rice on the coffee table, upsetting the container and sending rice and vegetables spilling onto the wood floor.

'Goddammit,' I muttered, sitting up and rubbing my face. I stood up to go get the dustpan when I heard a faint click echo in the hallway. I frowned a bit, and looked at my door. I was still groggy from sleep, and struggled to understand the sound.

Chuck usually didn't bother to hold the exterior door when he came in; it didn't close quietly. And then I'd hear the sound of his uneven gait on heavy, tired feet upon the stairs. But no sound came from the staircase, and my skin prickled. I took one step toward my umbrella stand, to go for my trusty golf club, but I didn't make it.

The door flew open in a bewildering crash and flurry of spinters and hardware, and I cried out in surprise.

Kevin barreled into my living room, his face red with fury and horror, and I had no time to counter when he landed a perfectly aimed kick to my chest. I was hurled across the room, and landed, thankfully, on Becky's massive beanbag, which I realized later, probably saved my fucking life.

Gasping, I reached my good arm out for anything I could grab, and landed on a heavy vase, which I heaved in Kevin's general direction. He dodged it easily as he charged toward me, and I only had enough time to roll out of the way before he threw another kick, which hit dead center of the beanbag, swallowing his lower leg for a second or two.

He tripped when his foot caught on the fabric, which gave me just enough time to stumble to my feet. I tried to make it to the door but was stopped when Kevin managed to grab my hair, and rip me backwards. I don't know how I stayed on my feet. He left me no room or time to get to my bedroom, to my closet, to unlock and load my safely stored revolver.

I threw my right arm out and clawed his face, which made him howl. I pulled back and managed to land half a blow to his cheek, but didn't have time to counter or block his right, which hit me directly in my fucking ear.

A high pitched ringing began instantly, adding to my inability to coordinate a counter attack and I felt my ankle get kicked hard. Before I knew it, I was on my side on the floor with my good arm pinned under me. All I could do was use my weak left elbow to block punches. I was only successful a few times; I felt a crack around my eye, a tearing of the flesh inside my mouth. I heard one of Kevin's blows land on the floor beside my face and he cried out- the crunch of bones against the planks told me he'd broken something in his hand, but it still wasn't enough to save me. I scraped and clawed and swung wildly once I managed to wiggle my good arm out from under myself, but his clothes were thick, he had on gloves (the smell of that leather will never leave my nostrils) and I never got through to his skin.

I was aware of the way the grit on the floor felt under my bare heels, as I kicked my legs in futility. I was aware of how cold the floor was. He was so heavy; he was compressing every molecule of air out of me.

That stupid, stupid stupid letter 'I', half-painted, half missing, was all I could see. I'd never see the northern lights, I'd never learn to speak French, I'd never meet my grandkids, I'd never get that stupid letter repainted.

I kicked hard and managed to lift him a bit, throwing his balance off, but his elbow slammed my mouth and blood gushed into my throat. I coughed and spit, splattering it across his face, and he hurled a slew of insults. He lifted his right knee and pinned my bad arm, flattening me onto my back, which made me scream through the blood, wildly blinded by the pain. His gloved hand gripped my right wrist and I was fucking done.

'That's enough Oshtrovsky,' he growled. 'That's fucking it. You fucked up everything. I had a nice little gig going, I was making bank. Absolute bank. I had my hobbies. My boat. I was going to cash out and retire somewhere nice and fucking beachy. Someplace nobody knew me. Stanhope had no idea his little girlfriend was gone, I told him she quit, and he believed me! *He* was easy. But you had to go and fuck it all up!' He'd been pushing his clenched right fist harder and harder into my cheek, and he pulled back, to deliver another blow, then, 'FUCK!' he screamed. 'Why are you *laughing*?'

I was out of breath and my face and hair were soaked with spit and blood. I smiled through the pain and the fear, blood in between my teeth and running down my throat. 'Chuck,' I gurgled.

Kevin didn't have time to register his confusion, before Chuck's Thanksgiving-turkey-sized fist was slamming into his right temple. He collapsed on the floor to my right, where he lay still except to twitch a few times, out colder than cold. Apparently, Chuck was, in fact, home from work. 'You alright?' my beautiful friend asked, kneeling beside me. 'No, I am definitely not,' I grimaced, rolling over on my right side and cradling my battered left arm to my chest. I was starting to cry from the agony I was in. 'But I will be, thanks to you.'

'Don't move. I'm calling an ambulance.'

'First, get my old cuffs and secure that asshole.'

'You got it.'

I heard Chuck digging around in my kitchen drawer, and once the cuffs were secured on the very unconscious Kevin, I closed my eyes. I must have passed out, because the next time I opened them, Beth Thompson's concerned face was leaning over me, the fluorescent lights of the ER overhead, and the doctor standing at the foot of my bed was rambling something about head trauma. Sigh. Back to sleep.

Robbie Wants Me to Find a New Hobby

'Hey, there you are,' Robbie's voice, calm and gentle, came through the fog of my brain.

'Hi Dea,' Becky this time.

'Hey,' I tried to reply, but my throat was very dry. I coughed a little and Becky held a cup of water out to me, straw aimed toward my face. 'Here, take a little sip.'

'How are you feeling? I'm going to call the doctor,' Robbie said, standing up. It hurt to try to look at his face, framed by the lights on the ceiling.

'Can we... can we dim the lights?' I whispered.

'Yeah, of course,' Becky said, jumping up and moving a switch on the wall. 'How's that?'

'Much better.'

Robbie returned a moment later. 'The doctor will be right in. How are you feeling?'

'I'm okay.'

'You're very injured.'

'Besides that. I'm okay.'

Robbie shook his head. 'Mom, can you admit it's time to hang up this particular hat?'

Becky shot him a look. 'Babe, leave her alone, she just woke up.'

Robbie rolled his eyes. 'I know. But Mom, like, this case, it's been so... so dangerous. You were nearly killed! More than once! I love you, but it's terrifying. I mean, I'm sorry! I know I sound selfish right now. But I'm tired of being scared you're going to die!'

'Rob, there is a time and place for this conversation and it's not right now.' Becky's voice was firm. I wondered if I was going to get a word in. Becky was patting my hand energetically, but I don't think she realized it.

'I just wish you'd get like, a hobby or something. Fucking tap class. Making jams or something. Grow some vegetables.'

I opened my mouth to reply but Becky cut me off. 'Leave her alone. She's fine!'

'She's not fine!'

'She'll be okay! Not all our cases are like this!'

'But you can never know, can you?'

'Rob, I love you, so so *so* much, but *shut* the fuck *up*.'

Rob opened his mouth to continue arguing, but I took the opportunity to speak. 'Um, can I say something?'

They both looked at me, their faces immediately softening. 'Yes, Ma, what is it?' Robbie pleaded.

'I've always wanted to learn how to play bridge.'

They both looked confused for a second, and I smiled weakly. Then I regretted it, because damn, my mouth fucking hurt.

Their fear and anguish left their countenances and they both laughed. 'Okay, let's all learn,' Becky said, sighing deeply. 'I bet Chuck will be our fourth.'

The doctor walked in. 'Ah, you're awake,' she said, smiling in a friendly way. 'How are you feeling?'

I was really tired of hearing that question, but then Inez strode in behind the doctor, her face lined with worry. She came around to the other side of the bed, held my unoccupied hand and asked, 'How are you feeling?' and I thought, I didn't mind hearing it so much, anymore.

A Good then Awful Morning

There's satisfaction in knowing you did the right thing, despite the risks. There is also a great deal of comfort in the knowledge that you've closed a case, solved a mystery, brought some bad guys to justice. A few less people- who hurt other people- out on the streets is a good thing, a job well done.

And then there are mornings like this one. It had started out good. Maybe even great. I'd woken up with Inez's leg draped across my body. I was warm, safe, I was the little spoon. Sometimes life is okay.

My wounds were healing; the bruises had reduced to ugly yellow splotches, the stitches had been removed, I was back in physical therapy for my arm.

I'd fallen asleep last night in her arms, after being unable to stop the flow of tears. 'I was right there,' I'd cried, 'I was right there, I was so close.'

But then this morning, both of us solemn, despite wanting to stay in bed, to be affectionate, to linger for a few precious moments, each of us knowing what was expected to transpire this morning; the late night calls Inez had taken mere hours ago on her work mobile, the updates she'd received, the arrangements that had been made. She had to be somewhere, and I was allowed to accompany her, as a courtesy.

We left from my place, but took two cars to the location: the end of Valmer Boulevard, previously known as the Walen Bros. Wharf, apparently, a few decades ago when it had been in business.

I stood a bit off to the side of the crowd of officers, supervisors, engineers and other assorted officials. A rig was hauling up its objective, slowly but surely. I could hear water pouring out of the ins and outs of the chains and the compact car that was hooked at the ends of them. I recognized the vehicle from the descriptions on the impound lot receipt that Shanks' landlady had given me. The color, the make, even the spot on the bumper that was black from being patched and sanded, but never repainted.

Anger mixed with sadness flowed through me.

The departments to which I'd handed over all the evidence in my case were under no obligation to keep me informed. But Inez had been given permission to give *me* permission to watch them pull up the wreck, and when she'd received word that the divers had found it, the engineers had approved the process and arrangements for the necessary heavy machinery had been made, I almost didn't want to be there. There was no gladness in this errand; the satisfaction from getting answers was far outweighed by the pain and horror this case had wrought.

Kevin had pleaded out in exchange for protective custody, and he'd spilled every gut he had left inside his festering carcass for the prize of solitary confinement for life. Every errand he'd run for the heads of the operation, every meet he'd arranged, every goon he'd hired, everyone he'd personally taken out, and the names of the girls he used, abused, hurt and killed, and finally, what happened to Janelle.

Inez succeeded, sort of, in convincing her chief to bring me in as a temporary consultant. Apparently, he didn't need too much convincing but Bowman was against it completely.

She told me that since they had use of all my work, and it helped in building their case, it was the least they could do; additionally, she said, I deserved to know what happened to the woman I'd been paid to find.

The chief allowed me to come in, but taking Bowman's advice, only to be compensated for the work I'd provided (detailed forms and paperwork all completed) and to view edited portions of Kevin's interview tapes under supervision, and then, to be an onlooker at the location today.

On the videos, Kevin's face looked weary and sallow. He was wearing tan prison scrubs and was cuffed to a heavy table in a plain gray room. The whole scene was surreal. He spoke slowly, clearly, he didn't mince his words, or appear remorseful. If anything he seemed annoyed.

According to his story, he'd been supervising the trade off of crates of money disguised as car parts. For every two crates of actual product, one crate was full of cash. He was only supervising personally because, the movies don't show you this, but goons get the flu too.

Shanks had no control over his alcoholism. He'd been a problem for a while. He'd been demanding more money for the late night shifts, and that night, he'd been in poor form. He'd nearly dropped a couple crates already, and Kevin was about to bench him and do the loading himself, when Shanks was pulling one down from a high shelf, didn't have it securely on the forks, and dropped it. The crate crashed open, spilling shrink-wrapped blocks of US currency all over the floor.

Janelle, apparently, had forgotten her mobile phone in her desk. Kevin said later, after everything was done and handled, he'd gone to scrub the CCTV and had ascertained what she'd been doing when he watched the files- he saw her moving through the warehouse and up to the office empty handed, then out again, her phone in hand. (It was going to be a long weekend, and I guessed she didn't want to leave it for three days.) She'd gone in, unseen, through the unlocked side door. Kevin accused her of being sneaky; of spying.

I suspected it was more likely that, with her natural shyness, she just didn't want to talk to these strange men who were working late at night. The chaos the forklift operator was causing had kept their attention on him.

When the crate crashed, all eyes were on the money. Kevin and the goons knew it was there obviously, but Shanks didn't, and he began yelling about it, trying to grab it, trying to run. In the commotion and tension, no one noticed Janelle had come up behind them, and was looking, wide-eyed, at the pile. Until she screamed.

Kevin told the Agents, in a voice that was so flat, so lacking affect that it chilled me, he'd struck the operator, once, twice, 'maybe three times' to silence him and stop him from grabbing up the money.

Janelle's scream was the first time any of them even knew she was there, and according to Kevin, it only took one hit to take her out.

He didn't have the time or materials to dispose of her in the same way he done to the working women. Her murder hadn't been carefully planned, unlike all of theirs.

With the help of the hired guys, he'd put her and Shanks' bodies into Shanks' car and drove to the Valmer Boulevard wharf, where he moved her body to the driver's seat, bashed her head against the steering wheel a few times and pushed them in.

'Why there?' the interrogating Agent asked.

'I'd scoped out that place before as a possible location for handoffs or use for moving crates. But there was too much debris in the water, and the wharf was too rotted. But, that's how I knew about it.'

'What about her family, or coworkers? Stanhope? Weren't you worried they were going to wonder what happened to her?'

'We only hired people to work in the offices who had few connections. No family. No lives. We were careful but Stanhope was stupid. He got caught up with her, but he was easy to manipulate. He believed me when I told him Stevenson had quit. I'd used her phone to submit the vacation request, I'd cleaned up her apartment, everything.

He saw with his own eyes she'd chosen to leave. Everything was fine and would have stayed that way but that bitch aunt hired Oshtrovsky.'

Then I watched as Inez had come into the interrogation room. She asked one question only: 'How did the incident involving Detectives Perkins and Oshtrovsky at the property, currently Blue Wave Imports, previously operating under the name Grayhawk- fit into all of this?'

Kevin snorted a small chuckle out of his nose. The sound went through me like a spear. A laugh. A *laugh.* 'I was wondering when someone was going to bring that up,' he said, sarcastically. 'That was just some... loose ends.'

'Elaborate.'

His demeanor changed in an instant. Anger and mania flashed through his eyes; even watching it on the video it was terrifying. He did not like to be given orders.

'I remind you that your deal is predicated upon-'

'You don't need to remind me of shit.' He paused. 'I'd only just gone into business with Robinaux. I'd invited a handful of good guys from the force, including Perkins, to join up; but he turned me down. He said if I didn't close down the security biz, he'd report me for a conflict of interest. I told Robinaux to sort it out, and well, apparently he did. He and his guys set the stage pretty well. They called in anonymous tips about drug and transient activity in that area for weeks.

None of the uni's ever found anything but the rumors were moving through the department. I wasn't on vice so I didn't hear about the call that sent Perkins and Oshtrovsky to the warehouse until the whole thing had already gone down. I had to spin it hard to stay away from it. But everyone believed what I said.' He stopped speaking, interlaced his fingers and leaned back in his chair.

'What happened next?' the Agent next to Inez asked.

'Robinaux's solution was more...rigorous than what Linhurst and I had had in mind. We didn't need that kind of heat. So we got a new crew and started fresh. Linhurst shuttered Grayhawk - before it really even got going- and we started The Solution. We kept my name off it. Clean slate.'

'What happened to the guys Robinaux had do the job?'

'I took them for a boat ride.'

The groan and squeal of the metal car frame echoed off of the crumbling walls of the brick structures, bringing me back to the present moment.

A snowstorm was quickly approaching, and the sky hung heavy with dense clouds. Large, thick snowflakes had already begun to fall, they came in waves, sometimes coming down for a few minutes, sometimes longer, here and there they ceased completely. The people on the wharf were working quickly, with a palpable sense of urgency to get the job done, evidence collected and stored, and get back on the road as expeditiously as possible. The amount of people who needed to be coordinated at a single time in this one spot to do this job was immense- so despite the weather reports, the plan moved ahead beginning at daybreak. I knew, because I felt the same, that everyone wanted to be tucked up in their homes before the expected worst of the storm rolled in later today.

The vehicle had been settling on the uneven bottom in frigid water for weeks, and was now being set down as carefully as the crane operator could manage. The noise was louder than I was prepared for it to be. The water pouring out of the vehicle spread out everywhere, some of it making its way back into the deep below. Inez, wearing rubber boots, went over to the driver's side and took a few moments to observe the remains. She turned around and gave me a nod to indicate the body showed some markers that it was indeed Janelle (I definitely couldn't take Kevin's word for it) and I nodded once in reply, then turned to wipe a few tears that had formed in my eyes that I didn't want anyone to see, which was silly.

I climbed into my car and sat for a few moments, watching my breath make small puffs of steam. I didn't need to watch the coroners remove the remains, I didn't need to see the rusting, warped car get loaded into the waiting trailer, or for the photographers to flurry around documenting the entire scene. The cold hadn't bothered me while I stood outside in the wind, but now my shoulder and left arm were aching, and I wanted nothing more than a giant coffee and the biggest pastry the bakery could legally sell me.

Maybe I should just buy a whole damn cake, I said to myself as I started the engine and let it warm up for a few minutes before I put it in gear, and hurried the fuck out of there.

Jasmine Gets Her Car Back

The tv was on mute with the captions going, and I glanced up to see a live news report about my recent case. I even thought I caught a little glimpse of Inez in the background. She had stayed over last night, and brought her court suit with her, dressing early this morning in front of my tall bedroom mirror.

'Looking dashing as ever,' I'd said, like a dork, but she'd laughed so it was okay.

I unmuted the tv and watched the news anchor speak about the arrests while the network played video clips and showed snaps of courthouse drawings, listed various high profile names- and look at that, it turned out that Carter Linhurst was real after all. The words 'federal indictments' 'corruption' and 'RICO case' floated around in various blurbs and through on-screen text.

The chyron that had been running for days on multiple news platforms included the names of our illustrious Congressman George Harrison Hackerman, Miles Stanhope, Carter Linhurst, et al, and showed pictures of all of them from better times. I was so glad they'd all been arrested, I forgot to be mad at how flattering the photos were that the media used.

Smiling, I clicked off the tv and grabbed my coat. I had a car to steal.

An hour later Chuck and I were camped out a block away from a shitty rental house surrounded by a chainlink fence, with a driveway that ended beside the back door. A car matching Jasmine's missing vehicle was parked in the driveway. I held up a picture- taken of her during a summer block party in her parents' neighborhood, where she was leaning against her car, long legs shining in the sun, and compared it to the vehicle we were looking at. Spot on, down to the decals and stickers that were still in the back window.

The license plates were different, but according to Jasmine, her ex wouldn't have thought twice about using some 'borrowed' ones. I'd also done my own homework, like any good, legally operating P.I. would. Jasmine had all the paperwork on the car, including the deed from when she paid it off, and a copy of the police report she'd filed when her ex took off with it. And this morning, she gave me the one thing that would leave nothing to doubt.

We watched as roomates, or friends or girlfriends left for their jobs, or went for coffee at the convenience store at the end of the block.

'That's him.' Chuck said, when another tenant emerged from the house.

'You're sure?'

'Yeah, he came by the club a couple times. His hair's longer now but that's definitely him.'

'Okay you ready?'

'Yep.'

We climbed out of the car and hurried up to the young man, who was clicking the unlock button on the key fob in his hand. He had a backpack and a coffee. He didn't realize we were there until Chuck took hold of his backpack and spun him around, achieving the desired effect of disorienting him. The coffee went flying and I heard it splatter against the pavement of the driveway. Flattened against the side of the car, he cried out 'What the fuck?' Then he saw who had a hold of him and his eyes went wide, and he decided compliance was best. Good choice.

'Shut up, give me the keys,' I said. He let them go and they fell, but I caught them before they hit the ground.

'Don't you start yellin',' Chuck warned him.

'Fuck you!'

'Clever.'

From my pocket, I pulled out the key fob that Jasmine had given me today- her spare- and clicked the unlock button. The car beeped in response. There was no question this was Jasmine's stolen vehicle.

'Well, well, well, I don't think this car belongs to you,' I said. He groaned. 'C'mon man, I'm just borrowing it. That stupid bitch told me I could keep it!'

'Which is it, you're borrowing it or she said you can keep it?' I asked.

'Aw fuck off, you little-'

'Enough,' Chuck said, shoving the man hard to the side, causing him to stumble and fall, landing in the dirt beside the house's front steps. 'Stay there.'

I handed Chuck both sets of keys and he climbed into Jasmine's car and slid the drivers seat all the way back.

I moved around to the passenger side and got in, as Chuck hit reverse and whipped the car out of the driveway. He dropped me off back at my vehicle, followed me as I pulled out of the neighborhood, and we headed back home. We paused in parking lot of my building, and Chuck took off the stolen plates. I got some satisfaction out of taking Jasmine's fob off of the ex's keyring, and throwing the rest of his keys into the trash. I was pretty sure he learned a solid lesson, and Jasmine had my number if he gave her any more trouble. I doubted he would. I dropped the stolen plates in a postal box on our way to Jasmine's neighborhood.

At Jasmine's apartment, she met us in the parking lot, wearing a robe that wouldn't stay closed over tiny nightie that was working hard to stay where it was supposed to be, and her hair was piled up atop her head in an impossibly messy bun. We were both hugged and kissed excessively as we handed over the keys. Chuck and I climbed back into my car, as Jasmine stood beside it, glancing backward periodically to gaze affectionately at her newly returned vehicle, which was surprisingly in pretty good condition. 'How much do I owe ya?' she asked, leaning into my window, filling the entire frame with her ample bosom.

'No charge,' I said, 'happy to help.'

STEPHANIE ELLIOTT

Made in United States
North Haven, CT
30 September 2023

42175034R00200